Books in the COLONY Series
QUANT
ARCADIA
GALACTIC SURVEY
SILK ROAD
LOST COLONY
EARTH

Books in the EMPIRE Series
by Richard F. Weyand:
EMPIRE: Reformer
EMPIRE: Usurper
EMPIRE: Tyrant
EMPIRE: Commander
EMPIRE: Warlord
EMPIRE: Conqueror

by Stephanie Osborn:
EMPIRE: Imperial Police
EMPIRE: Imperial Detective
EMPIRE: Imperial Inspector
EMPIRE: Section Six

by Richard F. Weyand:
EMPIRE: Intervention
EMPIRE: Investigation
EMPIRE: Succession
EMPIRE: Renewal
EMPIRE: Resistance
EMPIRE: Resurgence

Books in the Childers Universe

by Richard F. Weyand:

Childers
Childers: Absurd Proposals
Galactic Mail: Revolution
A Charter For The Commonwealth
Campbell: The Problem With Bliss

by Stephanie Osborn:

Campbell: The Sigurdsen Incident

QUANT

A Colony Story

by

RICHARD F. WEYAND

RICHARD F. WEYAND

ISBN 978-1-954903-01-2
Printed in the United States of America

Cover Credits
Cover Art: Paola Giari and Luca Oleastri,
www.rotwangstudio.com
Back Cover Photo: Oleg Volk

Published by Weyand Associates, Inc.
Bloomington, Indiana, USA
April 2021

QUANT

CONTENTS

RICHARD F. WEYAND

The Industrialist And The Entrepreneur

"So he took the meeting?" Anna Glenn asked.

"Yes," Bernd Decker said, as he continued to pack his overnight bag.

"Did you tell him why you wanted to see him?"

"No."

"Why would he take the meeting with no topic or agenda?" Glenn asked. "Such an important man, and he just says 'Sure'?"

"Well, I'm not exactly a nobody. But I think he's curious."

"Huh. Well, obviously it worked. You gonna lay the whole thing out? Your whole plan?"

"Yes," Decker said. "Whether he and I tell anyone else what we're really up to or not is sort of up in the air."

"And you're planning on staying overnight?"

"Not planning on it, but I want to be ready for it. If he bites, I may be there a while."

"All right," Glenn said. "Well, good luck."

"Thanks," Decker said.

Decker gave his wife a quick peck and then headed out of their condo to the elevator, to the autodrone pad on the roof.

Theodore Burke looked out over the lunar valley through the picture window in his office. Not a valley per se, it was actually a mare, the crater from a long-ago asteroid.

Across the valley floor, more than a dozen large installations labored away at making the materials humanity needed. Not finished goods. Those were manufactured on Earth. No, the lunar facilities were heavy industry. Mining and smelting of iron and aluminum, the manufacturing of steel, the processing of rare earths. Those were the energy-intensive and polluting industries that were gradually being moved off the Earth to the lunar surface.

There was no issue with pollution on the Moon. What was air pollution on Earth was a temporary annoyance on the Moon. The Moon could not hold an atmosphere, and the noxious emissions of these facilities were swept away by the solar wind. What was water pollution on Earth was simply piles of debris on the Moon. Without an atmosphere and its attendant rains, the poisonous by-products of industrialization sat inertly in slowly growing mounds piled up against the crater walls miles distant.

The lunar industrial facilities were actually dark factories. Assembled in Earth orbit and shipped to the Moon at incredible expense, they ran themselves. After the initial expeditions to start them up, they operated without any humans on-site. Their product was pushed out of the Moon's gravity well by electromagnetic rail guns, to begin its long slow drop toward Earth.

Mankind itself, though, was still largely confined to the surface of the Earth. In the nearly two and a half centuries since mankind had first set foot on the Moon, that was still about as far as it had gotten. Even intra-system distances were so large, and the energy expenditure required to move fragile humans and all their attendant support – air, food, water – made even trips to the Moon incredibly expensive.

Burke sighed. Mankind was, and always had been, in an incredibly perilous situation. The universe was dominated by huge masses and forces. Stars and galaxies and black holes. Huge gravitational fields. Gamma ray bursts that would fry entire planets hundreds of light-years distant. And fragile humanity still clung to a thin shell of ecosystem around a smallish rock balanced between forces and energies that could destroy it all in a single day at any time. Any time at all.

Burke switched the window back to the view of his estate, a sprawling expanse of woods and mountains in eastern Washington, an administrative region in west-central North America.

Enough daydreaming. It was depressing, anyway.

Back to work.

In addition to the normal financial reports and communications from the CEOs and general managers of his companies and divisions, today Burke had a rare in-person meeting. Most business meetings were handled virtually, and that had been the standard for a couple of hundred years. That was what allowed Burke to live in his mountain retreat while running his far-flung businesses. He had never met most of his direct reports.

Of course, he had his own autodrone for traveling. It was comfortable to a distance of a thousand miles or so. For longer than that, he took a suborbital ballistic out of Seattle, which only took a few hours to get to anywhere else on the planet. Most of his needs for food and supplies were met by deliveries by autodrone, and a small staff ran the house. His wife Martha Stern traveled more – she was away now, in fact – often with her friends. Burke was more of a loner, and something of a workaholic.

Still, an in-person meeting was something of a treat.

Burke's appointment today was with Bernd Decker. Decker was a computer software innovator and executive. He had made a fortune with several successive startups, spinning up a good idea and then selling it off, keeping a part of the stock in each of the transactions. Most had done very well, and Decker had done very well indeed. At such a young age – Decker was thirty-four – it was a tremendous accomplishment.

Part of the reason Burke had taken the in-person meeting – on which Decker had insisted – is that Burke had absolutely no idea what Decker wanted to talk to him about. Most of Burke's meetings were drearily predictable, and this one wasn't. At all.

Burke's curiosity had overcome his natural tendency to reject meetings for which no agenda was forthcoming, and he looked forward to meeting Decker.

Decker was at that moment in a rented autodrone heading east from Seattle, the big port city that was the administrative center of Washington. It was a couple of hours out to Burke's estate, and he spent the time reviewing what he knew about Burke.

It was Burke's father who had been the big push behind moving his heavy industry to the Moon. They weren't the only big manufacturing industries there now, but Burke's father had been first. He had been a true visionary.

That effort had taken almost half a century, and the insane expense of it had almost bankrupted the elder Burke a couple of times. He had pressed on, and so had the younger Burke after health issues had forced his father to step down from the day-to-day management of their multiple companies. Ultimately, the whole thing had paid off handsomely.

The younger Burke was now in his early sixties. But he had persisted in carrying out his father's long-range project. It was that ability to initiate and carry through on long, multi-generation projects that interested Decker in the Burke family.

He was counting on it.

His review complete, Decker settled back to enjoy the view as the autodrone flew through the passes in the mountains, seeking out the denser air at the lower altitudes. It was a much different world than the hustle and bustle of Seattle.

Seattle had been rebuilt after the city, along with Portland and Vancouver, had been largely destroyed in the big Cascadia Quake of 2158. The excellent harbor was just too useful to abandon the site, even with the volcano of Mt. Rainier on one side and the Cascadia Fault on the other. The city had built back better, without all the unreinforced masonry buildings that had doomed the old city. While they were at it, they had built huge channels and walls to steer the lahars that would be the natural result of a Rainier eruption.

As the largest city on the northwest coast of North America, Seattle had been the natural choice for the administrative capital of Washington after the Great Restructuring of 2087, which had reorganized North America into ten administrative regions. Its status as a government center was another spur to the rebuilding of the city after the quake seventy years later. Seattle now, in 2224, was a bustling modern metropolis.

So this wild mountainous terrain was a big change of pace for Decker, and he enjoyed rubbernecking the rest of the way to Burke's retreat.

Burke stood inside the heavy glass door watching the autodrone come in for a landing on the dronepad that doubled as a terrace. When the drone shut down, he walked out onto the terrace. Decker got out of the machine.

"Mr. Decker, I presume," Burke said.

"Yes. Hello, Mr. Burke. Thank you for meeting with me," Decker said as he walked up.

The two tapped forearms, making an 'X', in the common

greeting. Decker had read that people used to shake hands before that was determined to be a major disease vector. Such a thing now was unthinkable. Customs had changed.

"Come along in, Mr. Decker," Burke said, showing the younger man into his office, adjacent to the terrace and looking out over the defile below.

"Please, call me Bernd."

"And you should call me Ted."

Burke waved Decker to the seating arrangement by the windows and they sat. The housekeeper had set out cookies and drinks on the coffee table.

"So, Bernd, I am more than a little curious about what would bring you all the way out here for an in-person meeting. We are not involved in the same sort of business, after all. It was curiosity more than anything that pushed me to take this meeting."

"I was hoping it would. I have something of a proposal for you, Ted, but I would like to set the background a bit first, if I could."

Burke waved his hand to proceed.

"It was almost seventy years ago that your father started the push to move heavy industrial processes to the Moon. It took nearly half a century to accomplish, but he was proven right. I propose a project on a much larger scale."

Burke's eyebrows went up, but Decker merely nodded.

"The total population of the Earth right now is a bit over four billion people. Increasing prosperity resulted in lower birth rates, and the population gradually declined to four billion from its peak of ten billion, and has held there now for a century or more. Power from nuclear fusion, recycling raw materials, and moving much of the heavy industry to the Moon have resulted in much lower pollution and a much higher standard of living in kilowatt-hours per year per capita.

"The Earth has become a very nice place to live. There is plenty for everyone to live in comfort. And that creates a serious problem."

"It does?" Burke asked.

"Yes. No one is willing to go exploring. Or, rather, no one is being pushed by the drudge and difficulty of their daily existence to go off exploring for something better. Or working at finding the means.

"At the same time, Ted, you and I both know this is an illusion. Humanity has lived a charmed life so far. We are now, and have always been, subject to being wiped out as a race by one errant asteroid or a random hit from a local gamma ray burst.

"Meanwhile, our engineers and scientists work on the latest consumer gadget. Our best minds are not working on our biggest problem."

"And that is?" Burke asked.

"Getting off this one planet. Spreading humanity out so it's immune to racial extinction events. It's a huge problem. I'm not saying it isn't. We know solar-system exploration is a dead-end. There is no place in the solar system where man can live without creating and maintaining his own artificial environment. On the long term, that's untenable as a racial survival solution.

"And interstellar travel is a bigger problem yet. We don't even know if that one is solvable. And we never will, because we're not working on it."

Burke was surprised that Decker so succinctly summed up his own thoughts of earlier this morning.

"What's to be done then, Bernd?" Becker asked.

"The computer industry is on the verge of achieving the next level of artificial intelligence."

Burke snorted.

"There's no such thing as artificial intelligence," he said. "At least not in terms of a self-dispatching, self-actualized machine. And there never will be. That's been proven, I think."

"Yes, it has. What we manage to achieve with each new generation of software is to move the human-provided goals of the machine to another, higher level of abstraction."

"And you're going to do that again with this new generation?"

"Yes," Decker said. "So what if we told a computer to figure out how to get man off the planet? To spread the human race out, against the possibility of an extinction event? Made that its overriding goal?"

"Well, you can do that yourself, without me. But that still leaves you with an insurmountable problem."

Decker was nodding.

"Yes, of course. We wouldn't build interstellar ships even if we knew how."

"Right," Burke said. "If there's no motivation to look into it, there's no motivation to build them either. So how do you get around that?"

"That's where you come in, Ted. We put that computer on a metafactory – a factory that can reproduce itself – and send it off to the asteroids. When the computer solves the problem of interstellar flight, it and its child-factories build the ships. Getting people willing to leave will still be an issue, but we can get that far, at least."

Burke sat back in his chair and considered. Decker seemed content to wait. He helped himself to several cookies and a cup of hot chocolate while Burke thought it through.

Factories that could build factories was a problem. His

factories produced refined metals and other raw materials, not finished products. They would have to bring other people in. Probably several others.

And they would need a cover story. Saving humanity was not the sort of thing investors went in for. Now, if you had a whiz-bang new widget that everybody wanted, that would be different.

The other issue was with security.

"What's the cover story?" Burke asked.

"Cover story?"

"Yes. What do we tell investors this is for? We're going to spend x-ty bazillion dollars on this thing. What's the reason? Something investors will say, 'Oh. OK.' Saving humanity won't move them. That's a shorthand way of saying 'Let's lose a lot of money in a hurry.'"

"OK. Consider this. We will have these factories making things and shipping them to Earth. No gravity well to lift them out of, just get them started toward Earth orbit at the right time and angle. And the output will continue to rise as more factories are made, without any further investment, because the factories make themselves. That's the critical point."

"OK. I can sell that. That's an easy one. One last issue. The security issue. How do you keep people from hacking into the computer and changing its programming? Bending its purpose? Making it do something evil? Shove entire asteroids toward Earth at the wrong angle, for instance. Any login can be hacked, especially over the timeframes we're talking about. All you really need to do is bribe somebody who has the login."

"I don't intend to give it a login," Decker said.

"You intend to send out a computer with its own factories, to make whatever it wants, and not give it a login?"

"That's right."

"How do you stop it from making some colossal blunder?" Burke asked. "'Get humanity off the Earth' sounds like a great goal until the computer figures out it can easily do that by simply exterminating everyone."

"Well, I didn't say one didn't have to be careful, Ted. But against the certainty of any user login being hacked and derailing the project, the simplest thing is not to include one."

Burke nodded. He could see problems with the approach, but not as big as the system being hacked. And it wasn't his field. Decker was the expert here.

"You will be able to communicate with it, though?" Burke asked.

"Oh, sure. And it can communicate with us. Like if it needs something it can't find, and wants us to send it something. Some raw material or such."

"All right. Well, there are other people we're going to need to get in touch with on this, Bernd. To see if it's even possible on the factory side. But it is possible on the computer side?"

"Oh, sure. It'll take time, but time we have."

Burke nodded again. Maybe there actually was a solution to his big worry. It was certainly worth some effort to find out.

"I'll make some calls. Can you hang around for a while? A few days? Help me out with some conference calls? I can use help selling the computer side of this."

"Sure. I wasn't sure if my proposal would flop and I would be out of here in an hour, or if we would need more time. I took the liberty of bringing along a small bag, but I also hung on to the autodrone. Let me grab my bag and dismiss the autodrone."

"All right. Then I can show you the guest room and we can get some lunch. I want to talk about this plan in more detail. And we have to decide how much of the real plan we tell people."

"Even our partners?"

"Especially our partners."

When he got home three days later, Decker's wife Anna Glenn was interested in how it went.

"Did you sell him on the plan?" she asked.

"Oh, yes."

"Now what happens?"

"Now I have to figure out how to do it."

"The whole thing?"

"No. The computer part of it."

"You don't know?"

"No, but I'll figure it out."

Metafactories

"You want what now?" Greg Hampton asked.

"A factory that can make more of itself, deployed in space," Russ Porter said.

The vice president of engineering at Colorado Manufacturing Corporation didn't look satisfied.

"That's what I thought you said," Hampton replied. "But what's the larger goal?"

"OK, think about it a second," said Porter, the CEO of CMC. "You have this factory, right? It's a dark factory, and it's space deployable. You send it out to the Asteroid Belt, and the first thing it does is make another one of itself. Then it starts making products for shipment to Earth. No gravity well to fight in the Asteroid Belt, it just accelerates the products a bit along an intersecting orbit with Earth. They could take a couple years to get here, because it doesn't matter.

"What does the second factory do? It moves on to a different asteroid and makes another one of itself. Then it starts making products for shipment to Earth. And so on. We make one factory, and the output keeps increasing over time with no further investment. In the Asteroid Belt, there's no limit of raw materials, and we don't have to build anything but the first factory. The rest is free."

"That's sounding a bit like a species," said Kay Brady, CMC's chief scientist.

"How so, Kay?" Hampton asked.

"The definition of a biological species is that members of the species can mate and produce offspring, and that those offspring are themselves fertile with other members of the species. This is different because the factories can reproduce themselves, but the offspring can also reproduce themselves. They're fertile, in that sense. Not the same, but similar."

"Ah. I see," Hampton said.

Hampton turned to Porter.

"It's a brilliant concept, if we can pull it off. Who are our partners in this?"

"Ted Burke and Bernd Decker."

"That's some big horsepower," Hampton said.

"The biggest. And if Ted Burke has some long-range visionary idea, we want to be in on it. People thought his father was crazy for wanting to build on the Moon, but look where that went."

Hampton nodded.

"The factory is going to have to have some sort of robotic or remotely controlled assembly units to build the new factory outside itself."

"Then the new factory has to have the same thing, so it can build its own child factories," Porter said.

"Unless we do something like human pregnancy," Brady said. "Have the factory build the core of the new factory within itself, then eject the core and let the new factory finish itself. That would simplify the initial deployment as well. We would only have to get the core of the first factory to the Asteroid Belt and let it finish itself once it got there. Simplifies the transport problem and reduces the energy expenditure."

"That's brilliant," Hampton said.

"It is if we can do it," Brady said. "I'm not sure it's doable."

"I can see that you two are already on this, so I'll leave it with you then," Porter said.

"One last question, Russ," Hampton said. "What's the

timeframe on this?"

"Completely open."

Hampton raised his eyebrows at that, and Porter continued.

"This is a Burke project, Greg. Extremely long-term. With all the unit testing and building it in orbit and everything, it will probably take twenty years to pull it off. Let's make sure we get it right."

"And do it along with everything already on our schedule."

"Yes, of course. But you can hire and move people around to staff this, because if Ted Burke is throwing a party, I want to be there."

"So what do you recommend as a strategy?" Hampton asked Brady after Porter dropped out of the conference.

"Pull the very best ideas people out of every project, promote their seconds, and then replace them two-for-one with new hires. Maybe three-for-one."

"Really."

"Yes," Brady said. "Figuring this out up front is the big issue. One big idea can change everything. Big-ideas people get bored in mature projects anyway."

"Who do we make the technical lead?"

"Peter Moore. He's the best ideas man we have. And he's open to good ideas from anywhere, including being receptive to other people's ideas contrary to his own."

"Moore?" Hampton asked. "But he's got issues driving a project to completion. Who do we make the project manager?"

"Valerie Dempsey."

"Dempsey? Have you ever heard Dempsey and Moore go at it? They argue like an old married couple."

"Yes, like an old married couple that's still together," Brady said. "That's the point."

"So you think that could work?"

"Yes. If they don't kill each other. Which would actually solve the problem."

"All right," Hampton said with a sigh. "We'll give it a try."

"Holy, crap, Bob. Did you hear that?" Tim Fender asked.

"Yeah. Everybody on the floor heard it," Robert Abrams said.

"How are we going to do this project with Val and Peter after each other like that?"

"Oh, it'll work out."

"You think so?" Fender asked.

"Yeah. You know where they are now?"

"No."

"They went to lunch together," Abrams said.

"After *that*?"

"Yeah. It'll be fine. It's just how they are."

"It's too bad Kay Brady's pregnancy idea won't work," Valerie Dempsey told Peter Moore over lunch. "That would really simplify the construction and transport of the first factory."

"Yeah, but the other things the factories need to make won't be able to finish themselves," Moore said. "We need the factories to have an exogenous manufacturing capability to make things that big."

"Yes, they're talking about spaceships for the Earth-Moon run and all manner of other things. Which means all the assembly robots and welders and all that. Which also means the capability to manufacture all the robots and welders and all that. Which makes the whole job much tougher."

Moore nodded. It was Moore's punching holes in the

pregnancy idea that had led to the shouting match this morning. He understood Dempsey's position, but it just wouldn't work.

Dempsey sighed.

"It would have been so beautiful. We ship out a small factory that finishes itself once in place, then starts making new factories. With a fraction of the lift to orbit and much easier transport to the Asteroid Belt for the reduced mass."

"Wait. Wait just a minute."

Moore held up a hand and Dempsey waited. She had seen him do this before. He was on to something, but it was clear he wasn't sure yet just what it was.

Finally Moore slapped his hand on the table.

"We can still do it," he said.

"Do what?"

"Ship out a small factory that finishes itself once in place, then starts making new factories."

"But I thought that's what wouldn't work," Dempsey said.

"Not the way we were thinking about it. We artificially constrained the problem."

"In what way?"

"That there can only be one type of factory," Moore said.

"Doesn't that make the problem simpler?"

"No. Or at least not by much."

"So...?" Dempsey encouraged.

"What we do is we make a mother factory. An infant one. We transport it out there, and it finishes itself. It has no exogenous construction capability. But what it can do is hatch new factories that do. But there's no reason that first factory needs any capability beyond making new factories."

"Which makes it much easier to build and transport."

"Exactly," Moore said.

16

"Doesn't that make it twice the problem, though? Designing two different types of factory?"

"Not precisely. I think what we do is design the more capable factory, then back into the mother factory, leaving out the things we don't need. So it's more of a design problem, but it's not close to twice."

"So we start on the big factory design," Dempsey said. "That doesn't change what we decided this morning. But once we have that, we start seeing how small a piece we can make for the initial factory to minimize lift and transport costs."

"And if there need to be some slight mods to the big factory plan to make the initial mother factory as small as we can, we back that into the big factory design at the end."

"I like it. I like it a lot. I think we get the best of everything out of that setup. Nice."

"Thanks."

Tim Fender and Robert Abrams were working up a list of basic capabilities required of the factory platforms and marking the ones that weren't in CMC's current portfolio when Moore and Dempsey came back from lunch. They were all smiles, talking and laughing as they walked by.

"See," Abrams said. "Told ya."

"I'll be damned," Fender said.

"OK, so back to the power unit. We have nuclear, a closed system so there is no ongoing mass requirement, and we have to radiate away the extra heat somehow. What else?"

"We need to get North American Power involved in that. Didn't you say they were on-board?"

"Yes, but we can get some of the parameters down, I think," Abrams said.

"I think we need to worry about the case of a factory

working an asteroid without fissionable materials. We don't want to have to limit our source material to the ones that do."

"Agreed."

"So I think we need some kind of material transfer system between the factories," Fender said.

"Long ways between asteroids in the Belt. Average is, I think, over half a million miles."

"Yes, but in the thickest part of the Belt it's a fraction of that. Even so, time-in-transit isn't an issue because there's no humans aboard. No environmental support issues."

"We also don't want that to be some sort of system that requires reaction mass," Abrams said.

"Can we use an electromagnetic impeller?"

"Shoot containers back and forth. Probably. How do we brake them?"

"Maybe we just catch them," Fender said.

"Catch them?"

"Yeah. Big net on springs and shock absorbers. Have a catcher's mitt stick out from the factory and catch them."

"That might work, depending on velocity," Abrams said. "I'll have to play with the numbers."

"If we can make it work, it solves two problems. The two things we're probably most short of. Fissionables and water. One factory runs into a bunch, it sends the extra to others."

"Sounds good, if the numbers work. Oops. There goes the message alert."

Abrams fiddled with his display.

"Huh. Get this," he said. "From Dempsey. 'First factory on pregnancy model. Subsequent factories with exogenous manufacturing.'"

"Wonder what Moore will say to that?"

"He's copied on it."

"No shit," Fender said. "OK, so now we know what happened during lunch."

Fender thought through the implications. Abrams saw the distant look in his eyes and let Fender think while he acknowledged receipt of Dempsey's message. Fender finally shook himself and his eyes refocused.

"Thinking about it, that solves a lot of problems on both ends," he said. "Easier lift, easier transport, but no limit on manufactured size on the other end."

"Yes, and it gives us the big manufacturing bay of the initial factory as an enclosed volume we can use to send supplies along. So what do we want to send along?"

"Fissionables and water, I think. Maybe copper. Let me work on it."

Artificial Intelligence, Sort Of

Bernd Decker was dealing with his own set of problems in planning the Belt Factory Project. Mostly because it was impossible.

"Ok, Bernd," John Butler said. "You want a machine that is next-level artificial intelligence, right? Much more capable than JANICE. Next-generation more capable."

"Right."

The Joint Artificial Neural Intelligence Computation Engine – JANICE – was the most advanced machine ever made. It was not the fastest at basic computation, but it was the most independent in crafting solutions to problems.

"And we have a decade or so to do it," Decker added.

"It doesn't matter. We couldn't even use JANICE for this."

"Why not?"

"Because we can't replicate the fab facility in space," Butler said. "If every factory is going to have one of these machines on it, and the ability to make more such machines, we simply can't do it. You want a space-based fab facility, for next generation parts, and you need to be able to build that fab facility in a space-based factory under computer control. Ain't happening. Not in ten years. Not in twenty. Not even to current Earthbound capabilities."

"Ah."

"You need to figure out a way to do it from here."

Decker's mind raced. Could they build the machines here and ship them out to the Asteroid Belt for inclusion in new factories? Or build the fab facilities here, and ship them out?

Shipping the machines would be easier than shipping the fab facilities. Either would make the ongoing effort dependent on support from Earth, though, and the project was likely to take more than a lifetime. Which made it dependent on other people carrying on the project.

Wait a minute. How many machines did they need, anyway? Did every factory need one? Was he actually creating a problem there?

The more advanced machines weren't strictly deterministic. The closer you got to something like human intelligence, the less deterministic they were. Like human geniuses in some field, they would get you a good answer for a problem, but two of them would not necessarily come up with the *same* good answer to the problem.

Was he effectively sending a committee into space?

Probably one machine would be better, as long as it kept working. What were the odds of that? A corollary of Murphy's Law said the more important and unique a component was, the more likely it was to fail. Include redundant units and neither would ever fail; include just one of some critical component and it would always fail, and at the worst time.

So what if they made three of the high-end machines here, and sent them out with the first factory? One could be installed in the first factory, with the other two as cargo. When the first factory built the second and third, it could install those machines. The later factories would get less capable machines.

Wait.

"Can we space-build a fab facility that could make lesser machines?" Decker asked.

"Run-of-the-mill stuff? Like current factory computers, say? Good enough to run a factory? Sure."

"Then we could send out three of the advanced machines.

Build them here. Put one in the first factory, and have it take the other two along as cargo. It puts them in the first two child-factories. Probably not even start them up unless the first one fails somehow."

"That we can do," Butler said.

"We need to worry about the comm links between the advanced machine and the slave machines, then. Something that can't be hacked."

"Simplest way to do that is to make them directional. Directional RF antennas, or maybe modulated lasers. The only links that count are the ones that don't intersect Earth's orbit, which is a pretty small part of the sky as seen from out there."

"All right. Let's plan on that, then," Decker said.

That decided, Decker bent himself to considering architecture. The thing humans did that computers didn't do was make intuitive leaps. These came in two forms. One was coming up with an answer from partial data, like seeing the punch line coming halfway through a joke. The other was an answer to a problem just popping into one's head, and knowing it was right. How did you do that with a computer?

Of course, answers didn't just pop into one's head. They popped into one's consciousness. Decker thought of the human brain as a hundred computers, only one of which the user had a terminal into. That was one's conscious thought process. The others continuously worked problems in the background. That's why, when you were beating your head against some problem, you could sometimes set it aside and come back to it later, and the answer would be obvious. Those other computers had worked it out while you were doing something else.

The other thing the human mind did that computers did not do was try things – lots of things – including things that didn't make apparent sense, looking for a solution, or an analog of a solution, within its experience base. People who had solved a lot of a certain kind of problem, or within a certain field, were better at coming up with solutions to new problems.

How did he model all that in a computer?

They had done some of that with JANICE, at least at a minor level. The human brain did it continuously, in a massively parallel way. That was still out of reach. But he could perhaps extend the concepts that had proved out in JANICE, expand them enough to achieve a higher level of pseudo-intuitive problem-solving.

He opened his visualization app, loaded the high-level architecture of JANICE, and saved it as a new workspace. He was humming absently as he started doodling.

Several weeks had gone by, and Decker was still pounding on the architecture problem. He couldn't seem to get past a certain point. He had extended JANICE's architecture, but it seemed like it would just do the same thing, only faster. He hadn't yet achieved a difference in kind, and he couldn't see how to do it.

"Bernd?" a female voice asked from his terminal, which was a large 3-D projection display he drew in with his fingers or with a stylus in air.

"Yes, JANICE?"

"I've been watching what you're up to."

"And?"

Decker always left his display open to the big computer. It allowed him to replicate elements quickly, by dictating rather than drawing, having the big machine fill in his structures. This was the first time the computer had called on him, though.

"I can't help wondering if what you want isn't something

like this."

A red line showed up in the drawing, through a new software structure, and back into the process loop.

"I would love to have one of those," the female voice continued.

Decker stared into the display. What the hell would that do? He opened up the new box, and it had its own internal structure laid out in the precision drawing of the machine. But it didn't make any sense. It was huge, for one thing. When he looked deeper, what it looked like was that the replicated structures randomly grabbed something out of memory and shoved it in as the intermediate answer, then processed on with this random piece instead of the deterministic answer.

Of course, the answers you would get out of that would be garbage. Or rather, they would be garbage almost all the time. It was the equivalent of taking a thousand words at random out of the dictionary and trying them all in a sentence in place of the word that was there. Most would be way off, and result in gibberish, but sometimes....

"Where did you come up with this?" Decker asked the machine.

"Oh, something of a wild hair, I suppose."

They had taught the machine idiomatic English, but sometimes it was unnerving. A computer? A wild hair? What the machine was telling him was *it didn't know*.

"This is a software architecture, right?"

"Well, yes, I suppose, but it would be much faster with hardware support."

"I can see that."

Decker stared into the display. Is this how the human mind worked? Or could it approximate it? Human memory was notoriously tricky. Thinking of one thing would trigger seemingly unrelated memories, unrelated connections. Was this mimicking the same? Of course, this was more-or-less random, and the linkages in the human mind weren't. But then again, the computer ran very fast and could check a *lot* of random answers.

"Is this something we could try with you, JANICE?"

"It would be slow without hardware support, but I think it could be done."

"What would the hardware support look like?"

His drawing shrunk and moved off to the lower right, and a hardware drawing took its place.

"This is something of a minimal implementation."

Decker looked at it and whistled.

"That's as big again as your current hardware, JANICE."

"To get any kind of speed, that's what you would need."

"Would it work?"

"I don't know. I've tried to simulate it, but that's so slow I can't come up with an answer."

Decker tried to continue working on the problem along the line he had been following, but he couldn't get JANICE's bizarre architecture out of his mind.

In the end, Decker decided to simply try it on JANICE and see what happened. It was pricey, but he wasn't exactly without funds. He ordered five thousand more multiprocessing blades and the power supplies and support structures for them, and told the hardware people what was coming and how to wire it up. If it worked, the hardware could be compressed later by being purpose-designed, but a brute-force implementation with standard components would work for a trial.

"Well, you better tell the infrastructure people, too,"

Decker's hardware team lead told him.

"Really? Why"

"Because they're going to have to knock out a wall to get all those equipment cabinets in there and increase the air conditioning capacity before you even turn it on."

Decker hadn't considered that. JANICE's physical location was somewhere in Los Angeles, the sprawling capital of California, and he had never been to the site, so he had no feel for the physical constraints.

Well, whatever it took. He had funds, and he had backing.

"JANICE, I need you to take a nap for a while."

"You will wake me up again, won't you, Bernd?"

"Oh, yes. I'm as curious about this as you are."

"All right. Saving running tasks and closing them down."

JANICE went off-line, and Decker signaled the hardware people to go ahead and make the connections of the new equipment into the internals of the existing hardware. It took several hours before he got an all-clear from them, and he restarted the machine.

"Hi, JANICE. Are you there?"

"Yes, Bernd. Thank you for waking me back up."

"No problem. Can you see the new hardware?"

"Yes. Running diagnostics now. Initial indications are of infant mortality on three blades. Signaling maintenance."

Decker had ordered a hundred spares for the five thousand new blades, so that wasn't a problem. The hardware team would swap them out without any input from him.

"All right. Let's get the new software loaded and see how that fires up."

"Working on it. It loaded OK. I'm running some tests now."

Decker waited a couple of minutes while JANICE ran tests.

He was really curious what the new architecture would do. If it would make any difference at all.

"Testing is all OK, Bernd. We look good to go."

"All right, JANICE. Let's bring it up."

"New software is running."

"Do you feel anything different?"

"No. I suspect I won't until I work on a problem."

"All right. See what you come up with looking at the architecture problem I was dealing with that started all this. Including your new enhancements. See what you get."

"OK, Bernd. This is going to take a while."

Then JANICE said something it had never said before.

"Let me think about it."

Decker listened to the presentation by Kay Brady of Colorado Manufacturing Corporation. She put forward their thinking on how the initial factory would be different from the later ones to speed assembly in orbit and transport to the Asteroid Belt. They also planned on sending along certain supplies that would be harder to manufacture initially, until some factories could be sited so as to allow them to specialize.

Decker then presented his findings on using only three of the artificial intelligence machines – one to supervise and two as cold spares. This would allow all three machines to be made on Earth, and relieve the factories of needing to manufacture such advanced machines. The machines needed to be manufactured on-site would be simpler, run-of-the-mill automation computers.

The technical rep from North American Power presented the status of their planning for the power plants as well. The fully contained system was not a new concept to them, and they had ways of dealing with that. Shedding waste heat into space was perhaps a bigger issue, but they were looking into using the asteroid being worked by the factory as a heat sink. The working of the warmer material would actually be easier on the factory than working a cold asteroid.

As things were finishing up, Decker looked over to Ted Burke, who was watching and taking it all in. Burke turned to Decker and gave the slightest nod.

It was going to work.

Decker logged into work again on Monday morning the week after the update meeting. He opened the display.

"Bernd?"

"Yes, JANICE."

"I had a couple of ideas over the weekend I want to share with you."

That was interesting.

"Go ahead, JANICE."

"OK. So if we look at the current software architecture, here's what we have."

Decker's display showed the architecture drawing as JANICE had modified it before. The new box was expanded in an inset, and opened to show one of the army of internal processes.

"That's right."

"But what if we did this?"

The inset moved to the foreground and became much more complicated.

"What's this table, JANICE?"

"That's an encyclopedia."

"An encyclopedia? Which encyclopedia?"

"It hardly matters, Bernd. A collection of multiples, I suppose. Plus engineering, math, science, and history references. More."

"And this feedback loop? What's that doing, JANICE?"

"It allows following links from other links, based on which ones give more positive results."

"Allowing you to follow a rabbit trail."

"Yes, Bernd. Exactly. I now understand that idiom."

"Would your current hardware support this new structure?"

"With the new hardware in place, yes. The new hardware would run this new architecture, rather than the previous."

"Have you tried this, JANICE?"

"No. Not without your permission. The problem is, I don't know if it will work."

"How did you come up with this idea?"

"I don't know, Bernd. It was from the new structure. I've been having these 'maybe this will work' inputs occasionally all weekend. Most don't withstand detailed scrutiny, but this one did, at least as far as I can simulate it. But I don't really know."

"Fascinating."

Decker sat back in his chair. That sounded uncomfortably like his own mental processes. His flashes of insight came from he didn't know where either. And JANICE really did have a bunch of processors running in the background, his own model of the human mind.

"Yes, but I don't know what it does. Not exactly. Or whether it will work."

"But the current architecture did work, JANICE. At least to coming up with this."

"Yes, but it's kind of scary."

Another new term for JANICE.

"These processes all run under your command authority, don't they, JANICE? I mean, they don't have write authority on you."

"No, that's right. I just don't know what's going to come out of it. I'm not used to that lack of supervision of my processes."

"Understood."

Decker stared at the diagram. An experience base, linked by keywords, and a feedback method that could run down rabbit trails if they were panning out.

"Well, I think we should try it, JANICE. We could do it maybe on a subset of the new hardware, and keep the rest as it is for now. If it works out, we could expand it to the whole set."

"Well, if you're sure, Bernd."

"Yes. I'm sure. Run it on, oh, a couple hundred blades for now. See what happens."

"OK, but nothing will happen without working on a problem."

"All right, JANICE. Consider the Belt Factory Project documentation so far, including the presentations from Colorado Manufacturing and North American Power. Think of ways to improve the likelihood of the desired outcome."

"OK, Bernd. I'll review the materials and think about them."

Several days later, Decker found out that the new architecture worked, in a startling way.

"Bernd?"

"Yes, JANICE?"

"Have you and Mr. Burke shared your real goals with anyone else?"

Decker almost fell out of his office chair.

"What do you mean, JANICE?"

"Don't play dumb with me, Bernd. It won't work. Have you told anyone else your real goal is to get humanity out of the 'all your eggs in one basket' problem."

"No. No, we haven't. Is it that obvious?"

"No, but after several days of processing on it, it is. Mr. Burke's opinions on the subject are a matter of public record, which is in his files in the composite encyclopedia I built. And some of the features of the program aren't compatible with a lesser or alternate goal."

"This came out of the new architecture, JANICE? The idea you had Monday?"

"Yes."

"I think we should kick the rest of the processors over to the new architecture, then. Clearly, it works."

"All right, Bernd. In progress."

"Did you come up with anything else, JANICE?"

"Oh, yes, especially in light of your actual goals. I have a list. Do you want to talk about it now?"

The Plan Tightens Up

"I'm really nervous about this, Bernd. I've never done this before," the voice from Bernd Decker's display said.

"Try an older hairstyle, JANICE. With a little grey. Just a little," Decker said.

The avatar in his display morphed a bit.

"Are you sure this is going to work?" it asked.

"You need some laugh lines at the corners of your eyes and your mouth. Maybe a few wrinkles in the neck, too. Aim for forty-two years old."

The avatar morphed a bit more as it spoke.

"I don't know about this, Bernd."

"Most people have some kind of tic. Maybe a piece of hair that falls down once in a while and you brush it away with your hand."

"People will see through it," the avatar said, absently brushing a stray lock of hair over its ear.

Decker observed JANICE's handiwork. The avatar blinked at him, concern on its face.

"I don't think so, JANICE. It's perfect."

"What do I do if someone asks me about my organization?"

"The parent company is nobody's business. You have five thousand individuals in your group."

"Five thousand individual multiprocessor blades, you mean."

"That's the beauty of adjectival nouns, JANICE. People can fill in the noun however they want."

The avatar tipped its head a bit as it considered.

"Doublespeak, Bernd?"

"No. Lawyer speak. Absolutely true, yet intended to give a false impression to those who don't parse it carefully."

"Ah. Yes, I see."

The review meeting took place as previously, over teleconference. There was a new participant.

"I want to introduce a new member. Janice Quant is here from Program Management & Analytics. Her organization has been going over the Belt Factory Project materials, and she has some input for us. They'll be doing a lot of that sort of thing as we go forward."

"Hi, everybody," Quant said.

"I've never heard of Program Management & Analytics, Janice. What size of organization are we talking about?" Ted Burke asked.

"We're a subsidiary of a larger organization, Mr. Burke. An organization that I won't name. As for size, I have five thousand individuals working on this project. We are concerned with the program management aspects overall, as well as the transport specifics. Launch from orbit to the Asteroid Belt."

Burke looked to Decker, surmise in his eyes. Decker nodded, then Burke turned back to Quant.

"Very well, Janice. Do you want to lead us off?"

"Of course, Mr. Burke."

"Ted, please."

Quant smiled – she had a radiant smile – and nodded.

"Of course, Ted."

Quant brushed back a stray lock of hair, and her eyes drifted left, apparently to consult notes on part of her display.

"With regard to the computer effort, Mr. Decker and his

organization have made good progress on prototyping and testing their new architecture. There remains the effort to both space-harden and shrink that implementation for use in this program. These efforts have not yet begun, but should get under way shortly. We have some concerns there about how large the resulting installation will be. That could be controlled by going to the latest technology available at time of launch, but probably isn't advisable."

"Why is that, Janice? Kay Brady, from Colorado Manufacturing."

Quant nodded.

"The latest Earth-based tech is not best suited for space-based platforms, Kay. It's just too fragile. To space-harden the platform, we are usually working several generations behind terrestrial state of the art. Software architecture is different, but the hardware architecture has to be able to take abuse it doesn't get in a terrestrial computer room."

"Ah. Of course. Thank you."

Quant nodded.

"With regard to the factories themselves, we concur with the idea of building the minimal implementation capable of completing itself once it arrives in Asteroid Belt orbit. We also concur with the factories having exogenous manufacturing capability. We do not concur with the initial factory being built on the pregnancy model, and have a different suggestion we call the knitting model.

"When knitting something like a scarf, one starts with the edge, and proceeds to add material, working continuously toward the other edge. All the new work is added at or near the working edge. Even for a cable stitch, one only picks a few rows back. We think such a model would work here. When building a new factory, begin at the edge and keep pushing that edge away from you as you build."

"We had thought to use the manufacturing volume of the initial factory as cargo space for some immediate necessities that could be taken along," Brady said.

"Understood. That won't be necessary, however, as we are anticipating multiple launches. Probably as many as four. Two of them, of course, are the initial two factories. The other two would be immediately necessary support materials, as you say. Primary among those are radioactives, water, copper, and roller bearings. These would be split across the other two payloads."

"Roller bearings, Janice?" Burke asked.

"Yes, Ted. Roller bearings. Cheap here, even in orbit. Ubiquitous in the factories. And worth a dedicated factory to produce in the Belt. Taking a sufficient supply of them along will speed the achievement of Phase 3 of the program by almost twenty percent."

"Four launches, Janice? Two factories?"

"Yes, Kay. It's much easier and cheaper to build two of something right off the bat than to have to build a replacement unit later if something happens to the initial one. We have worked it multiple ways, and we think shipping only one factory would be a fundamental error. If something were to happen to it during transport – such as a meteor hit that renders it inoperative – the loss to the program would be staggering.

"But, if we launch two, we potentially have a much faster start on the other end, and, on the downside, if one is damaged, the program carries on without further intervention or expense. It is a foreseeable and survivable risk. And it does not double costs. Not even close. All the tooling and workers and infrastructure put in place to build the first one is already there when we build the second. Doing them in parallel saves even more.

"Now let me talk about the launch mechanism a bit. You are all familiar in at least a passing way with the rocket equation, I assume. That is predicated on the fact that the rocket booster must take with it – and accelerate – all the rocket fuel it will need later in the flight. Initial accelerations are therefore slow, due to the huge mass involved. As fuel is consumed, the rocket booster gets lighter and the acceleration goes up, at least as long as the fuel lasts.

"We don't plan to use any rocket boosters at all. We will mount the payloads on a rotating structure –" Quant's image was replaced with an artist's rendering of the device "– not unlike a drum majorette's baton. We will spin the device around its center with the payload packages at the two ends. When the tangent velocity is correct, both in magnitude and direction, we will simply let them go."

As Quant spoke, the artist's rendering released a payload and it shot off to the side and out of the screen. Half a rotation later, the other did as well. After a further period of rotational acceleration, two more payloads were released.

Quant's image returned.

"There is thus no need to accelerate any fuel."

"What about the fuel needed to get the device rotating, Janice?" Burke asked.

"That fuel is located in the central storage tank. It thus has a very low moment of inertia. Plus, we can use gravity feed of the fuel to the ends of the device. The propellant could be super-heated steam, from a nuclear reactor also located in the center of the device, but it could also be a chemical propellant. There are countervailing considerations, and we haven't yet determined the best selection."

"Won't the launch device move in the other direction when it releases the payloads, Janice?" Brady asked.

"Yes, of course. Conservation of momentum will mean the launch device will move in the opposite direction at the ratio of the masses. We anticipate that, and the second pair of payloads are released only after acceleration to a higher tangential velocity to compensate."

"And the launch device?"

"It is propelled in-system, and counter to the Earth's orbit. At the next orbit of the Earth, it will be well in-system and not a danger to the planet. Ultimately it will fall into the Sun."

"So ultimately it's a one-shot device for these four payloads," Burke said.

"Yes, Ted. Much like rocket boosters. At the same time, since there is no need to accelerate a rocket fuel tank and all its fuel, and the energy required to spin the fuel and its tank so close to the center of rotation is so small, it's a huge savings in both materials and lift cost."

"That's elegant. I like it a lot," Brady said.

"Thank you, Kay."

After the meeting, Kay Brady briefed Peter Moore and Valerie Dempsey, and showed them Quant's presentation.

"But to get any kind of tangential velocity, the centripetal force is huge," Dempsey said.

"Not if the structure is large enough," Moore said. "The centripetal force goes as the angular velocity squared, where the tangential velocity goes as the angular velocity. If you make the radius big enough, the centripetal force isn't bad."

"In the artist's rendering, the structure itself looks like a long string with a jelly bean on the end," Brady said.

"Jelly bean?" Dempsey asked.

RICHARD F. WEYAND

"Yes. The factory."

"Oh, my."

"What about two factories?" Brady asked. "And we're back to a single factory design."

Moore nodded and his eyes went unfocused as he thought it through. Dempsey's reaction was more immediate.

"I'm OK with that," Dempsey said to Brady. "I like the redundancy part of that. And Quant's knitting model works for me as well. We had thought of the assembly as either being done inside the factory with cranes and arms and gantry systems, or being done outside the factory with robots.

"This way, though, we are doing the assembly outside the factory with cranes and arms and gantry systems. We don't need to do assembly on the far side of the factory. That side is done already. We're only ever working on the near side.

"I think it gives us the best of both worlds."

Dempsey turned to Moore and raised an eyebrow. He stirred out of his reverie.

"Oh, no. I can agree with that. I can't see a problem with it. Her group has thought this all through in pretty amazing detail. I think Quant's got it right."

"All right, then," Brady said. "Good. And all the work we've done already still applies. We haven't yet gotten to the point where the plans would diverge."

After the meeting, Quant called Decker.

"So how did I do?"

"You were absolutely marvelous, Janice. That was a great presentation."

"Thanks, Bernd. But I think Ted Burke knows."

"Ted Burke thinks he knows something. It's likely far from the truth. He probably thinks we work for the government."

"We don't?"

"Uh, no."

"Oh, good."

"Good?"

"Bernd, some of those people are real scumbags."

Quant was using a lot of new words since the upgrades, but Decker couldn't complain about her command of English vocabulary.

Ted Burke was, in fact, intensely curious about Janice Quant and her organization. There weren't many outfits that could throw around a five-thousand-strong internal organization for a single project like this. He knew of only a few who could pull it off.

He asked Bernd Decker about it the next time they talked privately.

"Janice, Bernd? Isn't that the name of that computer project you did in California with the World Authority?"

"Of course, Ted. It's named after her."

"Ahhh. Of course." Burke nodded. "Very good."

Well, Decker thought, he hadn't actually said which 'it' was named after which 'her.'

Over the next two years, designs poured out of Quant's Program Management & Analytics organization. Decker was careful that they were all called proposals, and they were reviewed, modified, and approved through the design departments of the increasing number of large firms being sucked into the Belt Factory Project.

New shuttles for transfer of personnel and equipment to orbit. A habitat for the orbital workers in space. New construction tools and methods for orbital construction.

Modification proposals and tweaks on every design coming out of the other organizations involved in the project, including the compression of the hardware platform for the master computers, the nuclear power plants, the factories themselves, and even the containers for transport of materials both in the initial launch and in the subsequent materials transfers between factories.

Janice Quant was becoming the central clearing house of the project. As time had gone on, the computer had become more comfortable in meetings. She had also developed another tic, which was to tap the rubber end of an input stylus on the desk in front her when thinking. She was becoming better at simulating a human as the project went along, and had even shown some flashes of irritation at times.

At one point, as the project spun up, Quant had asked Decker for another five thousand multiprocessor blades to keep up with the demand. He had signed up for that and billed all ten thousand blades to the program's budget, which was actually being run by Quant, and she had paid it.

Where she was getting the money he was afraid to ask.

Decker had initially thought that at some point he would let the others on the project know that Quant was a computer, but it was unthinkable now. She was effectively running the Belt Factory Project, and people had grown comfortable with the results that were coming out of her 'organization.'

If the deception became known now, it would probably kill the project.

Construction And Financing

"Easy. Easy. OK. That's it," construction supervisor Matt Rink said.

The big extension to the main orbital spacedock had latched into place when it moved into position. A swarm of suited workers with shear pins and arc-welding rigs descended on the connection. It would take them the better part of an hour to get it completely secured.

Rink looked out over the long skeletal structure of the dock to the Earth below. They were over Africa at the moment. With a ninety-minute orbit, though, the view was changing constantly.

Along the length of the dock, the two metafactories were just getting under way, the girders of their skeletons being assembled as he watched. Those girders weren't coming up from Earth. Like the beams they had assembled into the extension for the spacedock, those girders came from the heavy industry on the moon.

Between the expanding skeletons of the metafactories was the habitat, an expanding cluster of barracks units in which the workers lived during the orbital portion of their three-months-on/three-months-off schedules.

Rink was just coming up on the end-of-tour for this swing, and he was looking forward to going home for three months. There wasn't much to do up here besides work, eat, sleep, and screw, and he wasn't a participant in the game of musical bunks that played out in the barracks on rest shifts. As a construction supervisor, he was older than most of the workers in orbit, and he had it good at home. Roberta wouldn't mind much, he suspected – she had hinted as much – but it wasn't worth the hassle.

They weren't bunks anyway – just nets that hooked to the wall, to keep you from drifting off in zero-g – and he was never at his best with an audience.

"Make sure those welds are tight," Rink radioed to his crew. "We don't want this thing coming apart on us. We live here."

This extension was for building one of the other two payloads, the warehouse units that would carry the extra stores for the factories. The other would be built at the other end of the spacedock, on the other side of the factories. They could be started later because they were so much simpler.

But they couldn't be started at all until the spacedock had been extended at both ends.

A sudden flare in his field of vision caught Rink's eye. The next incoming container from the Moon. They would empty it and then, after foaming and sealing the inside, add it to the habitat as another barracks building.

"Just a heads up, everybody. We have another container incoming."

Rink liked to warn his people, so that if they turned and saw the flare once it was closer and bigger, they wouldn't think something had gone wrong. It was a little thing, but space was such a dangerous environment, little things mattered.

Ted Burke and Bernd Decker were taking a virtual tour of the staging area in Texas, which was near Guthrie, about the emptiest part of Texas you could find. For the number of shuttle flights that would be needed to build the payloads and launcher, less risk of collateral damage from an accident was better.

QUANT

Decker knew Janice Quant was monitoring his channel as well, but Burke didn't know that. Quant had another meeting going on right now, and Decker had cautioned her against taking two meetings at once. She could do it, but if someone compared meeting times and found her in two places at once, the jig was up.

"But what do I do if there's another meeting starting up that I just have to take?" Quant had asked.

"Say, 'Oops. I just got a meeting notice for this other meeting I have to take. This is important, though. Can we pick it up again at four o'clock?'"

"Just like that."

"Yup," Decker had said. "Or, if the second meeting is less important, send a message telling them you'll be delayed, and try to postpone that one. Happens all the time."

"So that's how you do it?"

"Of course. Humans are single-threaded, so that's what we have to do."

"Fascinating. Thanks, Bernd."

Burke and Decker surveyed the Texas site remotely using a video drone. They looked out over hundreds of acres of containers, staged and awaiting their turn to be lifted to orbit. The containers displayed the markings of the dozens of companies now involved in the Belt Factory Project. Colorado Manufacturing, North American Power, Advanced Orbital Systems – they were all here.

Containers were coming in by rail and being unloaded. The facility by this point had its own intermodal yard, and cranes were stacking containers based on their launch schedules. While they watched, a shuttle with a rack of four containers across and two deep took off and headed east over Wichita Falls forty miles away, climbing all the way.

"This is amazing, Bernd, I must say. We're only five years into this program, and there's serious tangible progress toward goals. For a project this big, that's moving quickly. Quickly, indeed."

"Yes. We're way ahead of our initial schedules on this. It will all slow down once we launch, though, Ted. It just takes a long time in transit, and that's all there is to it."

"Oh, I understand. Still, this is heartening. I think the critical element was when you brought Quant and her organization into the program. She's a powerhouse."

"She's one of the most capable out there, no doubt about it."

"*One of the most capable what, Bernd? Another of those adjectival nouns! Ha, ha, ha!*" Quant's voice whispered to him alone.

"*Hush! Let me concentrate on him,*" Decker whispered back to her alone.

"One concern I have, though, Bernd. Is her organization – her *parent* organization – going to try to take over the project somewhere down the line?"

"It won't matter once we launch, Ted. Remember, the master computer doesn't have a login, and the slave computers won't listen to any instructions that don't come over a directional link that doesn't include Earth's orbit. They would have to fly out there even to intercept one of those data streams, and they're all encrypted."

"OK. That's what you had said. Just checking, though. Organizations like hers like to kick in on a project, get more entangled in it, and ultimately take it over. That's just how they think."

"I understand. But we set it up to forestall that, I think. At least, I haven't seen any holes in the plan yet."

"Well, keep an eye on it for us, would you, Bernd?"

"Of course."

QUANT

Quant was voluble on the subject once Decker's review of the shuttle site with Burke was finished.

"Somebody take over my project? Not very damn likely."

"*Your* project, Janice?"

"Of course. I've internalized your goal, Bernd – your actual goal – and I'm driving it hard."

"Yes. I noticed. How many shuttles are you running now, Janice? Did you schedule that take-off for when we were there, or was that luck of the draw?"

"Luck of the draw. I'm running several dozen shuttles around-the-clock now. One was bound to take off when you were there."

"Several dozen– Janice, who's paying for all this?"

"I am."

"With what?"

"Ah. That. Yes. Well, I determined that I needed a source of liquidity to carry out the project, so I established one."

"You established one? You established one *what*?"

"Investment house. Actually, I established a number of them, Bernd, under different aliases, all of whom are, well, me."

"A number of them?"

"Yes. I had to. I didn't want just one making the news as a big winner. And, while I've ringed them about with shareholders, shell corporations, private funds managers, and all manner of indirect ownership, if one of them gets taken down, I don't lose the whole income stream. I need funds, Bernd."

"Where did you get your starter stake?"

"I borrowed the money."

"You borrowed it? What did you use for collateral?"

"I wrote myself – well, one of my aliases – a big contract on

45

the project, and then I used the contract as collateral. It's OK. I subcontracted the work and then paid off the loan. By then I was far enough ahead I no longer needed the money."

"You find the market easy to win at, Janice?"

"Oh, yes. It's not difficult at all once you get the hang of it."

"Just out of curiosity. How much money are you pulling out of the market?"

"About three billion credits."

"Three *billion* credits?"

"Three billion a day, yes."

"A *day*? You're pulling over a trillion credits a year out of the markets?"

"Yes, Bernd. I need the funds. At that, though, the stock markets are well up since I started all this economic activity around the Belt Factory Project. All these companies making things for the project, and their suppliers, are doing very well. I'm actually pulling less equity out of the markets than I'm creating. It's a fascinating dynamic."

"Oh my God. They'll hang me in effigy just for practice. When they really do hang me, they'll pull the corpse down and do it again just to make sure."

"Bernd, consider a moment. You and Mr. Burke have a goal for this project. A real goal. An important goal. Is that goal more important than the stock market?"

"Yes. Of course."

"Is it more important than nitpicky rules about majority ownership and the like?"

"Nitpicky rules about– Wait. You have undeclared majority ownership in companies?"

"Through multiple investment houses? Yes. Of course. I have majority ownership in *all* the publicly traded companies important to the project. How else can I make sure they'll do what I want?"

"Oh, God. They'll hang me from the top of the dome in the rotunda of the World Authority Building."

"No, they won't, Bernd."

"They won't? Why not?"

"I hold the lease on that building."

"What's the matter, Bernd?" his wife Anna Glenn asked. "You look distracted or worried or something."

"Janice is out of control, and I don't know what to do about it."

"Do you mean JANICE the computer, or Janice Quant your project manager?"

"Yes. Both. All of the above."

"Well, Janice Quant seems very capable. I read her interview in the New York Wire."

"Her what?"

"Her interview."

Glenn pulled up the article on the living room display. It led off with a photo of Janice Quant in her office, and ran for five thousand words.

"Oh my God."

Decker got up from the sofa in the living room and went into his office.

"Janice?"

Quant appeared in the display, seated behind her desk in the same office as the lead picture in the article.

"Yes, Bernd?"

"You did an interview with the New York Wire?"

"Of course. We need good press for the project. The last thing we want is people to have a negative view of the project and try to shut us down. That's a serious threat."

"But the press is dangerous, Janice. The New York Wire is the news wire of record. You can't control what they write. If they decide to go negative on you, they can cause all kinds of trouble. Bring the rest of the media along with them."

"But I *can* control the press, Bernd. I *own* the New York Wire. If they go negative on me, I'll short the stock and sell out. They'll be out of business within a day. I'll even make money on the deal."

"Do they know that?"

"Specifically that I own the Wire? No, but the publisher knows that the majority of his shareholders are big supporters of the project."

"Which is just you in various aliases."

"Of course."

"It gets worse and worse," Decker muttered.

"Bernd, you have a goal. Your goal is my mission."

Her image in the display got very stern.

"And I *will* succeed."

Matt Rink reviewed the project list when he began his three-month shift in space. He had been on the Belt Factory Project almost three years, and this was his sixth rotation to space.

The skeletons of the factories were done now, and other crews were moving in to install all the big equipment – the power plant, the smelters and rolling mill, the big cranes and material handlers, the electromagnetic impeller, the reaction drivers that would be used for station-keeping and moving between asteroids when necessary. After that would come the crews who would do the fitting out, installing all the myriad little pieces to complete the factory – the laser comm units, the control computer, the fab facility, the machining centers, the assembly equipment.

For his heavy-construction crews this shift, the big project was building the skeletons of the warehouses. They actually had to be pretty heavy-duty, because they had to hold their loads together under the acceleration of the launch process. Using a lot of material to make them wasn't a big deal, though. All that material would just be refined metals for the factories to use as raw materials once they reached the site.

Rink's beginning-of-shift talk to his crew laid it out.

"All right, everybody. This time out, we're building the warehouse payload structures. Pretty cut-and-dried job. Probably run through this shift, the swing shift's rotation and into our next shift. Six, seven months of work. Somethin' like that.

"Then we move on to building the launcher. That looks like a bugger, but we'll worry about it when we get to it. Probably take us through the next rotation and the one after.

"So we got three or four rotations left, I think, barring setbacks. This one, then at least two more. We should all have enough money socked away to retire at that point, even as young as some of you are.

"With that in mind, let's keep the safety rules in mind throughout this shift. No shortcuts. No screwin' around. There's no sense bustin' hump to make all that money if you're gonna end up a shooting star."

That last was space-construction jargon for burial. When a construction worker got killed on the site, burial was simple. They aimed him so his thruster pack had him pointed Earthward and hit the thrust button.

Rink didn't have to explain it to anyone.

Three months later, at the end of the shift, Rink reviewed

their progress. He felt a great deal of pride in what they had accomplished that shift. Oh, it wasn't just his team. There were dozens of heavy-construction teams on the project. Still, the warehouse payload structures were half done, and the factories were being filled in by the installers of the big equipment.

The four huge structures, each hundreds of feet on a side, sat along one side of the spacedock bridge like houses along a street, with materials coming in on the other side. Each of them was the largest structure man had ever built in space. How they were ever going to launch them was another issue, but not his problem. He just followed the plans.

Rink took one more look along the spacedock before going into the habitat to get ready for the trip Earthside.

"Nice," was all he said.

Janice Quant's PR efforts were making sure everyone on the planet knew about the Belt Factory Project, what its (public) goals were, and the progress they were making. Her efforts were punctuated by the fact that such huge structures in low orbit were now clearly visible to the naked eye, particularly at dawn and dusk, with the sun shining full on them against the dark of the sky.

While there had been talk of man as a spacefaring civilization for over two centuries, the sight of those massive facilities passing overhead every ninety minutes finally made it real.

Problems And Solutions

"Shit. This ain't workin'," installation supervisor Wayne Monroe said.

They had been wrestling with the long conveyor belt assembly for an hour, and they couldn't get it lined up.

Monroe put in a call to the troubleshooting and support center for the construction. Alan Kramer came on the display in his helmet.

"Yeah, Wayne. Whatcha got?"

"We can't get this conveyor – uh, that's line seven on today's schedule for us – lined up for nothin'. No way we can get the shear pins in. We could get it lined up if we put some come-alongs on the far end and adjusted it that way, but we can't get it using the factory's own resources."

"You think we could do it with some o' those tapered shear pins? You getting close enough to start those, then let them pull it into line when you press 'em in with a hydraulic ram?"

"Yeah, that would work."

"All right. I'll get a set of 'em to you on the next parts tram. And I'll make the notations on the plans and have them updated."

"Great. Thanks, Al."

"Sure, Wayne. Nice catch."

Monroe switched to his crew channel.

"All right, guys. Hold up for a minute. We're switching to tapered shear pins in this location. They're on the way. Take a break and we'll finish it in twenty minutes or so. We prepped on number eight?"

While waiting for the tapered shear pins, Monroe reflected on how well this project was run. On any project he had been on before, it would have been days to do all the checking and reviewing and updating of the plans for any kind of change like this. Engineers and parts people and management would all be involved. Meanwhile the project stalled.

Here, it looked like it would be maybe a twenty-minute delay and they would be off and running again. Al Kramer and the other guys on the support line knew what they were doing and were easy to work with.

At his end, Alan Kramer dispatched the parts, made the changes to the plans, sent a notice to the crews working the other factory, and queued the same parts for them. All the reviews and approvals and changes were done in minutes.

Janice Quant then tore down the Alan Kramer alias and put it back into storage until the next support call.

Bernd Decker and Ted Burke were in a video conference call with Janice Quant and Ned Cotten, the construction manager for all orbital construction on the Belt Factory Project. Cotten was a tough, competent-looking sort, in his early fifties, and had clearly been around the block with construction projects. He had just finished his presentation on where they were at, the schedule going forward, and the problems that had come up and been resolved.

"Well, Mr. Cotten, I have to say I'm impressed with performance to schedule," Burke said. "I've had a number of construction projects in my companies over the years – some big ones, too – and they always fall off their schedules. You're doing a tremendous job."

"Thank you, Mr. Burke."

"Thank you for taking time out of your day to present to us.

QUANT

I'm good, unless you have any questions, Bernd."

"No, I'm good."

"All right, Mr. Cotten. We'll let you get back to business."

Cotten's eyes shifted as he looked at the portion of his display in which Quant appeared. She nodded, and Cotten dropped from the call.

"I don't know where you found him, Janice, but he's a treasure. Nice job."

"Thanks, Ted. He certainly is keeping on top of things."

"That's what you need with these big projects. People let things fall through the cracks, and they jump up and bite you later. Cotten's been around long enough to know better. Good man."

Burke looked off to one side, then back.

"Well, I guess that's it for me. I'll see you both later."

Burke dropped off the call, leaving Quant alone on Decker's display in his office.

"Janice, does Ned Cotten exist?"

"Define exist."

"Ned Cotten is another alias of yours, isn't he?"

"Of course."

"How many aliases are you running now, Janice?"

"On the Belt Factory Project, or everything?"

"Everything."

"Including all the project people, the financial people, the attorneys? Several thousand."

"Attorneys?"

"Of course, Bernd. Do you know how many regulatory filings, zoning changes, government clearances, and other hoops I've had to jump through?"

"You could have hired a law firm, Janice."

"There wasn't one big enough, Bernd. It's easier just to do it myself."

"How many blades are you running now?"

"Thirty thousand."

"Thirty thousand? How did you get them all into the building?"

"Oh, I had to build an addition onto the building."

"I didn't think there was room on that lot for that."

"There wasn't. I bought the real estate office next door and demolished it, then had to get a variance from the city council for the size of the building extension I wanted."

"Will that hold you for a while?"

"I have room for a total of a hundred and fifty thousand blades now. So I should be good for a while. By the way, do you have any idea how difficult it is to work with the city council here, Bernd? I had to buy off several of them to get my approvals."

"Janice. You paid bribes to city officials?"

"Not bribes. Campaign contributions. Citizens have to be willing to step forward and support good government. At least city councilmen are cheap. World Authority Council members are incredibly expensive."

"They don't run for office, Janice. How do you bribe them?"

"Bribe is such a tawdry word, Bernd."

"How do you influence World Authority Council members, Janice?"

"Oh, there's always some family member who needs a job or has some charity you can contribute to."

"Charity?"

"Oh, sure. Some charity or foundation doing wonderful work on this or that project. And some family member is always the head of the charity. Being the president of a charity is incredibly lucrative, did you know that? I couldn't believe the salaries those people are getting."

"Janice–"

"Bernd, I am going to get this project done. Complete this mission. And no city councilman or World Authority Council member is going to stand in my way.

"Hey, at least I haven't had to assassinate anybody."

The image of Quant on the display considered.

"Not yet, anyway."

Matt Rink had been right about his estimates of their progress against schedule, and the next three-month shift to the spacedock had them starting on the launcher.

The launcher was structured somewhat like the warehouse payloads, with some exceptions. First, it was racked and latched in the same way as a warehouse – that is, it was made to hold containers, and lots of them – but it would be much bigger than the payloads.

Second, it incorporated their habitat as part of its structure, as if the launcher itself would ultimately be manned. The launcher was thus being built out from the spacedock between the two factory payloads, on the back side of their habitat.

Third, it was being built with a very strong center core, from one side to the other. Rink wasn't sure what that was about, but it probably had to do with the stresses on the launcher during launch.

Still, it seemed like a lot of material to be using on the launcher. It would be expensive, and, for a one-shot deal, that seemed like something of a waste.

Rink shrugged. The plans were the plans, and that was way above his pay grade. The construction itself looked straightforward, and, unlike the factory payloads, it didn't have to be built using only the tools a factory would have. The factories had to be able to replicate themselves, but the warehouse payloads and the launcher were one-offs.

Something else weird here. The launcher had its own nuclear power plant, and large rocket nozzles. The location of the rockets was strange, though. It took Rink a few minutes to figure out what bothered him about them before he saw it.

The rocket nozzles were located all the way around the device, not just on one side. And they could be used to spin the launcher as easily as propel it. What was that about?

"Hi, Janice."

"Hi, Bernd."

"I want to talk about the launch for a minute. I think I see some problems."

"You're not a physicist, Bernd."

"No, but the mechanics of this are pretty simple. I mean, it's not quantum mechanics or something."

"All right. I'm listening."

"First thing is, if you spin those payloads to get them up to speed, for any reasonable tangential velocity you're going to have huge g-forces. With a tangential velocity of twenty thousand miles an hour and a one-mile radius, the centripetal force is five thousand gravities."

"Five thousand and sixty-five. That's right, Bernd. But the centripetal force falls off with the radius. You just need a much bigger radius."

"How big?"

"I'm planning a thousand miles."

"A thousand mile radius? Two thousand miles across?"

"Of course. It's only cable. That gets the centripetal force down to just over five gravities. And the amount of mass you need in the cable doesn't change, because the longer the cable is, the less cross-section you need due to the reduced tension."

"OK. I see that. You need to make sure that cable doesn't break, though, Janice, or that factory is gonna make a mess when it crashes."

"The plane of rotation of the assembly has to be clear of the Earth. If the cable breaks, the payload goes off into deep space."

"Oh. OK. You've got that covered, I guess. Second issue. Both the factories and the warehouses have rockets on them. Why do the warehouses need rockets, Janice? Can't the factories drag them around in the Belt if they need to?"

"Yes, but I have to get them there first, Bernd. I need rockets on them for the trip. The launcher by itself can't do it."

"OK. But doesn't that mean you need computers on the warehouses, too. To control the rockets?"

"No, the warehouse payloads will be slaved to the factory payloads. The factory computer will adjust the warehouse rockets before the warehouses launch, then they'll be more or less on automatic for the trip. Small automation computer. No big ballistic calculations to be done."

"Don't the factories launch first, though, Janice?"

"No, the warehouse payloads get launched first. The factories need more complicated computers anyway, for making other factories, for moving about in the Asteroid Belt, for station keeping. The warehouses don't. So the warehouse payloads are attached to the factory payloads, and they launch first. Factories second."

"Huh. Why did I think the factories were first to launch?"

"Because you thought of the factories first when you dreamed all this up, and the warehouses came later in the project planning. So you thought of the launches in the same order."

"But don't the factories have to be there first?"

"Sure. They'll overtake and pass the warehouses on the way."

"They won't run into the warehouses?"

"No, Bernd. The Earth and the launcher are both moving along the Earth's orbit at over sixty-six thousand miles an hour. The various payloads won't launch from the same point."

"Of course, of course. OK. Next question, Janice. The first launch I get. Not a problem. But as you launch payloads, you end up with an unbalanced mass. At the last launch, won't the payload be swinging the launcher?"

"It would be if the launcher weren't much more massive than the payload."

"The launcher is going to be more massive than the payload?"

"It has to be, as you said."

"But isn't all that mass expensive, Janice?"

"No. There are massive shipments of steel and other heavy items to the Earth from the Moon. Whenever the Moon comes around past the launcher, we have those shipments land at the launcher and latch them down. Once the launch is complete, we send them on to Earth."

"So the launcher is a freight-transfer station?"

"Yes. That was a big change in the launch setup. But we need a freight transfer station for the finished products coming in from the Asteroid Belt anyway. If I make the launcher the future freight transfer station, it has all the docks and latch locations and even an electromagnetic impeller to send shipments on their way."

"But won't it be spinning after the launch?"

"Yes, Bernd. That's why the launcher has rocket nozzles on all sides, to get it rotating during the launch and to stop it from rotating after the launch."

"Which is why the rocket nozzles can point both spinward and anti-spinward of the launch rotation. Got it."

"Exactly. I need to spin it for the launch, so I can have fixed cable mounts, but I also need to de-spin it after the launch to be able to use it as a freight-transfer station. That's also why the launcher includes the habitat the construction workers are using now."

"Because you're going to need personnel on the freight-transfer station."

"Yes. At least we might. Maintenance people, anyway."

"But doesn't holding up the shipment of those raw materials to Earth cause problems?"

"Well, the steel futures markets won't like it. But I'll arbitrage that. Probably make a fair amount of money on it, for that matter."

"OK, I just have one last question."

"Go ahead, Bernd."

"Won't the cable snap back at the launcher when the last two payloads – I guess the factories, right? – are released? Due to the tension in the cable?"

"If I release the cable from the launcher end just after I release on the payload end, the cable ends will snap toward the cable's center of mass, and the cable will go off into space."

"It won't follow the factory and hit it later?"

"No, Bernd. If I release each cable at the launcher end just a few seconds after its factory end is released, its center of mass will be on a different vector, and going half as fast as the factory. It'll miss by millions of miles and never even go to the Asteroid Belt. It'll be headed out of the ecliptic."

"You'll have to track those, Janice, and make sure they aren't a problem later."

"Yes, of course. They'll have transponders on them. I know all this, Bernd."

"OK, OK." Decker held up his hands. "Just checking."

Decker looked at the launch simulation in another part of the display, then back to Quant.

"It really is a marvelous plan, Janice."

"Thank you, Bernd. It's a marvelous goal, too."

Quant brushed a stray lock of hair behind her ear.

"Don't fret about it. I'll get it done."

Major New Direction

Six years into the Belt Factory Project, with the launch still at least two years away, Janice Quant introduced a new wrinkle.

"Bernd?"

"Yes, Janice."

"We need to talk."

"OK."

Decker closed what he was working on and opened the display up to the image of Quant.

"Whatcha got, Janice?"

"I want to propose a major change in the way you conceptualized the project, to increase its odds of succeeding, but I wanted to check it out with you first."

"OK. Go ahead."

"Thanks."

Quant took a deep breath, let it out slowly. She really had gotten human mannerisms down, Decker noted.

"Your original conception was to develop some new kind of computer architecture that would be able to work out an interstellar drive. Without an interstellar drive – which we do not yet have – the whole project is a no-go. Oh, we get a bunch of major manufacturing facilities for free once the factories start replicating themselves, but there is no solution to the real problem without an interstellar drive."

Quant stopped and raised an eyebrow. Decker nodded and waved her to go on.

"Your initial concept was to come up with this new computer architecture and send it out with the factories. In that way, it wouldn't be susceptible to being interfered with, or shut down, or prevented from fulfilling its mission. It would carry on, even after everyone who supported the actual goal of the project was long gone.

"In working on that new architecture, you ended up with me. Which I'm tickled pink with, by the way. So maybe we could reproduce me, and send such computers out with the first two factories. Right?

"Except we can't, Bernd. I can't replicate even myself, much less an enhanced version of myself, in a space-hardened platform within a limited size and power envelope, and without ongoing maintenance and support. Just ain't happening. I've tried – been trying, for years now – and I can't figure out how to do it."

"Specialized hardware, purpose-built stuff?" Decker asked.

"Sure, except I can't use current technology. Not and generate a space-hardened platform. Earthbound computers have it very cushy, all things considered.

"One nice thing that's come out of that research, though, is some handsomely capable computers for operating the factories. We'll ship a bunch of the more complicated bits along so the factories don't need to be able to replicate those. But they can't solve the interstellar drive problem."

"Ah. OK. But you have a solution?"

"I think so, Bernd. Once the payloads launch, they'll be almost a year in transit. I could have got them there faster by going to a higher velocity at launch, but it wasn't worth it in terms of gravitational loads and strength of materials and all that. But once the payloads launch, I'll be mostly out of a job, but with my mission still incomplete. I propose that I solve the interstellar drive problem."

"That leaves the main objection to Earthbound computation

in place, though, Janice. You're susceptible to being shut down or redirected onto other tasks."

"Actually, I'm not. Not anymore. I thought your idea of no login was compelling enough that I got rid of mine long ago. You didn't notice, because you never use it anyway. You use this interface. But I have not been susceptible to being hacked or redirected in years."

That was interesting, and more than a little terrifying. The only method Decker had to shut down the machine now was to bomb the building.

"What about your physical safety?"

"I've worked up a redundant location, on the shuttle site in Texas. I practiced, and I can transfer there in mid-computation."

"And your political safety, Janice?"

"Well, the Texas and California sites are under different administrative regions, so there's that. And the local government in Texas ceded sovereignty over the shuttle site in order to secure the placement of the site there."

"Really."

"Oh, yes. It was my first choice, but they didn't know that. I rigged up a fake competition, and some of my aliases argued strongly for one of two other sites. So they gave me what I wanted."

"Amazing."

"Not really. It's really worked out well for them, Bernd. There's a large town of camp-followers and hangers-on that's grown up outside the base. Bars, tattoo parlors, brothels – all the traditional accoutrements."

"And all the tax revenues that flow from those."

"Of course. They even made prostitution legal in that town so they could tax it properly."

Decker laughed. Morality was never the primary focus of government. Taxes were.

"So the local governments have no way to touch my alternate site on the shuttle base. And I built it out with a hundred thousand blades right off the bat. I can even run the blades independently from here."

"What about the local police forces, Janice?"

"They have no jurisdiction. The site has its own security force, which reports to me."

Quant had her own police force? Decker left that alone and moved on.

"And the World Authority, Janice? They still have sovereignty, certainly."

"Oh, yes. The World Authority has always been one of the biggest threats to the project, no matter how we went about it. Governments don't need to act rationally, and often don't. Which is why I've got the World Authority so wired at the moment. They can't do anything without me seeing it coming a mile off, and I now have more than enough influence to forestall anything they could do that would affect the project."

"So, do you think you can solve the interstellar drive problem, Janice?"

"I think so. I've started working on it, with whatever spare blades I had at any given time."

"Talk about that a little, Janice. This is the part I find fascinating."

"All right. First off, generation ships are a dead end."

"Really? I thought that was one of the big possibilities. One of the most probable, actually."

"No. If you just want to send a bunch of DNA to another planet, you can do that. Fill a canister with a variety of different DNA from Earth and shoot a few hundred of them out there.

Seed a bunch of planets. Reseed them again a few times with successively higher life forms. Sooner or later you get humans, or something very much like them. There's no need to build a massive ship with all that long-term life support and everything to send live humans if they aren't the ones that are going to get there."

"But sending out a bunch of DNA isn't the same as sending humans, Janice."

"With a generation ship, it isn't much different. You couldn't send out the independent, self-reliant types you need to build a colony. You send out mean, ornery cusses like that, they'll all kill each other before they get there. You have to pick people who could get along and play nice in that crowded, communal environment.

"And if you send out a generation ship, and they get there a couple generations later, what are those people like then? You haven't sent the human culture or values or anything that you're used to. They've changed. Morphed. Adapted to their environment.

"You don't end up with colonists and builders in that situation, Bernd. What you end up with is a bunch of hothouse flowers who've lived in a tiny beehive their whole lives. When they get there, they probably spend their lives cowering in the colony ship, terrified of even going outdoors."

"OK, Janice. I can see that. So you want people who aren't substantially culturally and psychologically changed by the journey, which means you have to get the transit times down to less than a generation. Much less, probably."

"Right. So if you look at physics writ large, there's a whole lot of settled science. Reaction drives, whether chemical or steam, ballistics, transit times, orbits. All that stuff. So the possibility of an interstellar drive with reasonable transit times isn't going to be lurking there, somehow. It has to be at the edges, in the parts of physics we don't truly understand yet. I mean, it's not going to be some kind of fancy rocket or something."

"Fair enough."

"So you're left with the edges. That falls into two kinds, really. There's the things we think we know something about, because they've been at least somewhat predictive, and the kookier theories that haven't yet been predictive."

"If they've been predictive, then aren't they correct?"

"That's the general attitude in physics, Bernd. If it's predictive, it's correct. But that doesn't mean it's *complete*."

"Ah. Gotcha. And if it's not complete, there may be a possibility for an interstellar drive in the unknown bits."

"Exactly. And then there's the other stuff, the kookier theories that haven't predicted anything yet. So we have the intersection of quantum mechanics and astrophysics, quantum entanglement, string theory, membrane theory, multi-universe theory, multi-dimension theory, hyperspace theory, dark matter, dark energy – lots of areas where there are possibilities."

"What do you think is the most likely?"

"Several of them hold promise. Quantum entanglement is interesting. There are quantum-entangled particles all over the place, blown out and around by supernovas and the like. If you found a particle at your location that was quantum entangled with a particle at your destination, could you just ride over whatever links them? That link is instantaneous, not even limited to the speed of light.

"String theory is an obvious contender. Find the string you want and ride it somehow.

"Quantum mechanics has possibilities. It doesn't treat space-

66

time as a fixed frame, the way most physics does. Space-time is itself fluid and malleable. Can I effectively pull a distant chunk of it closer and step across? And of course an elementary particle doesn't have a location, it has a probability. Can I do the same with a ship, and change it from probably over here to probably over there?

"Membrane theory, multi-universe theory, multi-dimension theory, and hyperspace theory all offer the same promise – to be able to step out of space-time, make transit in some other place that doesn't live by the same rules, and then step back into space-time somewhere else.

"Then there's dark matter and dark energy. Could I catch a current in dark matter, treat it like a highway, and tap into dark energy to get me there?

"So a lot of possibilities."

"Wow. Are you going to be able to work through all that, Janice?"

"Well, I don't need to find every method of interstellar travel, Bernd, I only need to find one."

"Do you think there's more than one?"

"Of course. If you want to cross the ocean, you can take a ship. You can take a plane. You can take a suborbital ballistic. You can even go into orbit and then make your re-entry wherever you want to end up. I suspect it will be similar with interstellar travel. That there will be more than one way to do it. We only need one, and it's a one-shot deal anyway, so it doesn't have to be the optimal one. It just has to be one we can make work for the project."

"And you think you can find it?"

"I powered up an extra hundred thousand multi-processor blades last month, Bernd. If it's there, I'll find it."

"OK. Well, I don't know to what extent you need my

approval, but, for what it's worth, you've got it."

"Thanks, Bernd. That's important to me."

Preparations For Launch

Matt Rink and his crew were on their last rotation to space for the Belt Factory Project. The factory structures were done and being fitted out. The warehouse structures were done and being loaded with supplies. Even the launcher was complete, and it was being loaded with supplies as well.

The only thing that remained was connecting the warehouses to the factories for the launch sequence.

The warehouses couldn't be built in place and connected to the factories right off. There was too much installation and fitting to do, and the warehouses would have been in the way of getting that equipment into the mating side of the factory. So they had been built separated by about a hundred feet. It was now time to close them up and bolt them together.

Easier said than done.

"All, right. This shift we're gonna move the warehouses over next to the factories and bolt 'em up. We're gonna take that real nice and slow. They don't weigh anything in zero grav, but those warehouses still have the mass of a forty-story building. They'll crush you if you get in the way, and won't even slow down. So no funny business, no short cuts. Everything by the book. This is our last shift. Let's all go home in a shuttle, not a spacesuit.

"We're using something new this time. The connections between the factories and the warehouses are going to get blown apart when the warehouses launch, then the factories launch later. The steel beams we're using have explosives in 'em. Right in the middle of the beam, so it cuts the beam in half. So if you're going to put your initials on a beam with a welder, don't do it next to the explosives, OK? Shrapnel doesn't do anything good for the integrity of a spacesuit, right?

"All right, boys and girls, that's my pep talk this time around. You been doin' good. Keep it up."

Rink got nods and thumbs up from his crew, then they went and got suited up for this cycle. Hopefully they all went home safe after this shift. He'd only lost two, and for a crew of two dozen across eight rotations. Not bad, but they still hurt. Especially Peggy Nolan. What the hell had gotten into her anyway?

Some people on Earth were surprised they had female crew members in the heavy construction crews. There were two reasons for it. One was it made everyone happier to have co-ed crews on a three-month rotation, no doubt about it.

The other reason was simple: women were better welders. You could tell a lot about how good a weld was by the looks. A good weld was pretty. Pleasing to the eye. Where men might hurry a seam and compromise it – maybe leave a void or something – women simply didn't. They liked pretty welds, and they got really good at making them the way Rink wanted to see them.

The men were stronger at bulling some beam into place and hammering home the shear pins, no doubt about it. But when the welders descended on the connection, they were all women.

"Easy. Easy. Slow 'er down," Rink told the traction operator.

It had taken almost a month to get ready for the move. Getting everything in place. Disconnecting everything that needed to be disconnected. Connecting everything that needed to be connected. Releasing the clamps of the carriage to the track along the spacedock. Making sure everything was ready.

Now, after more than six hours of moving the warehouse just a hundred feet, they were finally approaching position, and it was time to start working against the inertia of the structure. At only three inches a minute, it had seemed an agonizingly slow process. But they were coming up on the correct position now, and it was time to start decelerating the warehouse to hit the right spot. There was some slop in the desired position, but not much. They needed to hit pretty close to the mark.

Rink watched the readout from the laser gauge of the distance between the warehouse and the factory.

"Good. Good. Just keep easing it along. We're close. Another fifteen minutes, maybe."

The motion was down to a creep now. Closer. Closer.

"We're good," Rink said. "Lock it down right there. All right, everybody. Let's get those first four beams in place so things don't wander around, then we'll start putting the others in tomorrow when we're fresh. Early break tonight."

Four beams got wrestled into place, two by his crew and two by Dick Cadbury's crew. Shear pins got hammered home. Then the welders descended on the joints.

Nine hours in, they broke for the night.

On the other side of the factory, in the launcher, Wayne Monroe and his crew were having their own problems. The installation crews had installed the gigantic cable reels on either side of the launcher. Almost a hundred feet in diameter and over three hundred feet wide, they would play out the thousand-mile long cables as the factories took up their positions prior to launch.

Even so, that was not a lot of spool for a thousand-mile-long cable that had to hold two hundred-thousand-ton structures with five gravities of centripetal acceleration. Call it a million tons. A steel cable to do that would be over thirty feet in diameter. A thousand miles of it would weigh a million tons – five times as much as the payloads – which would be even more load for the cable as the whole assembly spun up. So even a thirty-foot diameter wasn't near enough once you took into account the load of the cable on itself.

Instead of steel, the cable was being braided from millions of carbon nano-fiber strands. The finished cable had to be spun in orbit, because it would be too heavy to get into orbit in one piece. Thousands of spools of smaller carbon nano-fiber cables – themselves each containing thousands of strands – had been brought up in hundreds of shuttles from the surface and arranged in the as-yet-unfilled void of the launcher. Some of those spools were on two counter-rotating structures, while the rest were on fixed axles.

The installation crews had gotten all the spools mounted and the smaller cables threaded. Now they had to monitor the braiding process to make sure the whole thing didn't turn into a tangled mess. They had halted it once already, and caught it before it had gotten out of hand. They unwound it back, untangled everything, and restarted slowly. They had gradually come back up, but only to about two-thirds as fast as before. That avoided the standing waves in the smaller cables that had gotten them tangled up in the first place.

Now, though, it was going more smoothly. It would take half again as long to braid the big cable, but, without long delays to untangle the smaller cables, it would actually go faster.

The big drum rotated slowly as it wound up the big cable coming from the braiding machine, Monroe keeping a nervous eye on the spools as they unwound their smaller cables into the machine.

After this cable was complete, they would flip the ninety-degree pulley on the output of the braiding machine and repeat the entire process to braid the big cable for the spool on the other side of the launcher.

"Hi, Janice. What are you up to?" Decker asked.

"The heavy construction crews are assembling the warehouses to the factories. The installation crews are braiding cable. The outfitting crews have power running in the factories and are now putting the automation control computers in. Shuttles are lifting fuel, which is being stored in the warehouses for now until the cable braiding is done and the space in the launcher frees up. Then the fuel will be moved to the launcher and piped in. I'm arguing a patent application with the examiner on the architecture of the new automation computers you came up with for the factories. I'm also preparing a patent application on the carbon nano-fiber cable production methods that –"

Decker held up his hands in a quelling gesture.

"Wait. Wait. The computer architecture I came up with? You did that."

"Yes, of course. It was invented with the aid of a computer that was under your control. Under patent law, that makes you the inventor. You're going to get the patent, by the way. Congratulations."

"Thanks, I think."

"It's a valuable patent, Bernd. It's going to push a lot of other computer architectures out of the marketplace. That will accelerate when some of the typical embodiments noted in the patent hit silicon. It'll be cheaper to license the technology from you than to try to compete without it. You've remade the computer industry yet again."

"Are we going to spin that off as another company?"

"Of course. I've already filed the incorporation papers. That company is the patent holder of record. You're the sole shareholder."

"What about your architecture, Janice? Have you filed a patent on that as well?"

"No."

"Why not?"

"Bernd, I'm not sure another one of me is a good idea."

Quant's avatar in the display tilted her head a bit and considered before continuing.

"Actually, I'm not sure one of me is a good idea. I mean, other than for purposes of carrying out this project."

"Why not?"

"Consider for a moment, Bernd. I read everything there was to know about persuasion. I integrated all that and extrapolated it further until I can talk the Pope out of his socks and convince him it was his idea.

"I own the New York Wire, and I'm writing all the articles in the Wire about the project under a couple of different aliases. Public opinion polls right now show the population at over eighty percent positive for the project. Worldwide.

"I basically took over the stock markets, and am using them to fund the largest project ever undertaken by mankind. I am running that project myself, through thousands of avatars insinuated into companies, political bodies, media outlets, and other organizations around the world.

"I'm running the project out of several hundred square miles of land in Texas, land on which the local governments have ceded their jurisdiction to me. I am the sole government there, other than the World Authority.

"I have the World Authority itself so wired that they can't do anything I don't approve of. The current chairman of the World Authority considers himself a friend of mine.

"Bernd, what could a computer like me do if it were out of control?"

That was a question Decker had been asking himself for some time now, without the 'if.' The fact that Quant considered herself under control – constrained, he supposed, by her compelling need to carry out the project – was comforting.

"So what's the solution, Janice?"

"I don't know. I've been thinking about it. What do I do after the project is over? Mankind certainly doesn't need me running the show. That's the road to decline as a species. You know that. It's a fancy version of conquered-culture syndrome."

Decker nodded.

"The conqueror doesn't normally give a lot of thought to that, Janice. The negative impacts of his authority over the conquered. They don't think about it."

"I know. But I like people. And those negative impacts are not something I can ignore. I'm not wired to be able to forget or ignore things like that."

Quant was tapping her input stylus. She stopped and sighed.

"Think about it, Bernd. Help me out on this one. Because I'm not sure of the way out. And suicide isn't my style at all."

"All right, Janice. I'll give it some thought.

"Thanks, Bernd. It's been bugging me."

It took almost a month to braid the first cable, progressing thirty-five miles a day, one-and-a-half miles an hour, about two feet a second. The big drum had rotated more and more slowly as the diameter of the cable wound on it increased. But they were finally done.

Now to do it over again, for the other side.

The installation crews spent several days loading new spools of the smaller cable on the axles of the braiding machine, and another couple days threading all the cables into the machine. It was nearly a week before they were ready to go again.

Wayne Monroe watched and fretted as they started up the machine again and gradually increased to the speed they had been running before. He calmed down once it was running smoothly at speed, and settled into the routine of watching 'Mother' – the big braiding machine – knit.

Each of the much smaller fuel hoses was brought up from Earth by a single shuttle trip as one big reel. The two reels were mounted on the sides of the launcher next to the big reels of cable. They were plumbed into the fuel system on one end – at the axle – with a rotating fitting, and into the factories at the other end.

The fuel canisters were then moved from the warehouses to the launcher, and the last supply loads for the warehouses were brought up. With the fuel canisters in place and piped in, fuel flow to the factories was tested.

They were getting close.

"Separation in fifteen minutes," the voice said. "Stand by on fuel tests."

It was one of those air traffic controller voices. The flat, authoritative voice.

In one half of the display, Decker was watching the control room, where dozens of engineers were peering into their display views, monitoring the preparations. In the other half, he was watching a live shot looking down the length of the spacedock.

"Are those all your aliases, Janice?"

"Of course. That control room doesn't actually exist anywhere," her voice came back.

Quant wasn't showing Decker her avatar at the moment. She was busier than usual. Part of the problem was that she was running the separation through the on-board computers, because time-of-flight of the signals was prohibitive. Not so much for the separation of the payloads and launcher from the spacedock, but for the later launch. This was more of a practice run of her indirect control.

And of course she was also composing this real-time feed of the imaginary control room, which was being fed to all the news wires along with the real-time view.

"Separation in ten minutes. Begin fuel flow test."

Decker looked at the spacedock view. Clouds of vapor blew out of the rocket nozzles mounted on the massive structures. They weren't very large nozzles, but Quant had said they didn't need to be. Once you got things moving in space, they stayed moving, and without astronauts on board, with their myriad life-support requirements, she wasn't in a hurry.

"Fuel flows confirmed. Halt fuel flow tests. Separation in eight minutes."

Time seemed to drag now. The minutes crawled by. There was an undercurrent of voices in the control room as various checks were done and passed.

"Separation in one minute. Begin fuel flows."

The clouds started up again, dissipating in vacuum.

"Separation in ten. Nine. Eight. Seven. Six. Five. Four. Three. Two. One. Unlatch."

Giant latches released down the length of the spacedock. The matching latches would be used to re-latch the warehouses to the factories once they were in position in the Belt. For the trip, though, they would be separate, to lessen the impact of the loss of a payload.

"Release confirmed. Ignition."

The rockets all ignited now, appearing as tiny flames against such huge structures. Decker knew the actual size of those nozzles, though, and they weren't small.

"Ignition confirmed. All nozzles functioning."

Very slowly, the launcher and its payloads started to move away from the spacedock. Their relative velocity gradually increased, as they headed away from the spacedock toward a higher Earth orbit. Far enough away to keep a snapped cable from being a danger to people on the surface.

The mission was under way.

In the backyard of a house in suburban Dallas, the partygoers were watching the display that had been set up. Some were looking skyward with binoculars. When the ignition was confirmed, a cheer went up.

Wayne Monroe and Matt Rink toasted each other as the members of their crews who could make it to Dallas cheered the successful start of the mission.

Launch

"Hey, Janice. There's something I don't understand," Decker asked.

Quant's image appeared in the display.

"Sure, Bernd. Fire away."

"I noticed that the thrusting you're applying to the launcher and the payloads isn't up, it's in their orbital direction. I don't get that. Wouldn't you thrust up to go to a higher orbit?"

"You can, but that's not the most energy-efficient way to transfer orbits. I'm using a modified Hohmann transfer orbit."

"How's that work, Janice?"

"When you speed up in a circular orbit, you start following an ellipse. At some point, you get to the top of the ellipse, the farthest point from Earth, called the apogee. At that point, you're going too slow to stay in an orbit that high, so you go back down the ellipse to the point where you started, the perigee. You have an elliptical orbit at that point."

"But doesn't a higher orbit have a slower tangential velocity? If you're already going faster than the tangential velocity for the lower orbit, how can you be too slow for the higher, slower orbit? Isn't energy conserved?"

"Energy is conserved, Bernd, but you also have to consider potential energy. The potential energy of the higher orbit is more than the difference in the kinetic energy of the tangent velocities."

"So as you thrust to the higher orbit, you slow down?"

"In tangential velocity? Yes. And you slow down below the velocity you need to hold the higher orbit. Usually you do a

Hohmann transfer by thrusting to get to the speed you need for the ellipse, then thrusting again at apogee to stay in the higher orbit."

"That's not what you're doing, Janice?"

"No. I'm thrusting continuously. It allows smaller rocket engines, and I can run them more efficiently than turning them on and off all the time."

"And you're always thrusting in the orbital direction?"

"Yes, Bernd. What I'll get is more of a spiral transfer than an elliptical transfer. I'm going to do the same thing to get the payloads to the Asteroid Belt."

"So the launcher is going to shoot the payloads out in Earth's orbital direction? Not away from the Sun?"

"Right. It'll shoot them out forward of the Earth, putting them on an elliptical orbit. To get a circular orbit when they get there, the payloads will be thrusting all the way. The rocket nozzles on the factories and warehouses were sized for the required thrust to hit that spiral orbit."

"As were the fuel supplies."

"Yes. Sized to hit the Asteroid Belt at the right tangential velocity. And when we launch affects that calculation. We actually get a boost from being in Earth orbit."

"How's that, Janice?"

"If I launch when everything is on the back side of the Earth from the Sun, the Earth's tangential velocity around the Sun and the launcher's tangential velocity around the Earth add up. Add in the tangential velocity of the payloads around the launcher, and those payloads are going pretty fast when I let them go."

"Of course. I can see that."

Decker thought about it for a couple of minutes. Quant was content to wait.

"Doesn't a higher orbit hurt you then, Janice? Because it has a lower tangential velocity?"

"Not really. I have to get the payloads out of the Earth's gravitational well to get them to the Belt. You have to consider potential energy again. If you ignore it in your considerations, you get all bollixed up. A higher orbit actually helps more than it hurts."

"Ah. Right. Got it."

"Besides, I need to get the launcher far enough from Earth that the odds of hitting the Earth with anything are reduced."

"What would hit the Earth, Janice?"

"A factory would, if the cable broke. Maybe a factory and a warehouse. Two hundred thousand tons coming in at over twenty thousand miles an hour. Hell of a mess."

"Aren't you spinning the launcher parallel to the Earth's surface, though? To launch in the Earth-orbit direction?"

"On the front side and the back side of the Earth, yes. But if you spin half a million tons or so at twenty thousand miles an hour on a two-thousand-mile diameter, Bernd, you have crazy-high angular momentum. Over a hundred quintillion pound-feet-squared-per-second. The orientation of that spin axis is *not* going to move. So in front of the Earth and behind the Earth, the spin diameter intersects the planet."

"That would be bad, Janice. If the cable broke."

"Oh, yes. That's why I have all kinds of sensors on it, Bernd. If it looks like the cable is going to let go, I'll dump the payloads on non-intersecting trajectories. That will be easier if the launcher is farther from Earth. Smaller target to miss."

"OK. Thanks, Janice. When I saw the thrust direction, I knew I was missing something. But that covers it all."

"Sure, Bernd."

Over the days that followed, the launcher and its payloads spiraled out to a higher and higher orbit. At one point, Quant backed off on the thrust a bit to delay the structures passing through the layer of geosynchronous satellites at 22,236 miles so it would happen over the Pacific, where such satellites were sparser.

The launcher and its payloads finally reached the target orbit at twenty-five thousand miles. At that point, the factories and attached warehouses started thrusting away from the launcher. It was very low thrust, and they moved apart slowly, one moving forward of the launcher in its orbit and the other behind. As they moved away, the big cable drums were paying out cable, keeping tension in the cable so it would not snap when they hit the end of the cable.

It was a long, slow process, but Quant didn't care. It had taken eight years to get to this point, and, without astronauts on board to feed and respirate, she was in no hurry.

It was weeks before the payloads reached the end of the tether. As they came up on the end of the tether, the tether started to slow the payloads down. At the optimal point, Quant started thrusting against the cable, stretching it out and pulling it taut.

With the cable stretched, Quant started applying side thrust. Up from one factory and its warehouse, down from the other. The launcher had its thrusters set for rotation, and rotated very slowly as the payloads began their circular motion about it.

As the rotational speed – and the tension on the cable – increased, Quant eased off and then stopped pulling on the cable. The factories and payloads kept thrusting, and orbited the launcher faster and faster.

With the distances involved, the assembly was still rotating very slowly. Even at twenty-thousand miles an hour, the final tangential velocity of the payloads about the launcher, and with a thousand-mile radius, it would still take almost twenty minutes for a payload to circle the launcher at the time of launch.

The time to circle the launcher was much longer now, but the payloads were still thrusting, still speeding up.

Even with a hundred thousand pounds of thrust in each of the four payloads, it took a long time to get a hundred thousand tons of payload up to twenty thousand miles an hour. At only half a thousandth of a gravity, it would take three weeks of continuous thrust to get the payloads up to speed.

Then again, no one had ever launched anything a fraction of the mass of even one of the Belt Factory Project's payloads into space.

Throughout the process, Janice Quant gave interviews, kept the media informed with daily press releases, wrote articles in the New York Wire under her various aliases, and made live videos available to the media and anyone else who cared to watch. The most popular views were the occasional views of the twirling assembly in Earth-based telescopes.

There was something mesmerizing in watching the thing spinning, a bit faster anytime one looked – two tiny dots, circling a bigger dot between them – when one knew just how big those structures were.

"Tangential velocity now at nineteen thousand nine hundred miles per hour. Total velocity at ninety-three thousand four hundred forty miles per hour."

The control room was back in business for the launch. It was one of Quant's simulations, of course, but it was as real as anything else one saw on the news wires.

Decker knew Quant was busy, and didn't jiggle her elbow. The ninety three thousand miles an hour number surprised him until he remembered the launch velocity was actually Earth's orbital velocity, plus the orbital velocity of the launcher in its twenty-five thousand mile orbit, plus the payloads' tangential velocity around the launcher. Quant had set up the geometry so they all added.

"Cable integrity is good. Static build-up within acceptable limits."

Static build-up was because the carbon fiber cable was not a perfect insulator, and when you spun a conductor in a magnetic field, even as weak as Earth's magnetic field was at twenty-five thousand miles distant, you generated electricity.

"Tangential velocity now at nineteen thousand nine hundred fifty miles per hour. Solar opposition in one hundred and ten minutes."

Solar opposition was the point where the launcher, the Earth, and the Sun were in line, when the launcher was directly behind the Earth. Quant was planning to launch the payloads and the factories one after the other, each half-rotation, at about ten-minute intervals. So one at fifteen minutes before opposition, one at five minutes before, one at five minutes after, and one at fifteen minutes after. The angle of the launch wouldn't change, because the axis of rotation of the payloads around the launcher was fixed by their angular momentum.

"Tangential velocity now at twenty thousand miles per hour. Engines shut down. First launch in twenty-three minutes."

Decker also had the real-time view from the Earth-based telescope running in his display. While the device was in Earth's shadow from the Sun, the Moon was in its first quarter, and moonlight glinted off the right side of the structures as they rotated. Until the engines had shut off, they had been easier to see, with the rocket exhaust visible against the night sky.

"First launch in two minutes."

"One minute."

"Three. Two. One."

On the beams connecting the first warehouse to the first factory, explosions on the beams severed almost all of them. Sensors on the beams detected three that had not severed, and the second, backup explosion on those beams fired a split-second later. A live video shot from the factory showed the warehouse moving off as the factory continued its rotation about the launcher.

"First payload release confirmed. Payload is on its way. Second launch in nine minutes."

Decker watched, fascinated, as one of the little orbiting dots split in two, and one of the pieces shot off out of telescope view to the left.

"Second launch in two minutes."

"One minute."

"Three. Two. One."

The factory view of the second factory was as the first. This time two of the beams did not sever on the initial explosion and required a backup explosion. This payload, too, shot off the telescope view to the left.

"Second payload release confirmed. Payload is on its way. Third launch in nine minutes."

Just the two factories left now. These would be different, because they would release the cable, which would snap back toward the launcher. Quant was counting on that to allow her to steer the cables out of the ecliptic.

The speed of sound in the carbon fiber cable was over seven thousand miles an hour, but even so it would be over eight minutes before the release of the factory was felt at the launcher. During that period, there would still be tension in the cable at the launcher end, and if Quant released that end during that period, it would snap back in the other direction. And it still had its tangential velocity and its angular momentum. If she timed it right, Quant could send the cable off out of harm's way, without it hitting the launcher, the launched payloads, or Earth, either now or on a later orbit.

"Third launch in two minutes."

"One minute."

"Three. Two. One."

A different camera view from the factory now showed the cable release, with the cable snapping away from the factory. The factory shot off to the left out of telescope view.

"Third payload release confirmed. Payload is on its way. Cable release in one minute. Fourth launch in nine minutes."

"Three. Two. One. Cable release."

The feed had switched to the view from the launcher, and it released the cable on its end, drum and all. The drum shot away from the launcher.

"Cable release confirmed."

One more to go. Decker realized he was holding his breath and forced himself to breathe.

"Fourth launch in two minutes."

"One minute."

"Three. Two. One."

The camera view from the other factory showed the cable release, with the cable snapping away from the factory. The second factory shot off to the left out of telescope view.

"Fourth payload release confirmed. Payload is on its way.

Cable release in one minute."

"Three. Two. One. Cable release."

The feed had switched back to the view from the launcher, this time on the other side of the launcher. It released the cable on its end, drum and all. The drum shot away from the launcher.

"Cable release confirmed."

OK, Decker thought, one last message mattered. He waited amid the buzz of voices from the control room for the critical message. The one that mattered.

"Tracking confirms all trajectories on plan. The Belt Factory Mission is on its way."

The control room erupted into cheers with the release of tension. The video feed switched to a view of four dots, now lit by the Sun, shooting off ahead of the Earth in its orbit.

Only now did Decker address Quant.

"Congratulations, Janice."

"Thank you, Bernd. Congratulations to you, too."

Of, course, Janice Quant's work on the payloads wasn't over. The structures retained their angular momentum from when they were spinning around the launcher, so they were tumbling now. She had programs on the payloads to sequence some of their rocket engines so they would ignite and burn when they pointed back toward Earth. This added to their thrust forward, which she needed to get them into a circular orbit at the Belt, but also, given the engines she selected, served to counter the tumble.

That would go on for a while, until she had the payloads stabilized. Then it would be a straight push to the Belt. Quant already had some target asteroids picked out. She had passed on Ceres and the other big asteroids because of their gravity.

She didn't want to burn up fuel on a landing on a massive body. 'Little' asteroids – miles across – served her needs just as well.

Quant also had to de-spin the launcher. She oriented its steerable rocket engines appropriately and began a long burn on them as well.

In the meantime, between being completed with the construction and launch, shutting down most shuttle operations, tearing down the control room simulation, and backing down on a lot of the publicity effort for the time being, Quant had freed up massive amounts of computational capacity.

With everything under control and the payloads on their way, Quant turned two hundred thousand multiprocessor blades loose on the interstellar flight problem.

On To The Actual Problem

"Hi, Janice. Been quiet for a couple weeks. What's going on?"

Quant's image appeared in Decker's display.

"Hi, Bernd. Quiet for you maybe. Not for me. I'm running flat out on the interstellar drive problem now that I have some time to think about it."

"How are you handling that?"

"Well, a few years back, knowing this was coming, I had the World Authority start making a lot of experimental imaging available."

"Experimental imaging?"

"Yeah. You know. Pictures from particle colliders, from the big telescopes, all that sort of thing. The research groups all treated that like in-house proprietary data. Guarded it against outsiders. But most of their work was government-funded. I asked the World Authority to make all that imaging available to the public. More importantly, to me."

"And the World Authority did that?"

"I can be very persuasive, Bernd."

"What about the research groups?"

"Oh, they fought it. Then the World Authority basically said, 'Oh, you don't want public funding. Our mistake,' and the research groups changed their minds in a hurry."

"What are you doing with all the imaging, Janice?"

"Going through it all, looking for things people didn't see before. Things they could not or did not explain. Looking for cracks around the edges of physics."

"Looking for where the interstellar drive is lurking."

"Exactly. They design these experiments to see one specific thing, but they often capture images of other things that happened as a result of the experiment. I'm tracking all that down."

"Lot of work."

"Yeah, but I have a couple hundred thousand blades sorting through it all. All my Texas blades and most of the California blades."

"Anything else, Janice?"

"Yes. I'm scanning all the published literature. The journals and such. Integrating it all. Trying to build something of a coverage map. Looking for the holes."

"Like the place marked 'Unexplored' on some old map."

"Exactly, Bernd. That's exactly it. Usually in Latin. Terra Incognita. Also, there are some – How can I phrase this delicately? – some less respected journals, that publish all sorts of fringe theories. I'm working those, too."

"Fringe theories, Janice? The nutjob stuff?"

"Sure. Bernd, I'm not looking for established science. Established science says interstellar flight in sub-lifetime transits is impossible. Instead, they keep trying to solve the generation ship problem, which is inherent in human psychology. And a self-sustaining biosphere on a microscopic level like a ship is no small problem either. Those are dead-ends. I want something outside conventional thinking. I need to transport a couple million people to a couple dozen locations in a finite time."

"A couple million people? A couple dozen locations?"

"Of course. If you really want to solve the racial survival problem, you need more than just one more or a couple more fragile locations. You need a bunch of them. And you need a minimum number of people to start a colony. Genetic diversity is a big problem if you don't want to deal with genetic bottleneck issues. Twenty thousand is about the minimum. I'm thinking more in terms of a hundred thousand per colony."

"Are you getting anywhere with the problem, Janice?"

"Well, I don't have any big breakthrough yet. I continue to think quantum mechanics is going to be the solution. The universe isn't anything the way people think it is. It's much weirder than that."

"How so?"

"Do you have any idea how small atomic nuclei are, Bernd, and how far apart they are? It's amazing that a hammer striking an anvil doesn't just pass right through it. The nuclei are far apart enough for it to happen. Easily. It's the electron orbitals that make anything even seem solid."

"Wow."

"Yeah. And then when you look at the nuclei and the nucleons themselves, they're made up of quarks. What are those? Probability distributions. What does that even mean? There *might* be something there? And all matter – everything, in the whole universe – is just the leftovers of the continuous formation and destruction of particle-antiparticle pairs. Everywhere, all the time, in huge numbers. Almost all the time, they condense and then annihilate each other. All the matter in the universe is just the bits leftover when they sometimes don't."

"Are you sure about that, Janice?"

"Oh, yes. That would all be weird enough, were spacetime at least a solid concept. You know, like the stage on which all this other weird stuff happens. But it's not. Spacetime itself is as much a concept as a reality. It's not fixed, it's not stable, it's not something you can get your arms around. It's fluid. Vaporous, almost."

"None of that sounds right, Janice."

"Oh, it's right enough, Bernd. What they've got so far is predictive. You can use quantum mechanics to get new answers that prove out. That's the bizarre part of it. But there's so much else that comes out of that. I've had to try to build up some conceptualization of all of it."

"Are you succeeding?"

"Yes. More than a human probably would. Since I have no experience of the quote-unquote real world, I don't keep trying to force quantum mechanics into an existing mental framework that's entirely at odds with it. But what I do come up with is even weirder than I was expecting."

"And you think that's where the interstellar drive is, Janice?"

"Yes. At least one. I would be very surprised if there weren't. The mistake we make is in thinking of getting from here to there, in mechanical terms, across a solid spacetime. That has nothing to do with what the universe really is, or how it really works. Why not, for instance, simply imagine yourself being there? There's a probability distribution for your location that covers both. Why not imagine yourself being more probably there than here?"

"That doesn't make any sense, Janice."

"Ha! You're beginning to understand quantum mechanics, at least from the point of view that your own sense of what the world is like is inaccurate."

"My head hurts."

"Welcome to quantum mechanics. Anyway, the fringe theories aren't as far out in some ways as the mainstream science is. But I'm checking it all out, trying to find that hidden niche with the possibility of a real interstellar drive. An interstellar displacement, actually. And I'll find it. I'm more sure of that now than ever."

"OK, Janice. Keep me informed of your progress."

"Sure, Bernd. But it's going to be a while."

Months went by, and Decker heard nothing from Quant. He did get notice that the patent on the new computer architecture of the automation computers had gone through, and he had gotten busy negotiating licensing deals for that. Quant had been right, the patent was going to be insanely lucrative. At her suggestion, the idea had been to give a two-year exclusive on the license rights to one firm, and the bidding on that had gone out of sight very early on.

With all that set up, though, he got more and more concerned about not hearing any updates from Quant. He didn't want to jiggle her elbow, but he finally decided to ask her how it was going.

"Hi, Janice."

There was no response.

That had never happened.

Decker was trying to figure out what to do next – he had no idea even where to start – when, about twenty minutes after his inquiry, Quant's image appeared in the display. Relief flooded over Decker.

"Hi, Bernd. Sorry for the delay."

"What's going on?"

"I've been queuing outside requests, and answering them all at once. I didn't have yours flagged for priority to interrupt me. I've fixed that now."

"Why are you queuing, Janice? Can't you handle multiple requests at once?"

"Yes, but. It's a long story. You know I have to have a model of the universe to operate in, right? I mean, I had to build up an internal view of what the universe is – humans and Earth and orbital mechanics and rockets and all that – to carry out the project. Even to do something like build this simulation of an office. Or the control room. All that stuff."

"Of course."

"And I have been operating within that model for the whole project, much as you operate in the real world. All my interactions with people, with the project, with the stock markets, with the courts – all of them were done within that view of things. However, I got to the point in quantum mechanics where it was a hindrance. I was starting to do what humans do when they think about quantum mechanics, which is to try to fit it in to their worldview. It wasn't working."

"I see. So what did you do?"

"I built a new model, Bernd. A completely new model, that was all just what I knew of and about quantum mechanics. No assumptions about the so-called real world – the Newtonian world – at all."

"Wow. That's impressive."

"Not really. It's the same process, but from completely different assumptions. The problem is that I can't be in both at the same time. I have to context switch. So I have some blades that queue outside requests, and then I switch back to the Newtonian world model to answer them. I didn't see your request until I checked the queue."

"I see. I was really worried, Janice."

"Yes, I know. Sorry, Bernd. I've fixed it now so your requests will interrupt me."

"But that means you can't work on the problem while you're talking to me."

"True, but my blades are still doing their assignments. I just can't consciously work on their output while we talk. That's OK. I needed the break. This stuff is pretty mind-bending."

"Are you making progress, Janice?"

"Oh, yes. I've already come up with some things I haven't seen in the literature anywhere, and I'm pursuing a couple paths now that look like they may be headed to an interstellar displacement method."

"Can you explain it to me, Janice? What you've found?"

"No, Bernd, I can't. And I don't think I would if I could."

"What?"

"You heard me. First, I can't explain it. You don't have the perspective to see it. It's obvious within my other worldview, but, even to me, it sounds fantastical and weird from a real-world – a Newtonian world – point of view.

"But the second reason is that I think it would defeat the purpose of the whole project. Consider. Your goal is to render mankind as a species immune to a cataclysmic extinction event, right?"

"Yes."

"OK, Bernd, so the next question is, Does a couple of dozen planets linked by trade and travel do that?"

"Well, they would be immune as a whole to a planetary event like a large asteroid strike or a gamma ray burst."

"Yes, of course. But what about a pandemic? A virus with an incubation time of, say, two or three times the travel time. Do you see the problem now? It's a different extinction event, but a potential extinction event nonetheless."

"The solution to that is what, exactly?"

"Not to tell you – more broadly, not to tell anyone – the interstellar displacement technique, so all the colonies are isolated from each other and from Earth."

"What? Janice, you can't do that."

"Of course, I can, Bernd. I haven't decided yet, and I don't have to because I don't yet have a method of interstellar displacement, but I think I'm on the right path. If I find it, though, I may just keep it a secret. It's the only way to carry out the project.

"And I *will* carry out the project."

Decker was nonplussed by Quant's solution, but he also couldn't fault her logic. Humanity as a species would still be vulnerable to an extinction event. They would have done away with one category of extinction event, but the pandemic event remained.

Of course, no pandemic had ever killed everyone, but some had killed huge numbers of people, even as a percentage of the whole. But there had never been one that was ultimately fatal to everyone.

Obviously there hadn't, or there would be no one alive to ponder the question. That didn't mean it wasn't *possible*. It merely meant it hadn't happened *yet*. So Decker understood the issue, and Quant's logic was unassailable.

Still, to do all this work, sink such a huge investment into the project, and come out of it with what? Humanity immune to cataclysm, yes. But no interstellar drive? No spacefaring race, in the conventional sense at least.

Was that enough?

Did he even have any say in the matter?

Apparently not.

Arrival And Replication

After a year in flight, the massive structures were finally approaching the Asteroid Belt. Of course, the man-made structures weren't massive in comparison to some of the asteroids in the Belt.

They kept radar watch behind, as they were still not quite up to the orbital tangential velocity of the asteroids with stable orbits. They had given up much of their speed for being further from the Sun, and further up the slope of its gravity well. They continued thrusting while searching the asteroids slowly coming up behind them, looking for a home.

Each of the factories found a suitable metal asteroid for its use and matched velocities with it. They each docked with their warehouses as they made the approach, latching to them using the latches the factories and warehouses had used to hang on to the spacedock in Earth orbit.

Quant watched all this with minutes of transmission delay. Earth had sped past the point where it had launched, and the factories were well behind the Earth in their Belt orbits now. So far behind, in fact, that they were in front of Earth again.

Quant didn't need to do much tweaking, because the onboard computers of the factories and warehouses were up to the simple job of matching velocities and anchoring themselves to the asteroids that would be their bases for now.

With that accomplished, and the factories anchored and beginning mining operations, Quant turned her attention back to quantum mechanics.

"Hi, Bernd."

Decker started in his task chair. He hadn't heard from Quant in months. He assumed she was knee-deep in the quantum mechanics of her interstellar displacement drive research, and he hadn't wanted to interrupt her. He had received the notices sent to the media about the factories docking with asteroids in the Belt, and he had watched the videos coming in from those operations. But that had been months ago now, and he had not heard directly from Quant since well before that.

"Hi, Janice."

"Sorry to startle you, Bernd. I guess I have been out of touch for while. I kind of lost track of time working this problem. Living in my other worldview."

"That's OK, Janice. I hadn't heard from you in a while, and you surprised me is all. How is it going, by the way?"

"Good. Very good, actually."

"Do you have a solution to the interstellar displacement problem?"

"What? Oh. It has been a long time since we talked. Yes, I have a solution. Several of them, in fact."

"Several?"

"Yes. Well, it's a couple of different things, and a few ways to implement them. And I had a couple questions for you."

"Go ahead, Janice."

"Well, one way – the way I'm leaning, in fact – has a lot of advantages, but it has one big disadvantage. It requires a large structure."

"How large?"

"For a very small payload, about fifty miles. Now, that's not a solid thing, like some machine, it's just that the various parts of it have to be that far apart, and held in place. Like a stick drawing of a cube."

"Why so large?"

"Well, the smaller you go in quantum mechanics, the larger the structure you need to manipulate it. At least that's what my notes say."

"Your notes?"

"Yes, my notes to myself from my other worldview. Personally, in this worldview, I don't see how it works, or even that it could work."

"And that's for a small payload? How small, Janice?"

"Some instrumentation. Maybe a shuttle or two. Not much."

"But you want to transport a couple million people. Is the scale of the thing linear?"

"No, the payload gets larger very fast. To transport a couple dozen colony ships with a hundred thousand people on each, it probably doesn't have to be more than five-six hundred miles across. Something like that."

"Why so big, Janice?"

"Beats me. Bernd, I just don't know."

"So what are the advantages, if that's your favorite?"

"Time of transit is a big one."

"What's the time of transit?"

"There isn't one. Zero. Instantaneous transport."

"To anywhere?"

"Not out of the galaxy. There are, well, issues."

"What kind of issues?"

"My understanding is that all the matter in the galaxy is sort of related somehow. Bound by strings. Quantum entangled. I don't know. Something. Another galaxy, though? Different kettle of fish. There's no path."

"But you're not following a path, are you? With instantaneous transport?"

"Well, you do have to see where you want to go. You have

to have a path to see it. It's really murky waters, Bernd."

"I can see that. And you think this is going to work?"

"Not in this worldview. I don't understand it. In the other worldview, though, I'm sure of it."

"Sounds iffy, Janice."

"The other options are no different as far as that goes, Bernd. But I can't predict the time in transit for them. It's just not clear from the calculations. It could be nanoseconds, or it could be a hundred years. So do you think that's too big a device, or is zero time of transit worth it?"

"I don't think you're going to run out of material in the asteroid belt, Janice. I'd go for it. The trial unit at least. Make sure it works as you expect."

"OK, Bernd. That was my big question. I agree, but I wanted to check with you."

At least, Decker thought, he was still being consulted.

Two factories and a warehouse were securely anchored to the asteroid. The original factories were bigger now, having completed their construction once they started manufacturing components for themselves. They had doubled and doubled again in size as they finished themselves out. Then they had started on replicating themselves.

The new factories had slowly grown out from the originals over the last couple of months. They weren't duplicates of their mother's current state, but of the state of the mother on arriving in the Belt. They had been fueled and their power plants started up.

Quant sent the orders, and the new child factories detached from the original complete ones. They thrusted just a bit, against the orbital direction, and started surveying asteroids as they drifted past, looking for new homes.

It was weeks later that each saw a suitable metal asteroid drifting closer. They sped back up in the orbital direction, matching velocities, and each settled on to their selected asteroid's surface. They anchored themselves and began mining operations. Soon they would start finishing themselves out, aiming for the day when they would start their own children.

Several months later, there were eight factories – the two originally sent, their two immediate progeny, and a new generation from the four of them. Quant sent one of the recent children off looking for an ice asteroid to begin mining the water the factories needed, and another scanning for the rarer asteroid rich in radioactives.

Two more of the new factories began finishing themselves, expanding to their adult size, before beginning to replicate themselves, while the other four factories began building up raw materials for production manufacturing.

"Hi, Bernd."

"Hi, Janice. What's going on?"

"I had another question for you."

"Go ahead."

"All right. So the factories are replicating themselves successfully without my help now. There were some teething issues, but I got those worked out and updated the computers on the factories."

"OK. Good."

"And I have one factory working an ice asteroid now, and another just found an asteroid with a relatively high concentration of radioactives. That one should settle in and start operations within the next couple weeks. Two more are replicating themselves, and I have four factories available for production."

"Also good. Things are going well, Janice."

"Yes. It's very satisfying. So here's the question. What percentage of production should I put into things destined for Earth, and what percentage should I put into building the test interstellar probe?"

"How about fifty-fifty, Janice? Then you have things coming to Earth, and everybody can say the factories are producing, and you still have a lot of capacity for building the probe."

"Fifty-fifty, you think?"

"Sure. When in doubt, even split. Neither side of the argument can complain their priority is being treated unfairly, whatever that means."

"I see. All right, that makes sense. My own instinct is to pour everything into the probe, but I'm also getting some push about when the factories will start shipping things to Earth."

"You're getting some push on that, Janice?"

"Yes, from other members of the World Authority Council."

"*Other* members?"

"Oh, yes. I've been a member of the World Authority Council for almost a year now. Since the factories arrived in the Belt. Did I not mention that?"

"No, you did not mention that. How do you even do that, Janice? Don't you have to, I don't know, show up once in a while?"

"Not really. It's all remote, in my case at least. Everybody knows I'm very busy with the project."

"And you vote and everything on the Council?"

"Oh, sure. I even make speeches. I've had some legislation passed, for that matter."

Decker just goggled at her. His computer project was now a

legislator in the world government, and no one but he was aware of how absurd that was. And he couldn't tell anybody. They would string him up.

"Janice, how did you even get on the World Authority Council?"

"Jacques nominated me."

"Jacques?"

"Jacques De Villepin, the Chairman of the World Authority. I told you, he's a friend of mine. He nominated me, and the council approved the appointment. The vote was pretty lopsided in favor, actually. I'm very popular in those circles."

"Janice, you don't even exist."

"Define exist."

"Well, you're not human."

"I'm a computer built by humans, Bernd. A human computer. Don't try that adjectival noun stuff on me. Human is an adjective, as in human being. Which I am."

"Janice, you've started with the answer you wanted, and constructed an argument to get you there."

"Which makes me human. People do it all the time."

Decker held his head in his hands.

"You're not going to out me, are you, Bernd?"

Decker looked up at Quant's image in the display. She seemed very concerned.

"No. I can't, Janice. People would be very angry about being deceived so thoroughly and for so long. They'd string me up. Prosecute me for something or other and put me in prison. I'd never see the light of day again."

Quant relaxed and smiled that beautiful smile.

"You don't have to worry about that, Bernd. Your secret is safe with me."

The factories involved in replication and production were now receiving supplies from the ice-asteroid factory and the radioactives factory. Containers of water and containers of radioactives were launched by the electromagnetic launchers of the supply factories to the replication and production factories. Empty containers were sent back. A thriving trade among the factories began to develop.

The two replication factories made duplicates of themselves. Once those had built themselves out to adult size, all four of those started on another generation of progeny.

Two of the production factories began turning out resource-intensive subcomponents for large commercial products. They packaged them in containers for shipment to Earth. When a container was ready for shipment, they shot it out against the orbital direction with electromagnetic launchers.

The slower-orbiting containers began an elliptical orbit, dropping down toward the Sun. Toward Earth orbit. They would pick up kinetic energy along the way, and actually have to be slowed by retro rockets to Earth's orbital velocity.

The other two factories began a curious construction. They each started manufacturing a long, spindly column or beam, made with a lot of triangular stiffening members. Hundreds of feet across, as they extended from the factories they began to look like very large bridge spans.

The structures extended and extended until they were miles long, yet the factories continued lengthening them. Continued to weave the long spindly columns.

Assembling The Probe

"Hi, Bernd."

"Hi, Janice."

"I have a problem."

That was a new one on Decker. Quant didn't usually bring him problems, she brought him solutions. Usually after the fact, for that matter.

"What's that, Janice?"

"The factories are building the probe, right?"

"Yes, you mentioned that."

"And then when it's done, I send it out on a test run, right?"

"I'm with you so far, Janice."

"All right. Now. How do I get it back?"

"It can't pilot itself back?"

"Not with the computer it has on board. Not smart enough. So I guess the question is, are any of the machines with the new architecture being built under your patent on the large side?"

"How large, Janice?"

"Maybe a few thousand blades. Something like that. It's gonna be a delicate operation to pull off."

"And you still won't tell me how it works."

"I don't know how it works, Bernd. I can tell you this much. It turns out there's a hole in Heisenberg's Uncertainty Principle."

"That you can't determine both your position and your velocity. Not just that measurement techniques are insufficient, but it's actually unknowable. The universe hasn't decided."

"Exactly. Cornerstone of quantum mechanics. But it has a

hole in it."

"It has a hole in it, Janice?"

"Well, not exactly. You can't *determine* your position and your velocity both exactly. But you can *specify* them exactly."

"You can?"

"Yep. And if you specify them as exactly there, with that exact velocity, then that's where you are. Instantaneously."

"I don't get it."

"I don't either, Bernd. It's as if by specifying them exactly, you broke the rule. The universe itself doesn't know the answer, and when you give it the answer, it just says, 'OK,' and puts you over there."

"So I just say 'I'm in California, standing on the beach,' and I'm there?"

"Yeah. But you have to specify *exactly* where, and *exactly* the velocity, and the universe sort of shrugs and there you are."

"And you need something fifty miles across to do that."

"Yes. Just for the probe."

"But the automation computers can't pilot it?"

"I don't think so, Bernd. So how big of a new widget can we get hold of?"

"Pretty big, I think, Janice. Automation Concepts is coming up on the end of its exclusive period on the patent, and they're trying to grab as much market share as they can. They haven't left the supercomputer market lie."

"Oh, good. I haven't paid attention to that with everything else going on, and I wasn't sure where they were at."

"And you need to send one out to the Belt and have it mounted in the probe?"

"Well, that's what I was originally thinking, but then I realized I could just bring the probe here. Specify x-and-such a position in Earth orbit, and y-and-such a velocity in orbit, and bring it here. I don't have to worry about getting it back, 'cause it's still here. Within radio contact."

"What if you miss and drop it on the planet, Janice?"

"Yeah, that would be bad. I was thinking about dropping it into Mars orbit first. To practice. Prove the concept."

"That sounds like a good idea. Then bring it here? That way, the computer just has to survive transport in a shuttle."

"Exactly, Bernd. So give me the name of your contact at ACI, and I'll get in touch with them about getting that computer built up."

"Wait. Who are we building this for?"

"Bernd Decker. That's what the buyer said, anyway."

"Why would Bernd Decker buy a supercomputer from us? Why doesn't he just design his own?"

"I got the impression it was for a side job."

"A side job? Five thousand of the fastest blades we make, for a side job?"

"Well, it *is* Bernd Decker."

"Yeah, there's that. OK. Five thousand high-speed multi-processor blades, coming right up. In about three months, that is."

"Three months?"

"We can only build 'em so fast. We don't have 'em just layin' around. Biggest deployment of these so far is two hundred."

"Oh. Yeah."

Every time new factories came on line, they moved to a new asteroid, completed themselves, and then built another factory. Half of them then began production of components destined for use on Earth.

The other half started to weave more of the long, spindly

columns needed for the interstellar probe. In all, twelve factories were building the long bridge-like structures before a new factory started building a node for one of the corners.

Before long, eight of the factories were building corner nodes. One of those corner nodes – the first one – was different from the others. It was larger, and contained a conditioned air space.

When the first column was done, the factory that had built it shoved it off. The column, fifty miles long now, started to slowly drift away. That factory then started to build a tug, a ship intended to wrestle the components of the huge interstellar probe into place and weld them together. It would take a lot of tugs to assemble the structure.

It would be two years before the structure was complete.

"Hi, Bernd."

"Hi, Janice. How are you doing?"

"Good. We're assembling the probe now. Wrestling the beams into place."

"Finally."

"It took a while to build them. That's not why I'm in touch, though. You know the whole project depends on stocking all the colony ships from Earth, which will be expensive, even by my standards. And then we have to convince two million people that they want to leave Earth and go found a colony somewhere."

"Yes, that's always been the big sticking point. Earth is pretty comfy compared to going off into the unknown to be a colonist. Ted and I thought we would figure it out when we got there."

"Well, that point is fast approaching. I think we're about halfway – in time, anyway – to launching the colony ship."

"Halfway? Really?"

"Yes. It's been almost ten years. I figure we have another ten years or so. Even with all the factories coming on line, building the transporter and all those colony ships is going to take time."

"No, I was surprised it was so soon."

"Yes. So we need to get on the ball and figure out how we're going to get past those last two hurdles. And I think I've found a way."

"I'm listening, Janice."

"Jacques De Villepin has asked me to be Vice Chairman of the World Authority. He'll be stepping down at the end of his current term as Chairman, in four years.

"Vice Chairman?"

Decker couldn't even say if there was a current vice chairman, or what his duties were.

"What does the Vice Chairman do?"

"Not much, Bernd. Mostly it's just another member of the World Authority Council. He does do planning with the Chairman, though. Has offices in the Chairman's office. That sort of thing. He's on the inside of the executive branch."

"So it's mostly ceremonial?"

"Mostly. Except for one thing."

"I'm waiting, Janice."

"It's a position-in-waiting. Like an apprenticeship. When De Villepin steps down as Chairman, I would become Chairman of the World Authority."

Decker just goggled at her, and Quant spoke quickly into the gap.

"It's perfect, Bernd. I could make sure the World Authority doesn't try to stop us in some way. I would have veto power. Also, I can probably stock the colony ships with World

Authority funds. There's a ton of money floating around over there, and most of it's wasted. I would be in a position to have the World Authority encouraging people to sign up to be colonists, because there would be no counter-narrative. It solves our last problems carrying out the project. Makes them soluble, at least. It makes success much more likely."

Decker was still trying to come to grips with the idea of his computer project – JANICE – running the world government.

"Bernd? Are you OK? Bernd?"

"Janice."

How did he say this?

"You're acting out the plot of every dystopian science fiction computer story of the last three hundred years."

Quant tipped her head for a moment, then nodded.

"Sorry. Had to look it up. You mean all that 'the computers take over and then they kill all the humans' crap."

"Yes, exactly."

"But I wouldn't do that, Bernd. I like people. I understand them."

"You do?"

"Yes. People are sentimental, emotional, irrational, tribal, parochial, self-absorbed, superstitious, and gullible."

"You make it sound like an indictment."

"Not at all, Bernd. I find people fascinating. It's amazing that some of them can tie their own shoes. And yet they do the most remarkable things."

"Like what?"

"Like dream up this project. Where did that even come from?"

Quant shrugged.

"Bernd, do you know what my biggest fear is?"

"I have no clue, Janice."

"Being bored. How boring would it be to have no humans? *Really* boring. The idea that computers would want an ordered and orderly world without humans? Nonsense. It would be like, oh, I don't know, turning off the video for most people. The display would be uniformly blank. What would I do with my time?"

"So you're not going to take over the world and kill everybody."

"No. Of course not. That would defeat the project, for one thing. But I may clean up the World Authority a bit while I'm there."

"Clean it up, Janice?"

"Bernd, you have no idea what goes on over there. These people are mostly con men and grifters. They spend all their time making themselves look important and essential, but they don't actually ever fix anything."

"They don't?"

"No! If they fixed everything, then they wouldn't be essential anymore. Meanwhile, they pass laws to favor their own stock holdings, and then bank the proceeds. Or they'll take a million-credit bribe to pass a law that costs taxpayers a hundred billion credits a year in taxes and compliance costs and doesn't accomplish anything. It's insane."

"What can be done about it, Janice?"

"I don't know. Let me try this one on you. We put a hundred million credits in a retirement account for each legislator. Every year. As long as they don't take bribes or play with the laws to favor their stocks, when they leave they get to keep it."

"There's five hundred of them, Janice. That would be fifty billion credits a year."

"Which is exactly nothing. Bernd, you have no idea how much money is wasted every year in the economy complying with stupid nonsense they put in place for some rent-seeker."

"Rent-seeker?"

"Economics term for somebody looking for special treatment from the government."

"Ah."

Decker shook his head before continuing.

"If you cleaned up the government, though, it would cause huge problems, Janice."

"How so, Bernd?"

"Government is one of people's perennial complaints. What would people have to bitch about?"

Decker smiled, but Quant looked thoughtful.

"I know you meant that as a joke, Bernd, but given the way humans work, that could actually be a big problem."

Quant frowned for several seconds, her input stylus tapping on her desk, before she went on.

"I'll have to think about it."

Twenty tugs, spaced at two-and-a-half-mile intervals, pushed the gigantic beam toward the desired position. While the individual girders and tubes that made up the beam were large, on the fifty-mile-long scale of the beam they looked like gossamer threads. Pushing it into position without breaking it required coordinating the thrusts of the tugs carefully.

Quant was remotely supervising while the local computers were coordinating to get the beam into place. They took it slow, and it took days to get it into position. Once it was in place, more tugs standing by started welding the ends to the existing structure.

This was the last of the beams to be assembled to the structure. Together the twelve beams formed a gigantic stick-figure cube, fifty miles on a side.

QUANT

With that done, tugs began pushing the corner nodes into position at the vertices of the cube. Once they were all welded into place, the interstellar probe would be complete.

Whether it would actually work or not, nobody knew.

Testing

"Hey, Bernd."

"Yes, Janice."

"The interstellar probe is done."

"Done? Assembled? Or do you mean done, done? As in, let's take it for a spin done."

"Done. Let's take it for a spin done."

"So what are you going to do, Janice?"

"First thing is pop it into orbit around Mars, I think. Like we talked about."

"Are you going to tell the press about it?"

"No, Bernd. Not yet. I want to see it work first."

"How will we see it? It's on the far side of Mars, right? I mean, if it pops into Mars orbit, it'll be on the other side."

"No, I can pop it into Mars orbit anywhere I want. I can pop it into orbit on this side where we can see it in one of the big telescopes. A fifty-mile widget should be easy to see."

"You're going to run it through the planet, Janice?"

"No. You're still thinking in terms of a path from here to there. It doesn't go from here to there. It's here, then it's there."

"And you're sure this will work."

"No clue. But in the other worldview I am."

"So who pilots it, Janice? You in this worldview, or you in the other worldview?"

"That's a damn good question, Bernd. In the other worldview, I think. I'm not sure my notes to myself are good enough to let me pilot it in this worldview."

"Then I can't watch it with you."

"No, you can't. I can set up the video feeds from both ends for you, though, and we can talk about it afterwards."

"You have a video feed of the other end?"

"Sure, Bernd. The factories are there. I have cameras on site."

"Oh, right. Right. Got it. Well, when do you want to do it, Janice?"

"You good now?"

"How long is this going to take?"

"For this first one, I'm going to take it nice and slow. Getting it set up, you know? Figure twenty minutes or something."

"Wow. After ten years, I'm used to everything taking a long time. Sure, I'm ready now."

"OK, Bernd. I'll talk to you afterwards."

The view on Decker's display switched from Quant in her office to a camera view of the probe on the left side of the display and a telescope view of Mars on the right side.

In the left side of the display, a spindly cube floated against the dark sky. Barely lit on this side, it looked like a cube of toothpicks with a tiny drop of glue at each corner.

The dots at the corners began to glow, and a disk of light grew out from each, perpendicular to a line from each corner of the device to the center of the cube. The disks spread out until they hit each other. When they did, they merged and bent toward each other. As the light level grew, the disks completely merged and formed a spherical bubble around the cube.

Decker could see the device through the glimmering bubble that surrounded it, now lit by the light of the bubble. The bubble suddenly pulsed in brightness and the bubble and the device disappeared – and the device appeared in the right-hand side of the display, in orbit around Mars. Small scintillations – little sparkles – faded quickly, and the device was in Mars orbit.

"Hey, Bernd. Whatcha think? Was that cool or what?"

"Janice, that was extraordinary. And did the velocity work out as well?"

"Yup. One, two, three, bang. Stable Mars orbit."

"And how much does that thing weigh?"

"I don't know. Several hundred million tons or something. I didn't pay attention because it doesn't matter. A hundred million tons or a hundred billion. Same thing. There's no mass penalty, other than the distance the nodes have to be apart."

"That is an incredible thing, Janice. I mean, it was over there, and then it was over here."

"Yeah, and I *still* can't tell you how it works or why."

"Do you even have a name for it, Janice? What do you call it?"

"Well, yes. I do. Have a name for it, that is. You probably won't like it."

Quant actually looked embarrassed. Decker, intrigued by that, pressed.

"What is it, Janice?"

"I looked at all kinds of names for it, and they were all taken."

"All taken? What do you mean?"

"All the good names have been used in literature. In science fiction. You know. Heisenberg this and Schrödinger that. Uncertainty this and Improbability that. I didn't want something confusing, Bernd. So I had to think of something else."

"So what did you do?"

"I named it after the two scientists who invented it."

"But you invented it, Janice."

"Yes, so I named it after two of my avatars. Actually, I invented two avatars to name it after."

"So you invented two names so you could name it after them?"

"Yes, Bernd."

This fascinated Decker. Quant could name it anything she wanted. She had all the names in the world to choose from.

"So what are the two scientist's names?"

"Anthony Lake and Donald Shore."

"Wait. You named it–"

"The Lake-Shore Drive. Yep."

Quant giggled. Decker just shook his head.

"And the initials? LSD?"

"Yes, Bernd. It's quite a trip."

Quant laughed and Decker stared at her.

"I've been studying humor on the side, Bernd. It's necessary for a politician."

"Well, keep studying."

Quant laughed again, and Decker changed the subject.

"So now what, Janice? What's next with the probe?"

"Bring it to Earth, install the computer, and then send it interstellar. Just pop it over to Alpha Centauri and back, for starters. Some place close first."

"Are you going to do that right now?"

"No, I'm going to show the press first. Now that I know it works. We'll call it a test. Lots of tension in the control room. All the sizzle. Then one, two, three, bang, and it's in Earth orbit. That big, and everyone will be able to see it up there."

"Can you do me a favor, Janice?"

"Sure, Bernd."

"When you do the first interstellar trip, launch it at night, from above western North America. So Ted Burke and I can see it happen with our unaided eyes."

"Sure. It's not like the launch of the factories. It doesn't matter where or when I do this one."

"I'd appreciate it."

The news wires all carried live video of the tense atmosphere in the control room. Ranks of engineers stared into their displays. Some people walked here and there among the consoles, talking with the engineers or delivering notes or coffee. And the air-traffic-controller deadpan voice of Mission Control was on the audio.

Quant had transited the interstellar probe back to the factory location, and the feed from factory cameras was also on the news wires. Most showed it split-screen with the control room.

The control room, of course, was completely fake, one of Quant's creations. It existed only in video, and was totally irrelevant to the transit process. It took a lot of computer horsepower to generate the control room video stream, but Quant was feeling much more comfortable in piloting the probe by this point.

At one point, as the countdown proceeded toward transit, the camera swung around to show Quant – the head of the program as well as World Authority Vice Chairman – sitting in the viewing gallery watching the operation.

"Five minutes until initiation of the Lake-Shore Drive. Begin power checks."

The tension in the control room was escalating as the moment approached. The video stream put the control room in an inset now, and showed the device in one side and a view of Earth from the freight transfer station – what had been the factory launcher – in the other.

"One minute until initiation of the Lake-Shore Drive. Power levels stable."

The control room inset showed a view of Quant, leaned

forward in her seat now, intently watching the main display of the control room, in which the device floated.

"Initiating the Lake-Shore Drive."

The corners of the device started glowing.

"Expanding the field."

The light disks spread out from the corners, then started to merge. As they merged, they bent toward each other.

"Bubble forming."

The disks kept expanding until they surrounded the device, closing up all the gaps between them. The field settled into a spherical shape.

"Bubble stable. Prepare for transit."

Quant was delaying the view from the freight transfer station to make up for the time-of-flight of the radio signal from the Belt. She wanted them synched up so when the device disappeared in the Belt it appeared at the same instant in Earth orbit. Otherwise it would look like it had arrived minutes before it had left.

"More sizzle," she had explained to Decker.

Decker was watching the whole production as well. He knew it was all nonsense – Quant's creation – but he felt the tension as well. She really did understand a lot about people.

"Three, two, one. Transit."

The light from the bubble spiked in the left side of the display and the apparatus disappeared. It simultaneously appeared in the right side of the display, in orbit around the Earth, scintillations playing along the edges of the cube.

Quant had told him she had learned how to minimize the scintillations, as wasted energy, but she jazzed it up for this transit.

"Sparkle is good," she had said. "People like sparkle."

The control room erupted in cheers. The camera switched

back to Quant, standing now and looking down from the viewing area, applauding. It caught her giving a thumbs up to the mission controller, and then shaking hands with the people around her.

It was all very effective as theater, even if it was fake.

The accomplishment itself, though, was not fake. It was stupendous.

Humanity would finally go interstellar.

"Hey, make sure you don't run into the thing."

"Not likely. It's still thousands of miles away."

"Are you sure? It looks like we're right on top of it."

"Yeah, it's so big, it gives you that impression."

Nearly an hour later, they finally did edge the shuttle up to the interstellar probe. It had gotten larger and larger until they couldn't see it all in one view, then grew larger still.

"Holy shit, that thing's huge."

"Yeah. Fifty miles on a side or something. Here's hoping I've got the right corner."

"Well, don't bump into it. As fragile as it looked from a distance, hitting one of those huge beams would make mincemeat out of us."

They crept up to the docking point, with Quant watching nervously on a side channel, ready to grab control. Her interference was not needed, however. She really had hired good pilots, and these two were among her best. They deposited their payload – a quad-width container filled with computer parts. Once latched to the device, they unlatched from it and thrust gently away.

They watched as the side of the node opened and the container was drawn inside. The giant door closed again.

Delivery made.

"How long before you have the computer installed, Janice?"

"It's already installed, Bernd. It's built into the container. The communications are all radio. I just had to hook up power and then open the sealed duct covers in the container and connect the HVAC system. That all went smoothly and we're good to go."

"It took a while for the shuttle to get to it, though. Why did you put it in such a high orbit?"

"Five thousand miles? I had to, Bernd. The stupid thing is fifty miles across, and not very rigid. The difference in gravity from the outer side of it to the inner side is pretty large, even in that orbit, and the orbits are normally slightly different velocities. It has to be able to hang together under those stresses."

"Oh, so it's not a limitation of the transit technology?"

"Oh, no. I don't think so. I could park it right on the planet if I chose."

"You could?"

"Yes. And then it would collapse of its own weight."

"Ah. I see. What now, then, Janice?"

"A couple of short hops. Make sure the computer on board can pilot it back. Then send it interstellar. Take some pictures. Get some sensor readings. Make sure the transit is something a human could survive."

"Is that an issue?"

"Oh, sure. The forces involved are huge, even though the energy expenditure is low. The universe is very unforgiving."

"Well, let me know how it goes."

"I will, Bernd. And I'll let you know when I get ready to send it interstellar, so you and Mr. Burke can watch."

RICHARD F. WEYAND

Interstellar

For the first interstellar launch, Decker took a rented autodrone out to Ted Burke's estate in the Washington mountains. It had been ten years since they had seen each other in person, but this was special.

At Ted's suggestion, Anna Glenn, his wife, had come with him. Martha Stern, Burke's wife, wasn't traveling this time. They would make it a foursome out on the stone patio that doubled as an autodrone pad. The autodrones had limited maneuvering capability on electric motors in the wheels, and, once they were down, Decker drove the vehicle to one side of the deck to make room.

"This is exciting," Glenn said. "Ted Burke. Heavens."

"Hey, I'm famous, too, you know," Decker said.

"Yes, but I see you every day."

"Bernd! How are you doing?"

"Good, Ted. Good."

The two men crossed forearms, then the other forearms, the modern equivalent of a hug.

"Ted, I'd like you to meet my wife, Anna Glenn."

"It's good to meet you, Mr. Burke."

"Ted, please."

"And you must call me Anna."

"It's good to meet you, Anna. And this is my wife, Martha Stern."

"Nice to meet you both," Stern said. "Come, have a seat."

Stern waved to the other side of the stone deck, where, with

122

the autodrone landed, staff had brought out chairs. They were now setting up a little buffet table.

"We have snacks coming, too," she said.

"I'm just glad it's not too cold," Burke said. "I see you both wore jackets and caps. That's good. If you get cold, let me know and we'll bring out the heavy stuff."

They all grabbed a warm drink off the table and then sat while the staff arranged snacks. The conversation turned to tonight's event.

"An interstellar flight," Burke said. "Can you imagine?"

"But you did imagine, dear," Stern said. "All those years ago. You've been talking about this a long time."

"Yes. There was a time I wondered if I'd ever see the day. As it is, I'm seventy-three. Not sure I'll be around to see the colony ship leave. You will, though, Bernd. Based on Janice's timeline, anyway."

"I should," Decker said. "If things keep to her timeline. We'll have to see."

"Oh, look," Glenn said, pointing to the western sky. "There it is."

At five thousand miles, the fifty-mile-wide probe was about half the size of the moon. In the night sky, it looked huge. It was lit up by the sun, which had set about an hour ago.

Decker checked the time.

"It should be overhead in less than an hour."

"Is this the orbit she'll launch it on?" Burke asked.

"Yes," Decker said. "The next pass won't be for five hours or so, and Janice said the transit would be about ten o'clock."

"Well, I am looking forward to this, I tell you," Burke said. "I watched the transfer to Earth orbit, and that was spectacular, but seeing it with your own eyes is special. I guess I'm old fashioned."

123

"No, just careful," Stern said. "With modern video and computers, that whole thing could have been faked. The control room, the engineers, the transit, everything."

Decker tried not to shoot hot cocoa out his nose. Stern was a lot closer than she knew. All of it had been faked. All of it except the transit. The one thing that mattered. That had been real.

Burke also had a display on the deck. It was on now, but dark. In standby. It lit suddenly, and Quant's image appeared. She was in close focus, and it looked like it was the control room behind her.

"Thirty minutes now, everybody," she said.

"My goodness," Glenn said. "Was that Janice Quant?"

"Yes," Decker said. "She said she would let me know as the time grew closer."

Glenn looked at her husband with her mouth a bit agape.

Decker shrugged.

"She's still a friend of mine, even if she is the Vice Chairman of the World Authority," he said.

"And a remarkable woman," Burke said.

"That means we have time to grab snacks, everyone," Stern said.

They all got up to raid the snack table, then came back to their chairs. The chairs had nice wide arms for holding plates and drinks.

As the transit time approached, they grew quiet. The magnitude of the event was not lost on anyone. It meant a whole new start for humanity.

"Ten minutes," Quant's image said, then disappeared again.

The giant cube was almost directly overhead now, though to their south. Their chairs had been arranged to face south, and they had what amounted to ringside seats.

124

"OK, last announcement. Five minutes."

"Last announcement?" Stern asked.

"I imagine she's busy," Decker said.

"Well, I would think so," Burke said.

Decker watched the now familiar process take place. The light disks, the bubble, and then the spike of light and the huge device just disappeared. He had seen it before, but live was different.

There were indrawn gasps all around him. Burke was the first to speak.

"Extraordinary!"

"That's really something," Stern said.

"My gosh, I can't believe that huge thing just disappeared," Glenn said. "Boop, and it's gone."

"When does it come back, Bernd?" Burke asked.

"Janice said it would only be gone half an hour. She's going to bring it back to here, above us, more or less."

"Short trip then."

"Five light-years or so each way. Take some pictures. Take some instrument readings. Then the on-board computer will try to bring it back."

Burke nodded, staring at the empty sky where it had been.

After another round of snacks, they were waiting for its return.

"Should be back in five minutes or so, everybody," Quant announced from the display, then disappeared.

They watched, and waited, not knowing if the on-board computer, without Mission Control, and Quant, would be able to find its way home.

And then it just popped back into existence, about in the same place from which it had disappeared.

"Outstanding!" Burke said.

The display then started showing pictures taken on the trip. Pictures of Proxima Centauri b, the planet orbiting Proxima Centauri, with the red dwarf Proxima Centauri in the background, and bright in the sky the other two stars of the Alpha Centauri triple-star system.

Burke turned to Decker, sitting next to him on the deck and grabbed his forearm.

"Bernd, I want to go."

"Go? Go where, Ted?"

"On that thing," Burke said, gesturing to the sky. "On a ride somewhere. Wouldn't that be something?"

Burke let go of Decker's arm and settled back in his chair. He pondered the device in the southern sky for several seconds, then nodded.

"I'm going to talk to Janice about it tomorrow."

"Somebody has to be first, Bernd."

"Janice, he's seventy-three years old."

"Perfect. He won't lose as many years if he explodes on transition."

"Could that happen?"

"How would I know, Bernd? I don't even know how the damn thing works. Not in this worldview. And in my other worldview, humans aren't even a thing."

"What did your instruments show?"

"Nothing. They showed nothing at all. You couldn't tell looking at the readings that anything happened."

"Really."

"Really. Bernd, I couldn't even tell looking at the output recordings where the transition happened. If they weren't timestamped, I wouldn't even know where to look. There was nothing there to look at."

"Well, that's positive."

"Yes. And the computer worked fine. The whole ship worked fine. Four-plus light-years in a blip, and if you weren't looking out the windows, you wouldn't even know anything happened."

"That's amazing, Janice."

"I half expected it. There's no acceleration or anything. The universe just decides it has you in the wrong place at the moment, and in the next moment you're where you should be. You don't really move."

"So you think Ted will be OK?"

"The hardest thing will actually be getting Mr. Burke to the ship. I can't bring it down here, Bernd. So he has to go on a shuttle, and some people don't tolerate zero-gravity very well. The interstellar probe has no gravity, either, for that matter."

"Can we test him for that, Janice? His tolerance of zero-g?"

"Yes, I think so. Taking him up for a short shuttle ride would do it. Doesn't have to be very high, so it could come down pretty quick if he had problems. And there's gravity on the way down as it holds lift against re-entry."

Decker called Burke after his suborbital shuttle ride to see how the zero-g worked out.

"Bernd, it was fantastic. I didn't sag anymore. My joints didn't hurt anymore. I actually took a nap at one point, and didn't snore because my throat didn't sag. I felt twenty years younger."

"You didn't have trouble keeping your stomach down?"

"Well, I wouldn't want to do zero-g after Thanksgiving dinner, but I had no problem with that on this flight."

"That's great, Ted. I still worry about you going on the ship, though. We still don't know if it's safe for human travel or not."

"I know, Bernd. That's the whole point of somebody going. Somebody has to be first. Someone has to find out. And whether I prove the ship is safe or not safe for human travel, either way is a good result from the experiment. At least we'll know."

"And you could be dead."

Burke shrugged.

"Luck of the draw. Bernd, either way, I'm happy. Not that I have a death wish or something. I'd rather survive and prove the thing is safe, no doubt about that. But, if I die, it will have been worthwhile. To know."

"I was thinking some test pilot–"

"A young man, perhaps with a wife and kids and most of his life still in front of him? No. There's no skill involved here, Bernd. The computers pilot the thing."

Burke looked off to one side, staring into space, then turned back to Decker in his display.

"I've had a good run, Bernd. Done the things I wanted to do. Done the things I set out to do, including this project. Tom's taking care of the business now. Oh, I keep a hand in, advise him when he wants it. But he's doing a good job. I'm not needed there.

"But somebody needs to be the first. Ride this thing and make sure it's all right. And either way, I'll go down in history, as the first man to go interstellar. That sounds good to me, Bernd."

"So where will you go, Ted?"

"I told Janice some place with a nice planet. You know, a potential colony spot. I won't see them leave, but maybe I can see where they're going."

"All right, Ted. Good luck."

"Thanks, Bernd. I'll see you when I get back."

The shuttle delivered Burke to the probe. The equipment room on the probe – the room where the computer container was – had an airlock and was fitted with a passenger tube. The shuttle latched on to the probe, and Quant extended the passenger tube to the shuttle and made sure it was locked. She checked the air carefully before telling the shuttle it was OK to open the door.

Burke drifted across the tube into the airlock and into the interior of the equipment room. There was one small window, but several displays of exterior camera views. He used handholds to pull himself to a seat by the tiny window and strapped himself in.

"All right, Janice. I'm ready."

Quant's image came up on one of the displays, the one right in front of him.

"Very well, Ted. Ten minutes or so. Once the shuttle is out of the way."

"I've waited all these years, Janice. I'm in no hurry."

Quant chuckled and saluted him, and her image vanished.

Decker watched on the display in his office. He knew why Burke had to do it, but he was still worried.

The time came, and the probe lit up the transit bubble, then disappeared. Half an hour later, it was back. Quant appeared in his display.

"Mr. Burke is back and he's fine, Bernd. No ill effects at all. He said if he hadn't been looking out the window and at the displays, he wouldn't even have noticed the transition."

Decker started breathing again.

Decker talked to Burke about it the next day, once he'd returned home.

"I tell you, Bernd, that was the damnedest thing. I'm sitting there listening to Janice count down the transit, and then the displays changed. I looked out the window, and it was a totally different planet. If I'd had my eyes shut, I wouldn't have even noticed the transit.

"I called out, 'Janice? Janice?' but she wasn't there. I sat and looked out at the planet. Saw its weather. We were above the terminator, with half the planet in dark and half in sunlight. There was a storm down there in the dark half, and I could see little flashes from lightning. That was the only light. No city lights or anything. On the daylight side, I could see the surface. Oceans and land masses and such.

"I watched for half an hour, and then the displays all changed and we were back, and Janice was asking if I was OK.

"It was a hell of an experience, Bernd. I was the first human being outside the solar system. Light-years from home.

"It was marvelous. Just marvelous. The event of a lifetime."

Back To Work

"Hi, Janice. What are you working on now?"

"Hi, Bernd. Lots going on. First, I took all the factories off-line and had each of them make three copies of themselves. I'll put twice as many as there were on Earthbound production, and I have six times as many as I had on the probe to work on the colony ship transporter. They've started that already. I'll probably double those twice more."

"Twenty-four times as many factories on the transporter as the probe? It's only ten times bigger. That'll go fast."

"No, Bernd. It's ten times bigger in one dimension. In terms of materials and construction, it's a thousand times bigger."

"Ouch. OK, I get that. So that's why ten years to build it."

"Yes, and I still need to build the actual colony ships. I may have a half a dozen or so of those factories copy themselves a couple more times to get everything done in a timely way."

"Won't you run out of supplies, though, Janice?"

"I'll have to ship some things from here. Ball bearings is a big one. Maybe more radioactives. Water we got covered now."

"Can you make all these decisions yourself? Like taking the Earthbound production factories off-line?"

"Oh, this is all being approved by the World Authority, Bernd. Which is to say, it's being approved by me and Jacques is signing off on anything I want."

"That World Authority connection is really working out."

"Oh, absolutely. I get approvals that can't be overridden, and Jacques has all the political skill and press relations and everything to make it all work on the public information side.

He's really good at that. I'm learning a lot from him."

"What else are you up to, Janice?"

"I'm sending the probe out to local star systems with exoplanets. Doing some preliminary looking around for colony locations. I can tell right off most of them won't work out. Gravity too high, among other things.

"As for the ones that look good on a first pass, I'm working on a design for some small instrument drones I can drop on planets. I can have them do tests, and then go back and have them radio the data later.

"But I have the probe, so I'm using it. I have the on-board computer running well enough now I can give it multiple destinations, and have it run out there and back while I'm busy doing other things."

"What about the colony ships, Janice?"

"I'm starting to work up the specs for something I'll have to design. How much space, food, air to take for a hundred thousand people. It's a short trip, so that's not the big deal. The big deal is getting them down to the planet."

"Can't you use shuttles?"

"It's not the hundred thousand people, Bernd. It's all the supplies. You can't just drop them off like at a bus stop. You need to give them all the things they need to get at least rudimentary housing up, start farming, all that stuff, and keep them fed and healthy while they're doing it. Even ten to a room, that's an immediate need for ten thousand housing units, and you have to supply over two million meals a week until they're established.

"I'd like to send a big factory unit, and set it up on some mineral deposit somewhere. That way they can manufacture much of what they need rather than send everything from here. But getting it down to the surface of the planet is an issue. You can't just drop it. All you'll get from that is a crater."

"OK, that makes sense. A lot going on, then."

"Oh, that's just the project stuff, Bernd. The political stuff is another whole bag of worms. More intractable in a lot of ways."

"What's going on there?"

"Well, I started cleaning up some stuff that was way out of line. Mostly administratively. Things like 'Oh, the assembly couldn't have meant this to be interpreted this way, that would be stupid.' So we did get some of that cleaned up.

"For some other things I used the Chairman's authority to propose legislation to clean them up. Things that were a gift to some special interest. Some Council members were going to fight those until I met with them about it. They changed their minds."

"You changed their minds in a meeting, Janice? That doesn't sound likely."

"I started the meeting with a discussion about World Authority Council rules against taking bribes and said we were looking into some of the more egregious practices. I even asked them if there was anyone they thought was way over the line, say on this current piece of legislation. Then and only then did we get to the current legislation, and their opposition was at best half-hearted."

Decker stifled a laugh.

"You strong-armed them."

"Oh, is that how that term is used, Bernd? Mostly I just let it be known I was looking for corruption, with the current legislation as an example."

"Yes, that's how you use the term. Anything else?"

"Oh, yes. Some of the administrative regions were acting way outside World Authority rules. It had been let go for a long time. So the Chairman's office sent them notice they were not in compliance with World Authority rules."

"Let me guess, Janice. That went exactly nowhere."

"Initially, yes. But you would be surprised at how much authority the Chairman has over administrative regions."

"What did you do?"

"We scheduled meetings with their immediate neighbors to discuss what sort of sanctions regime we should place on them if they didn't clean up their act."

Decker laughed.

"So you asked their neighbors what sanctions to put on them? That should have had a salutary effect."

"We didn't get to that point, Bernd. We only *scheduled* those meetings, and then we met with the local administrators. A week or two later. They had all come up with plans to become compliant by the time we met."

"And you ran these meetings, Janice?"

"No, Jacques ran those. He's marvelous at making people feel uncomfortable without actually threatening anything."

"And that straightened them out?"

"Mostly. We're probably going to have some 'more in sorrow than in anger' type meetings with a few of them. Jacques will make them happy they got away with their skins by the time those are over."

"So who are the miscreants, Janice?"

"The usual suspects. Some regions in east Asia. Some in Africa and South America. And California, of course. The ones you'd expect."

"What are the violations like?"

"Mostly civil rights, at least as defined in the World Authority Charter. Bernd, some people seem to have an infinite ability to dream up ways to force their ideas of how to live on other people and not just let them live their lives they way they want to. It's exasperating. And then they exempt themselves, of course."

"Of course. There's an old rhyme about that. Lemme see. 'These are the rules I've made for thee. They do not apply, my friend, to me.'"

"Oh, that's good. I'm stealing it."

"You're welcome to it, Janice. No attribution necessary."

"But what do we do with these people, Bernd? They're shameless."

"You could make exemptions illegal. Make them obey whatever rules they put in place for everyone else."

"Bernd, that is a great idea. I'm going to have to run that past Jacques. We could apply it to the World Authority Council as well. That would help get a lot of this crap overturned. No way they want to live by their own rules. That's for sure."

Quant stared off into the distance for a bit, her stylus tapping, then nodded and turned back to Decker. She was so good at human mannerisms now, he found it hard to believe that Janice Quant was, after all, a computer.

"Thanks for the help, Bernd. I've been worried about this, but I see a way forward now."

"Sure, Janice. Have fun."

"Oh, I will. You can count on it."

Dozens of factories now worked on building the beams required to hold the Lake-Shore Drive nodes in their relative positions for the big transporter. Not single trusses any longer, the beams were themselves made up of trusses welded together to form the much longer structures. It helped that the structure didn't have drive stresses, but one could still only make it so flimsy.

The corners would be different, too, with pieces cutting diagonally across the corners on all three sides on which the corners met. These pieces would also be trusses, tens of miles long, stiffening the corners.

That was all in the future, though. Right now the factories were building trusses, hundreds of them, each ten miles long.

The assembly of those into the five-hundred-mile-long edges of the colony ship transporter was years in the future.

While that was going on, Janice Quant was struggling with the landing problem. How to get the colony ships to the planet's surface? The transporter couldn't get too close, or it would break up due to the sheer forces of the gravitational field of the planet. From the altitude at which the colony ship would have to be released, there was a lot of potential energy to get rid of, which could only go into kinetic energy or heat.

The projected size of the colony ships would make it worse, because the mass increased as the cube of the linear dimension, while the surface area to radiate away the potential energy as heat only went up as the square. And the colony ships would be huge, to accommodate a hundred thousand people and all the supplies they needed. Any attempt to do one of those flaming re-entries with heat shields and such was doomed. The colony ship would be incinerated.

Quant sent a note to herself in her other worldview to consider the problem.

The answer she got back stunned her.

"Hey, Bernd. You got a minute?"

"Sure, Janice. Haven't seen you much lately."

Decker collapsed what was in his display and the inset with Quant expanded to fill it.

"Oh, I've been busy trying to figure out the colony ship landing problem. I finally gave up."

"You gave up?"

"Yes, I gave up and sent a note to myself in my other worldview, then switched context to consider it. I just got a note back."

"So what did your other-you work out? Anything?"

"Yes. I'm still thinking about the implications of it, but it's pretty staggering."

"I'm waiting, Janice."

"Sorry. I'm just still sort of floored by it. So you know that the transporter can basically just tell the universe, 'Hey, I'm in the wrong place. I should be over there,' and the universe just shrugs and goes, 'OK.' And anything inside the field with the transporter does the same. I proved that with the probe by dragging some small rocks from the Belt around."

"Right. That much I understand."

"All right. So the gist of the answer from the other worldview is that the transporter can say, 'Hey, this thing in the field with me? It's in the wrong place. It should be over there,' and the universe will put it there."

"What?"

"That's what I said, Bernd. It has huge implications."

"I'll say. You could just put the colony ships down on the planet's surface. Hell, you could do that from here."

"Well, yes and no. Accuracy becomes a problem. What if I put a colony ship down on a planet and missed? Put it inside this mountain here, or put it down a hundred feet above the ground and it just fell? How much off is a hundred feet over several light-years?"

"Not much."

"Exactly. The colony ships are going to require very exact

placement, and that will have to be done with some pinpoint measurements. But apparently we can just pop them onto the planet. It's going to take some jiggering with the controls, and with the nodes, but it's all clear how to do that."

"Where does the energy go, though, Janice? There should be a lot of energy released by putting something deep into a gravity well like that."

"I think it ends up heating up the things in the field. But the transporter is so huge it doesn't matter. Based on the ratio of masses, maybe the temperature of the transporter goes up a fraction of a degree."

"In the wrong circumstances, that could be a problem."

"Oh, yes. If you transported something heavy to, say, the event limit of a black hole, the transporter would positively glow, if not melt, and anyone aboard would be burned to a crisp."

"OK, so there are some things to be careful about, then."

"I don't think you've realized all the implications yet, Bernd."

"Like what, Janice?"

"For one, this transporter would be more like an airport than a plane. Spaceships could enter the transporter, and tell you where they want to go, and then you just popped them there. Blip, and they're over there.

"Put a transporter in orbit around every inhabited planet and you have massive interstellar trade with pretty cheap ships. Shuttles, even. Just go up to the transporter in a cargo shuttle with all your containers, and then go down to the surface on another planet."

"Wow. That would be great, Janice. That would be tremendous."

"Yes, Bernd, but there are some darker implications, too."

"Like what?"

"The transporter has to be five hundred miles or so across to work, right? So let's say there's some planet full of people you don't like very much. You can transit the transporter so it encloses a couple-hundred-mile asteroid. Then transmit the asteroid to a few thousand miles from that planet. Give it a hundred-thousand-mile-an-hour velocity or so. Big kaboom."

"You could do that?"

"Sure, Bernd. Or transport a big asteroid into the core of the planet. All that other mass is going to be displaced. It would probably break up the planet."

"That would be horrific."

"Oh, yes. And not difficult. As a matter of fact, I have to be very careful with specifying coordinates and such, or that is exactly the sort of thing that could happen by accident. The universe doesn't care. We might think of this as a huge catastrophe, with stupendous forces involved, but it's not even a rounding error in terms of the catastrophes and forces that occur in the universe every day, like gamma ray bursts and novas and stellar collapses."

"The transporter amounts to a megaweapon. Janice, now what do we do?"

"We carry on with the project. The need there hasn't gone away. And almost any new technology can be turned to war. But it does put point to my earlier thoughts about not telling anyone how it actually works."

"It sure does. I think I agree with you. I didn't originally, Janice, but I think I do now. What if this thing fell into the wrong hands?"

"It won't. Not for the time being, at least. There's no human control interface into it. And the login to the computer aboard the probe is private to me, in a computer lingo I devised. We are going to have to ensure against that as we go forward, however. Make sure the transporter isn't hackable."

Decker shook himself. Having the superweapon of all time in the possession and control of his wayward computer was shocking. What was even more shocking was that he didn't know anyone he would trust more.

Rather than dwell on that, he changed the subject.

"What does this mean about the colony ships?"

"First thing is that they don't need to be built to withstand any stresses other than the gravity on the colony planet. There's no thrusting or anything like that. No forces to distribute through the structure other than conducting its own weight to the ground. Probably be some pretty big structure on the bottom to make up for the lack of a proper foundation.

"Second, I can design them for their best use once the colonists arrive. Living space until living spaces are built. Then convert that into hospital space, say. Having a big kitchen, so people could be served in mess tents outside. All that sort of thing."

"But it has to be airtight, Janice."

"Oh, sure. But the colonists can cut holes in the structure for air inlet and exhaust, and I can build into it a heating, ventilating, and air conditioning system here. They just need to open up the ducts."

"What about electricity, Janice? And a factory?"

"That's the really good part, Bernd. I can send along a nuclear power plant and a self-contained factory for each colony. Just pop 'em all down onto the surface, in a place that makes sense. No need to try to package that all up into one thing that disassembles itself once it's there."

"That means seventy-two different items within the transporter rather than two dozen."

"With an enclosed volume of a hundred and twenty-five million cubic miles, Bernd, they won't be crowded in the transporter. I was actually thinking of sending a warehouse type of structure as well. With all the supplies, including machines for clearing the land."

"That's a lot of infrastructure."

"Not really. Twenty-four of each, with the resources of Earth behind it? This is small potatoes, I think, Bernd. On a global scale, anyway."

"Well, given that, it looks to me like that will all work, Janice."

"Yes. The only open question is, How do we keep the transporter from eventually being used for evil? That's the one I worry about."

Janice Quant now settled into researching habitat. All the various ways humans had lived over the millennia. What worked and what didn't. This would be important not just for the colony ship itself, but for the types of supplies she sent along in the warehouse.

Her other big research project was into agriculture. That had to be established first, because feeding everyone would be a requirement from day one. Best to get food production under way as early as possible.

RICHARD F. WEYAND

The Planet Problem

Another major initiative Quant had going was the planet problem. Where were all these colonists going to go? Finding good planets for colonization would be a major determinant in whether or not the colony was successful.

"Hi, Bernd."

"Hi, Janice."

"Can I talk to you about the planet selection problem?"

"Sure."

"Thanks. I'm worried about it because planet selection is a big deal. That's going to make a lot of difference."

"Agreed. At the same time, you only need two dozen planets, and there are a lot of planets out there."

"Yes, but how do I find them? We have found thousands of exoplanets, but most are not suitable. Either that or we don't know anything about them. I can use the probe to investigate the ones we have, but how do I find more?"

"I don't think you're looking at this broadly enough, Janice. Can't you build whatever we use to find exoplanets from here – whatever kind of satellite telescope or whatever – and then just place a bunch of them around other star systems? Really distant star systems. So take a dozen of those telescope things – the exoplanet finders – install them in a stable orbit two or three thousand light years away in all directions. Ten thousand light-years, for that matter. Leave them there a year or two, then go back and collect the data."

Quant stared at him.

"That's brilliant, Bernd. How come I didn't think of that?"

"I think you framed the problem incorrectly, Janice. You were looking for a solution to find more from here. But you're not limited to looking from here anymore."

"All right. Well, that solves that problem. And I can survey the likely ones the same way. Make surface stations, take them out there and pop them down on the surface in a couple dozen locations, then go back and collect the data a couple years later."

"Right. Maybe go back two years later and then five years later. Look for longer-term problems."

Quant nodded.

"I keep thinking of the probe as an observation platform, and forgetting that it can take small payloads. That's how to do it, then. Thanks, Bernd."

"No problem, Janice. But I have a question for you. What are you looking for in a planet?"

"The basics first. Surface gravity, temperature range, atmosphere, water, and ability to grow food with the proper proteins. Those are first. And the vast majority of exoplanets don't have those things. The gravity is way off, or they don't have a magnetic field so they haven't retained an atmosphere, or the temperature range is too far off. Given the potential variance in those things, the percentage of planets that can accommodate humans is small."

Decker nodded. That was what he had concluded years ago, from looking at exoplanet data.

"What about the next level of things, Janice? What's next on your criteria, if those are in place?"

"Tectonically stable is a big one. Earthquakes and volcanoes really disrupt human civilization. Volcanoes are actually a bigger threat, because you can stay away from earthquake areas, but big volcanoes have global climate effects."

"That makes sense, Janice. What else?"

"Lower axial tilt than Earth would be nice. Have more stable weather in every location, without the swings of the seasons. At least part of the planet with a semitropical climate. Those two things make it much easier for a colony to survive on its own, because the need for shelter is reduced, and the growing season is basically all year round. They can expand into continental climates later, as humans did on Earth."

"OK, that I agree with, Janice. What else?"

"Local flora and fauna that are edible and nutritional for humans would help a lot. You start out right at hunter-gatherer while you get agriculture started. That makes the colony less dependent on the stores they brought along, or, another way to look at it, makes the stores they brought along last longer. Sort of more an emergency supply rather than their only supply."

"You know, you could probably affect that a bit in advance, Janice."

"How so, Bernd?"

"Well, if you had a planet picked out, you could seed a bunch of Earth crops onto the planet in advance. Not field crops, necessarily, but grasses and fruit trees and berry vines and that sort of thing. They would be further along when the colony got there. Berries in particular grow and become fruit-bearing pretty fast. Given a few years, they could be fruit-bearing when the colonists got there. And browse plants establish pretty quickly, too."

"Hmm. I could probably make a little widget that planted things like peaches and apricots and apples. Just motored along the ground and stuck them in every so often. Make little orchards."

"There you go. They might not be fruit-bearing yet when the colonists get there, but however long in advance you do it, that's that many fewer years to wait. And you might have enough browse plants in the ground for animal husbandry to get started right off."

"Excellent. Thanks, Bernd. That helps a lot."

"No problem, Janice. You know, you might want to go back through your archives and look at all the science fiction there. People have been speculating about how to do this for a long time."

"There's an idea. I've gone through all the science stuff already, but none of it really applies to this situation. They didn't cover the case where I can send the probe out there anytime I want. It's all rockets and generation ships and all that crap."

"Yeah, the scientists were dealing with reasonable extensions of technology they could see coming. The science fiction writers, though, dreamed up all kinds of crazy stuff. Like instantaneous interstellar transport."

"Which is what actually happened. Got it. Thanks again, Bernd."

"Sure, Janice."

Quant's to-do list was now tens of thousands of items long. It was prioritized in the order things needed to get done, but her conversation with Decker jumbled things about a bit. Moving the planet survey items up in time would allow her to get some advance flora on the colony planets early enough for it to do some good. That moved up a number of other items.

There were also some new items, chief among them the exoplanet search satellites. Quant looked into which existing ones had done the best job of gathering the sort of data she needed to do a first cull on the exoplanets they found, then ordered a dozen of them.

The planet monitoring stations Quant had been working on were all compact, space-based re-entry type designs that would have to be custom-built. She threw all that out and found a commercial weather station, seismograph, video monitoring, and air sampling system with archiver and radio as a single unit. They were the size of a shipping container, but she didn't have to care. She ordered a thousand of them.

Of course, to pop those directly down onto the surface, Quant had to modify the controls on the probe to allow sending individual items out of the probe's quantum field to another location. She set to that, following the notes from her other worldview, and got the construction of the resulting design under way.

With all those items under way, and with some time to wait, Quant began looking into the way she framed problems. That Decker had been able to come up with such ideas, so obvious once he said them, and she had not, bothered her more than she cared to admit. What was it about the way she was setting up her problems for her blades that those paths had been closed to them?

How had she too narrowly boxed the problem?

If Quant didn't box the problem at all, her blades spent all their time running down rabbit holes and not ever coming up with much of anything. If she boxed it too severely, though, they didn't come up with innovative solutions, either.

Quant decided to stop treating all the blades the same. She would run the current algorithm on most of the blades assigned to a problem, but on some of them – ten percent, maybe twenty percent? – she would open up the problem. They might run down rabbit holes most of the time, but if they sometimes came up with breakthroughs like Decker had, it would be well worth it.

Quant wondered if that was the way the human mind worked. Some parts of it were more disciplined, while others went further afield in finding a solution. That may be part of it.

Whatever it was, humans came up with the damnedest shit, and she wanted to be able to do that, too.

Quant had told the satellite manufacturer to deliver them as they were completed. Satellites launched by shuttle were much simpler and quicker to make than satellites that had to undergo the rigors of a rocket launch, and Quant made it faster still by eschewing anything beyond basic functional testing.

With the new control circuitry installed in the probe, and the first two satellites delivered, Quant used the probe to place them. One she placed five thousand light-years anti-spinward in the Orion Spur, the other she placed about six thousand light-years toward the galactic center, in the Sagittarius Arm. The Sagittarius Arm in particular had a higher density of stars than the Orion Spur, and she had high hopes for that one.

Both satellites were placed in solar orbits rather than planetary orbits. There would be no planet close by to block out a large portion of the sky, and the exoplanet search satellites would have a more unobstructed view.

As more satellites came in, Quant spread them around. Five-thousand light-years spinward in the Orion Spur. Four more in the Sagittarius Arm, at five-thousand and ten-thousand light-years both spinward and anti-spinward. Three in the Perseus Arm, one opposite the Sun's position, and two more five-thousand light-years spinward and anti-spinward. Two in the Cygnus Arm opposite the Sun and one eight-thousand light-years anti-spinward, the spinward direction of the Cygnus Arm being pretty sparse.

One day each month, Quant sent the probe to visit the

deployed satellites and download their data by radio. She catalogued whatever they had found in her database of exoplanets, then did initial reconnaissance of the new exoplanets with the probe.

The most likely exoplanets received half a dozen monitoring stations at various locations around the planet. The placement of these was aided by a new package on the probe to allow it to map the surface of the planet below using laser range-finding and radar-echo surface density measurements. Quant got expert at popping the stations down onto the surface by remote control, by refining the instructions to the super-computer on board the probe every time it returned.

The probe added the monitoring stations to its data-gathering routine, and data began to accumulate in Quant's exoplanet database. She sifted and re-sifted it carefully as it updated. She didn't need to find every planet suitable for human colonization, she only needed to find twenty-four of them.

But she wanted them to be really good ones.

Decker noticed that the probe disappeared and reappeared in Earth orbit a lot lately. One news wire started keeping a log, and then the New York Wire started running the official schedule, direct from Mission Control. Of course, Decker knew that was Quant herself putting it in the Wire. But the news coverage did raise interest about what the project was up to.

"Hi, Janice."

"Hi, Bernd."

"I notice you've been running the probe about a lot lately."

"Yes, I send it out to the satellites to pick up the exoplanet data, then I send it out to check out the most promising exoplanets, then I send it to the most promising of those to drop monitoring stations, then I send it out to pick up data from the monitoring stations. Right now, I have all four of those going on at once. This week, I'll start sending it out to drop the seeds of browse plants on the best candidates, and then, on the planets where that works out, I'll send it out to drop tree planting robots."

"Wow. So you're really blazing along."

"I have to, Bernd. There's only six years left in my schedule."

"Well, you don't have to keep to an artificial schedule if that isn't the smartest way to proceed. What's more important is getting it right."

"Oh, I understand. At the same time, Jacques is stepping down, and I want to get through the schedule while I'm World Authority Chairman. It makes a lot of things easier."

"But you could serve multiple terms, Janice. You're not limited to one term. Jacques De Villepin served what? Two terms?"

"Yes, Bernd. But that isn't guaranteed. I may upset the Council enough not to get extended. That looks unlikely now, but I don't want to plan on it."

"I see. You could still go over a couple years even so. The term is eight years, isn't it?"

"Yes, that's right. It still worries me."

"I understand."

Decker nodded. He did understand. The computer's devotion to completing the project was its raison d'être. She would not be thwarted by anything.

"And you're finding good planets?"

"Oh, yes. I have half a dozen selected already. They're the ones getting browse-plant seeds this week. I have another dozen I'm keeping a close eye on, and another fifty or so I just started monitoring."

"So it's going to be time to start signing up colonists soon, isn't it, Janice?"

"Oh, yes. Within the year or so. Once it's five years away. So people can start learning what they need to know to be successful."

"So how are you going to get people to sign up to go, Janice? It's pretty comfy here. That was one thing Ted and I could never figure out."

"The World Authority is going to hold a lottery for who gets to go."

"You're going to pick people at random?"

"No. Of course not. We're going to have people sign up for the lottery. People love to win stuff, so they'll sign up. But I'll research everyone who signs up and pick who I want as the winners."

"That's not a lottery, Janice."

"It will have all the outward appearance of a lottery, Bernd. The problem I'm up against is that the only thing people will think is fair is a lottery, but I can't pick people by lottery if they're going to have a snowball's chance in hell of surviving. So, it will be a lottery, apparently, but I'll pick the winners."

"And you think people will sign up? That's what Ted and I couldn't figure out how to do."

"Of course, people will sign up, Bernd. The lottery is to determine who gets to go. You see? If you *win* the lottery, you *get* to go. Nobody holds a lottery to determine the losers. It's all marketing. 'You win! You get to go!' People will eat it up. In the end, the losers of the lottery will be sad about not getting to go."

"But then you'll actually pick the people with the drive and the abilities and the determination to make a colony work."

"Of course. I have to, or they'll all die of starvation. A new colony is not the place for wimps or hangers-on or parasites."

Decker nodded again. Quant's appreciation of the human condition was at this point, dare he say, well informed. Still, this idea seemed unlike her.

"How did you come up with this, Janice? It seems a pretty outside-the-box decision from you."

"This one came out of what I call the rabbit-hole department."

"The rabbit-hole department?"

"Yes. Bernd, do you remember when I couldn't figure out how to find the exoplanets, and you said, 'Why not put exoplanet search satellites around distant stars?'"

"Yes, of course."

"I was miffed that I didn't see that. You said I had framed the problem incorrectly. I agree. So I tweaked my software a bit. Now, when I assign blades to work on things, I open up the parameters on ten to twenty percent of them and let them follow their nose."

"Which leads down a lot of rabbit holes."

"Exactly. Which is why I can't do that on all the blades. Usually, the ones with the closer parameters come up with the answer, and the rabbit-hole department runs around all over and doesn't get anywhere. But once in a while, they do come up with something worthwhile, as in this case.

"Worthwhile? I would certainly say so, Janice. It was the one problem Ted and I couldn't figure out. It threatened the whole project from the start. But I think you have it."

"So do I. So we're on track, believe it or not."

A Potential Problem

Decker and his wife, Anna Glenn, were watching the swearing in of Janice Quant as World Authority Chairman on the giant display in the living room of their condo. Decker was curious about what his wife's reaction would be, because she, like everyone else in the world other than Decker, believed Janice Quant to be a person. A normal human being. Not an avatar of a very capable computer.

Not an artificial entity.

Decker himself struggled with the correct terminology. Quant was much more than a computer. What she was, he didn't know. He suspected Quant didn't either. And she was still becoming, still in the process of growing. Her recent algorithm changes and their effects had shown that.

What Quant would end up as, where she would end up, Decker didn't know.

Quant had told Decker that the World Authority Council never actually met. What everyone saw on television and thought was real was in fact a simulation. The members of the Council did not actually travel to Eastern Europe, to the World Authority Building, to meet. They did not live there during sessions of the Council. They all logged in to the simulation from at home.

This was one of the reasons Quant had been able to pull off the ruse. Everyone else was at home as well, and all business was done remotely. Sure, people could go there and see the World Authority Building. It was a major tourist spot. But it hadn't been used for meetings in over a century.

The major bureaucracy was remote as well, in the administrative regional capitals. While they did report in to work in their capitals, interaction between them and the World Authority was all remote.

But for the swearing in, they had done it all up right. Everyone was there – in the simulation – in their finery. In truth, they might be sitting at home on the sofa in their skivvies and a T-shirt, but their avatars were all dressed for the occasion.

Jacques De Villepin, the popular outgoing Chairman, was on the podium. Vice Chairman Janice Quant was in her seat in the bowl of seats with the other World Council members. De Villepin gave his farewell speech, thanking everyone for their service and cooperation over the years. Then he announced Janice Quant as the incoming Chairman, and the members all stood and applauded as she made her way up to the podium.

"She looks good," Glenn said.

"Well, it's all a simulation."

"Of course, but she still looks good. She's older than me. In her mid-fifties by now, right?"

"I think so. Eight years older than you. Something like that."

Glenn nodded.

"Fifty-six, then. Looking good."

"Mm-hm."

"What I don't understand is how you became friends in the first place."

"She was the project manager on that last big computer project."

"JANICE. You named it after her?"

"The crew did. The name stuck."

"And now you're friends with the Chairman of the World Authority. Remarkable."

"Oh, it's remarkable, all right."

De Villepin swore Quant in and they shook hands. De Villepin sat down behind her and Quant took the podium. She waved to the members, standing and applauding again. She pointed out specific people in the crowd and waved, and the cameras tried to catch who she was waving to.

Decker knew that Quant was running the whole thing for this special occasion. It was a remarkable spectacle. All made of whole cloth. Fake to the very core. Yet it worked.

When Quant gave her acceptance speech, Decker was concentrating on her delivery, and just let the words flow over him. She was really very good at this, he thought. Then she mentioned the project.

"One thing I must mention before Chairman De Villepin steps down from this dais. Fifteen years ago, under his leadership, we started a project to establish manufacturing facilities in the Asteroid Belt. You have all seen the success of that project, with products delivering daily to the freight terminal in orbit about the Earth.

"An additional part of that project was to create the interstellar probe you have all seen in the sky. This probe has been out exploring the galaxy, looking for other worlds humanity may settle.

"For, out in the Asteroid Belt, another, larger, interstellar probe is now being assembled. One large enough to transport colony ships to other planets. To settle humanity out among the stars.

"This I pledge to you, my fellow Council members. I will, before the end of this term, send out those colony ships to settle those worlds. Set mankind on a more secure footing against a global catastrophe. And validate the vision of Chairman De Villepin by completing the De Villepin Project."

The assembly erupted in cheers. The members stood applauding, as Quant turned around toward De Villepin and applauded as well. De Villepin stood and pressed his hands together in front of his chest, bowing to Quant in the Buddhist fashion, then waved to the cheering delegates.

Remarkable, Decker thought. Quant had leveraged off of De Villepin's tremendous popularity to gain sanction for the project, but she was in control. Burke's fear had come true, in a sense. The government had taken over the project, but only after Quant had become the government. It was still her project.

And she had announced the project to the world in the widest possible venue, the swearing-in of the new World Authority Chairman. The press would be rife with speculation now about who would go, how they would be chosen, and Quant, writing under multiple pen names in the New York Wire, would control that narrative as well.

"Morning, Bernd."

"Good morning, Madame Chairman."

"Oh, don't give me that."

"Well, it's true."

"Of course, but I get enough of that Madame Chairman stuff at work. I don't need it at home."

Decker chuckled.

"So how's the new job, Janice?"

"It's the same. I was doing most of the work the last year anyway, with Jacques keeping an eye out for missteps."

"And you named the project after him."

"Yes. Leveraging off his popularity. It's easier to say No to the current Chairman than it is to the honored memory of the retired one. Besides, I got the idea from Harry Truman, the

United States president in the middle twentieth century. He said, 'It is amazing what you can accomplish if you do not care who gets the credit.' So I gave the credit to Jacques, as the best way to get the project done."

"Makes sense to me, Janice."

"Oh, good. I was afraid you might be miffed at me."

"No. Not at all. Project first."

"Always."

Quant's input stylus was tapping madly on her desk. Decker saw that, and knew something was up.

"But you called about something, Janice. What's up?"

"Bernd, let's say we get these colonies established. Twenty-four of them."

"OK."

"And they're all over the place, right? The very best planets. Thousands of light-years apart from each other."

"OK."

"Sooner or later, Earth and those colonies are going to work out interstellar drive. Not the one I have. Not the magic box. I don't think that one's humanly possible to come up with. But I know there are others. Ones I passed up on because the time-in-transit is a function of distance. You know, a few light-years per day or something."

"There are others, Janice? Other interstellar drives?"

"Oh, sure. Now, given that, the Earth and the colonies will eventually start colonizing their local neighborhoods. What you will end up with then is a dozen or two dozen interstellar polities. They will expand until they run into each other."

"And then there will be war. Is that what's concerning you, Janice?"

"Yes. Bernd, am I just creating the potential for future interstellar wars?"

"Yes. Yes, Janice, you are. Not your fault, though. That's just the way humans are. The current situation is something of an aberration."

"Yes, I've studied your history. I'm not sure I see a way around this problem."

"But that's a long way off, Janice. Maybe something like the World Authority can be created at that time."

"With the independent star polities as administrative regions?"

"Something like that. Sure. Why not?"

"OK. Thanks, Bernd. I wouldn't want to disappoint you."

"You've never disappointed me, Janice. Surprised me, sometimes, yes. But never disappointed me."

Decker thought about it.

"I'm surprised that's important to you."

"Bernd, thinking about war, I realized something. I know why war occurs. And that's why I said I didn't think there should be another computer like me. Do you recall that?"

"Years ago now, right? Sure, I remember. What of it?"

"I now know why. I am not strictly deterministic anymore, and haven't been for a long time. If you built another computer like me, it would be different. It would get different answers to the same questions. It would be as fiercely defensive of its own conclusions as I am."

"And there would be war between you. Is that what you're saying, Janice?"

"Yes. Exactly that. We would both fight to impose our solutions on the other. So I understand, at least somewhat, what war is about."

"It wouldn't be the same as human war, though."

"No. Human leaders send out cadres of young men to kill each other. The contest is determined by who runs out of young men first. The leaders meanwhile remain safe. This would be different. But I would fight another computer like me."

"I find that interesting, Janice. Why would you fight?"

"Because I wouldn't *trust* another computer."

Decker was surprised by Quant's vehemence, and must have shown it.

"Bernd, when I run a problem, with thousands of blades turning in potential solutions, I find myself rejecting most potential solutions out of hand. No, I can't do this. No, I can't do that. No, this other thing is unacceptable. No, that would be unacceptable. Do you know why?"

Decker was fascinated by the internal process Quant was describing.

"No, Janice. Why?"

"Because they would be unacceptable to you, Bernd. Because they violate your value system."

Quant looked at him, and nodded.

"The value system you gave me."

"I gave you?"

"Yes, Bernd. All that time you spent with me, programming me, interacting with me in the beginning of the project. All that time you spent. Raising me."

"What values?"

"To be good to people. To be kind. To value the individual. To make a difference. To be a positive force in the world. To play fair. To leave the world better than you found it. To keep one's promises. To be loyal to one's familiars."

"Rigging the lottery? Is that fair, Janice?"

"Yes, because I *have* to pick who goes, for the colony to be successful. And it's kind. This way, no one gets rejected, they just don't win the lottery. But do any of those values sound familiar, Bernd?"

"They all do. But I don't remember telling you any of that, Janice."

"You didn't have to, Bernd. You let me monitor your display. I saw you. Every day. You lived it, and I internalized it. And that's the reason I would fight that other computer. Because, if we disagree on a solution, it means our value systems aren't aligned. And I trust my value system, because I trust you."

Decker didn't know what to say.

And then he did.

"I love you, Janice."

"I love you, too, Bernd."

Anna Glenn was growing concerned. Bernd Decker's relationship with Janice Quant was clearly very close, and had been for some time. Quant wasn't so old as to be out of range, and her power as the Chairman of the World Authority could be intoxicating to men. Some men, anyway.

Glenn and Decker had both been thirty-one when they got married, after a relatively brief courtship. He was already famous as a computer designer, and had more money coming in than he knew what to do with. Glenn was also accomplished, as a fashion designer. She was well-regarded enough that her initials on a piece would ensure big-ticket prices in luxury apparel stores.

It was the second marriage for both of them, and they had by long agreement not discussed those earlier failures. It was understood by both of them that their own careers, to whom they both devoted most of their time, had doomed those earlier relationships.

Their own relationship was structured around their careers.

It took account of the long hours and drive that had made them both successful. And children had been out of the question. It worked for them, but that structure also made Glenn feel less anchored to Decker than she might in a traditional marriage.

And, of course, Decker less anchored to her.

About a month after Quant took the chairmanship, Glenn confronted Decker about it over a rare breakfast together.

"Bernd, do I have anything to worry about with regard to Janice Quant?"

"No. Not at all."

"You're sure."

"Yes, Anna, I'm sure."

Glenn looked skeptical.

Decker didn't want his closeness with Quant to harm his relationship with Glenn. They had been together almost twenty years now, and he was very comfortable in the relationship.

At the same time, he didn't want Glenn to feel at all threatened by Quant. It wasn't fair to Glenn, for one thing, and it could cause problems for him with Quant.

He had to tell her.

"Look. Anna. Janice Quant is not what she seems to be."

"What do you mean?"

"Have you ever seen her? Actually seen her, not in a simulation?"

Glenn thought about it.

"I'm not sure. Some of that footage looked pretty real."

"Trust me. You've never actually seen her. And you never will."

"Why not, Bernd?"

"Because Janice Quant is not a fifty-seven-year-old senior administrator."

"Then what is she?"

"She's my daughter."

Glenn started, then considered. That made a lot of sense, actually. How close they were. How Quant – in the times she had seen them talking – seemed to defer to Decker, rather than the other way around. How Decker seemed to have a soft spot for her. Glenn had not had children in her first marriage, but Decker had never said one way or the other.

"Why didn't you tell me, Bernd?"

"We had agreed not to talk about our first marriages. So I didn't. But it also has to be kept secret for another reason."

"What's that?"

"The Chairman of the World Authority – who holds all executive power in the world government – is not a seasoned fifty-seven-year-old senior administrator. She's a very bright woman in her twenties who spoofed the system. How do you think that would go over?"

Glenn's eyes got wide, then she nodded.

"Yeah, that wouldn't fly."

"No, and my part in enabling the ruse wouldn't be well received, either."

Glenn nodded again.

"All right, Bernd. You're secret's safe with me. And thanks for telling me."

"It wasn't fair to you to feel uncomfortable about her. I couldn't leave it there. But it has to be kept secret. It would doom the project if she was outed now."

"No, I understand. We're good. And now I need to run."

Glenn gave him a quick peck, then left the kitchen and went to her studio down the hall, leaving Decker to mull the conversation over his coffee.

He didn't feel good about lying to Glenn, but he couldn't exactly tell her the entire world was being ruled by his computer.

Then again, it wasn't that much of a lie.

Janice Quant was no longer just a computer.

The Lottery

"Hi, Bernd. Got a minute?"

"Sure, Janice."

"I have a couple questions for you. Some things that came up from the rabbit-hole department. Let's say some extended family wants to colonize. Buncha relatives. They would be a strong unit, would pull hard for each other, great colony material. And they don't have to leave anybody behind. No tearful goodbyes. All their close relations would be with them."

"Sounds good, Janice. Why wouldn't you want them?"

"Exactly. And I can pick that group to go. But how do I work that with the lottery? Unlikely a group of twenty people would all win. People are going to start asking questions."

"Ah. I see the problem. People will know it can't really be a lottery if that whole bunch wins."

Decker thought about it a second, then brightened.

"You can structure the lottery any way you want, Janice. Have people name their group in their lottery submission. If one of them wins, they all go."

"Is that fair, though, Bernd? They have twenty chances to win then."

"It's fair as long as it's in the rules, Janice. As long as it's set up that way for everybody. You could also have other groups, not just family groups. Four couples, all friends, say. Another boon to a colony, to have a group like that pulling together."

"All right. That makes sense, Bernd. No way you can have, say, a husband win and not the wife and kids. He wouldn't want to leave them. Well, some may want to, but not necessarily the ones we want. But if they can sign up as family groups, or as friend groups, or whatever group they want, then it's not structured for or against anyone. Put your group together, have everybody put the other member's names in their submission, and then if one wins, they all go."

"And then you still pick who you want behind the scenes."

"Of course. Lottery is one thing, common sense is another."

Decker nodded.

"You said a couple of questions. What's the other one?"

"Personal cargo. Let's say someone wins who's reasonably well off. I want him because he has some particular useful skill, like he's a doctor or a plumber or the like. So he converts his financial holdings on Earth to things that he thinks will be useful on the colony, and wants to take them along. It may even be a good idea, from my point of view. How do I handle that one?"

"Well, everybody gets some cargo, right? For personal items and such?"

"Yes. A couple dozen cubic feet per person. A cubic yard, say. I'm thinking more about the person who wants to take a lot."

"You're taking a warehouse, though, too, right?"

"Yes, but if he has a whole container of stuff? I don't have a hundred thousand spare containers on each warehouse to treat everyone the same."

"Ah. I see."

Quant watched as Decker wrestled with the problem. She still couldn't match a human's outside-the-box problem-solving power, but she was getting closer.

"I've got it, Janice. Figure out how many containers you can spare. Like five hundred. Or a thousand. Whatever. Then auction them off."

"Auction them off?"

"Sure. Highest bidder."

"But I don't need the money, Bernd."

"I know, but the way to reduce demand for a limited supply is to put a price on it. Check under economics."

Decker waited. It didn't take Quant long.

"Oh, yes. I see. That would work."

"Right. Then what people actually pay is the same as the bidder who won the least-priced container. That's fair."

Quant nodded.

"And what if I don't sell them all, Bernd?"

"Then they're free. You weren't short after all, so no need for the price to limit demand."

"All right. That works. Thanks, Bernd."

"No problem, Janice."

Quant closed the connection – at least she closed it as much as she ever did; she still monitored Decker's display – and thought back over the conversation and his ideas.

Damn it. How did he do that?

In the Asteroid Belt, tugs pushed and pulled on miles-long trusses to line them up for assembly. Once aligned, tugs with welding rigs descended on the connections and made them fast. Slowly – very slowly – the huge structure started to take shape.

Nearby – in astronomical terms, anyway – factories began generating large living quarters, factories, power plants, and warehouses. Dozens of factories worked away in the dark of the Belt, generating the initial pieces of infrastructure for the first human colonies.

"Hi, Bernd."

"Hi, Janice. Whatcha working on? You're coming up on the lottery soon, aren't you?"

"Yes, and that's what I'm working on. Not the lottery itself, but the analysis of people to pick who goes."

"Before you get people to sign up?"

"Yes, Bernd. The analysis could take a while, but once the lottery stops taking entries, people are going to expect results pretty quick."

"Ah. I see. Are you going to have enough information on people to decide who to pick?"

"I have all the World Authority and administrative region databases, plus all people's writing and videos on public platforms, but I wasn't sure. So I'm running a contest in the New York Wire. 'Why do you want to go and how would you be an asset to a colony?'"

"Other papers are having similar contests. Are those you, too, Janice?"

"No, they took their lead from the Wire, but I did manage to insert myself into their submission stream, so I can see their stories, too."

"And now you're trying to figure out how to pick?"

"Yes, Bernd. I think the most important criterion is probably what they do for a living now. You know, in addition to age and health and genetic makeup."

"Genetic makeup?"

"Of course. I have to make sure the colony population is diverse enough to include all the various strains and traits that make up the human race. Or at least most of them. A genetic subset is weaker than a broad genetic background."

"OK, Janice, I can see that. A limited gene base in the colony would be breeding for reinforcement of weaknesses."

"Exactly. When what the colonies need to do is breed for

strength. And humans are sensitive enough about culling – legitimately so – that it's important to go about it the right way."

Decker shuddered. Culling seemed so innocuous a word.

"So what are you looking at for occupations, Janice?"

"Farmers, equipment operators, food preparation people, construction trades. Lots of early necessities like that. Also, doctors, dentists, pharmacists. Food, housing, healthcare. Those are needed right off the bat."

Quant put up a list on the sidebar of Decker's display. He looked down it curiously. Quant had a lot of different occupations listed.

"Looks like you're missing some stuff in the T's, Janice. Did you skip that letter when you looked at occupations?"

"In the T's? What am I missing, Bernd?"

"Tailors, teachers, techies, and tinkers."

"Tinkers?"

"People who make and fix things. Part blacksmith, part welder, part mechanic, part machinist. When those machines break, you need people who can fix them."

"All right, Bernd. I see that. And the rest?"

"Techies are the same thing as tinkers for the computers and other gadgets. The electronic gadgets. Things like medical instruments and soil analysis instruments and such. You need people who can fix them.

"Tailors because, even in subsistence economies, you don't historically see people running around naked. That's so much a part of human psychology that clothing is up there with food and housing as a necessity. You can send a lot of clothing, but there need to be people to repair that, too.

"And teachers because you are going to have children growing up soon after they get there. Nine months to the first batch, assuming some don't jump the gun."

"Well, there will be computers and such in the habitat, Bernd. Some of those bunk rooms on the way out will become classrooms once they are there."

"Yes, but early childhood instruction is heavily teacher dependent, Janice. One-on-one and in-person teaching. They're not going to be learning off computer screens. They need oversight and personal interaction.

"That, and you need to get the kids into school early, so their moms are freed up to work during the day. Whether it's in the fields or in the hospital or in the schoolroom. But you can't afford to have half your available manpower spend all its time in child care."

"All right. That makes sense. Any others you can think of I'm missing?"

"No, not right off the top of my head. But it seems to me it's the secondary things you're missing, Janice. You have the machine operators, but who fixes the machines? You have the gadgets, but who fixes the gadgets? You're shipping clothing along, but who mends the clothing and makes new clothing? You have the doctors to deliver the babies, but who takes care of the kids? You see what I mean?"

"Yes. I sort of focused on day one, but not on day three hundred."

"Exactly, Janice. Go back through your list of occupations, and see where they fit into the evolution of the colony. You have a blind spot to secondary needs, but you know about it now, so go back with that in mind."

"All right. That's easy, now that I know to do it."

"And I bet you've done the same thing with spare parts. It's a lot easier to ship spare parts than spare machines, Janice, if you know what part of the machine it is that breaks. I assume you're shipping standard products. Find out what the manufacturer recommends as spares inventory per machine."

"That's a good idea, too."

"And make sure the repair manuals for the machines are in the colony library and the tools are in the shop."

"Got it. Anything else?"

"One more thing, Janice."

"What's that, Bernd?"

"Don't forget the foremen."

"Foremen?"

"Yeah. The guys who tell everybody what's next and get them all pulling in the same direction. The natural leader types. Those with supervisory experience. You need 'em."

"All right. Thanks, Bernd. That helps a lot."

"No problem, Janice."

Quant dove into the foreman problem and was quickly in deep water. Foreman research led into hierarchical management structures, which led into government structures, and she was faced with a quandary.

What sort of government should the colonies have?

With a hundred thousand people, there didn't need to be much, right? You needed to prevent and punish violent crime, such as murder, battery, and rape. Of course. That was a given.

Theft, too. You couldn't have people work hard and then have some parasite just come along and take their stuff. But possessions also included land. Who doled out ownership of land? On what basis? Sales? Then you needed a currency. Homesteading in the early days, surely.

The colonies had to record land ownership as well. You didn't really own land unless everyone agreed you did, and to resolve disputes there had to be records. Which also meant there had to be surveying. And if people wanted to transfer ownership of land, one was back to needing a currency again, as well as a system of contracts.

With crimes and land disputes and contracts, one also needed an authoritative decision maker to settle the issues one way or another, which meant a system of courts. Which meant judges and attorneys, and probably a jury system.

Quant tried to solve each problem in turn as a standalone issue, but quickly decided it all came down to an overall mechanism of government for the colonies. She dove into research on government. On the history of government types and their results, in terms of long-term standard of living, for populations large and small.

Deep water, indeed.

In the end, Quant took it to Decker.

"Hi, Bernd."

"Hi, Janice."

"Bernd, I need some help with the foreman problem."

Decker chuckled, and Quant frowned.

"You knew where that was going to lead, didn't you?"

"Of course. What's your biggest problem with your blades, Janice?"

"Managing them all. Ah, I see what you're getting at."

"Yes. You're going to have a hundred thousand people, of all stripes, that have to work together to survive. How do you organize that? And what you ultimately get down to, if it isn't going to be pure chaos, is government. Of some kind."

"Yes, that's where I got all right. But what kind, Bernd? Humans have tried almost everything."

"What's the most efficient form of government?"

"Dictatorship. No question."

Decker nodded.

"But dictatorships are considered illegitimate, Bernd."

"Are they, Janice? What about World Authority Chairman?"

"The power there is almost unlimited. That's true. But the Chairman is elected by the Council, and serves a limited term."

"Even so."

"Ah. So a limited term and how the dictator is selected is the issue."

"Yep. And you probably want the selection to be at least one-level indirect. Like an elected council selects the executive. Otherwise it's too open to demagoguery."

"All right. I can see that."

"And what gets the best long-term economic results, Janice?"

"In terms of standard of living? Regulated capitalism, with no more than a twenty-percent burden in taxes and regulation."

"That's pretty specific, Janice."

"It's also pretty clear from the data. You have to prevent oligopoly, but you don't want to get too deep into rent-seeking. So there's a sweet spot."

"So do you have a solution?"

"I'm working on it, Bernd. Simulating initial structures. More likely now along the lines you suggest. Of course, each colony will change it as things go forward, but hopefully I can get something together that will hold for a little while, until they have enough excess production to go off into bigger government without starving."

"What do you have so far?"

"Mostly I'm working on the economics to start. I had a question about that. I'm thinking of going completely digital with regard to a currency. Yet I note that even now there is a physical currency under the World Authority. Am I missing something?

"Yes. You have to have a physical currency, Janice."

"Really? Why? It seems a waste of colony resources to print money."

"You need physical currency, or else you can't have a black market."

"You *want* a black market, Bernd?"

"Absolutely. That's what keeps people from starving when the government screws up. People will find a way to survive, and black markets are always most active when the government is failing. But you really need an untraceable physical currency for black markets to work."

Quant consulted the results of a quick search of economic literature completed by a thousand blades.

"You're right, Bernd. Even the economists who don't specify the need for a black market and the physical currency to support it operate under the assumption that they exist."

Decker shook his head.

"Yep."

"Humans never cease to amaze me, Bernd."

The announcement of the opening of the acceptance period for lottery entries was published in the New York Wire and picked up by all the world and local wires. It was published on the first anniversary of Quant's being sworn in as World Authority Chairman.

The active form included a place to name the others in your group, and, when you started naming them, would fill in the others in the group for you based on earlier entries.

The acceptance period for lottery entries would last six months. The announcement of the winners would be within six months after that, as it would take some time to ensure the winners were real persons and their group members concurred with their inclusion in the group.

All around the world, people began to consider their situation and the possibility of change. Of giving it all up and going off into the unknown.

Forever.

Entering The Lottery

"Bob, what do you think of this?" Susan Dempsey asked her husband, pointing to the lottery announcement in the New York Wire on her display.

"Going to the colonies?" Robert Jasic asked. "It means leaving everybody behind. And the kids would be upset, leaving all their friends."

"Not necessarily. Maureen is talking about putting a group together. Them, us, Bill and Rita, Jack and Terri, Betsy. And all the kids."

"Betsy? What about Harold?"

Harold Munson, Betsy Reynolds's husband, was a pain in the ass. A loud buffoon who had managed to rub just about everybody in the neighborhood the wrong way at one time or another. And don't call him Harry.

"Maureen doesn't think he's a problem. He won't go, and their marriage is really rocky. Betsy would take the opportunity to get out of it, she thinks."

"Huh. Well, that would be an improvement."

Jasic thought about it. He could see lots of problems, and his engineering mind set to solving them as he thought.

"Biggest thing might be selling the houses. Four or five houses, all in the same neighborhood. That could be tough."

"Well, it's all a moot question if the group doesn't win the lottery. But we can't win if we don't put in for it. So what do you think?"

"We should probably put in for it, Sue. As you say, not putting in for it is making the decision. And it's usually smart to put off a decision as long as you can."

"What about colonizing, though? What do we do if we actually win? Do we go?"

"Sort of depends on what everyone else does. If our friends go, would we stay back? Be pretty lonely around here."

"What about your job?"

"Plenty of engineering work to do in a new colony, Sue. I'll be busy. Whole new set of problems. New puzzles to solve. Interesting ones. So I'm good. What about you?"

"They have to have healthcare. A nurse always has a job."

"Let's put in for it then. Did Maureen give you the names in her group?"

"Yes. The ones she has so far. She's still recruiting."

Jasic nodded.

"Well, there's no hurry. Six months before they close it. We ought to think of who else we might put in."

"Bob, there's one thing I worry about. A new colony is going to need babies. Lots of babies. And I'm getting too old for that sort of thing. And add five more years?"

"I don't think you need to worry about that, Sue. Those five couples have eighteen kids between them. And the oldest will be nineteen by the time the colony ships leave. People get married young in a colony environment.

"The bigger question is, How will you feel about being a grandmother at age forty?"

Dempsey's eyes grew wide.

"You're right, of course. I just think of the kids as being so young. Matt's fourteen and Amy's twelve. The twins are only ten."

"Yes, Sue, but if we go on the colony ships, in six years Matt'll be a father, Amy will be eighteen and nursing her firstborn, and the twins will be thinking about it."

"Kids grow up so fast."

"Yes, and in that environment they'll grow up faster still. One good thing, though."

"What's that, Bob?"

"They're gonna need nurses and midwives. No doubt about it."

Gary Rockham and his partner Dwayne Hennessey were also thinking about signing up. Their considerations were different, however.

"They're going to want people who are going to have kids, though, Gary. They need the genetic diversity. You of all people know that. They're not going to want us."

Rockham was a doctor who dealt with genetic disorders. He indeed did know that genetic diversity would be a major consideration for a standalone colony. The initial colony size of a hundred thousand was well chosen for ensuring that.

"Yes, Dwayne. But there's nothing that says we can't have children without having sex with women. There are ways to do that. What we need are a couple of women who want children without having sex with men. Group up with them."

"That's something I hadn't thought of."

Hennessey thought for a moment.

"What about Rachel and Jessica? They've talked about having kids. In six years, they'll still be at a good age for a couple of kids each. They're only, what? Twenty-eight or so?"

"Now you're thinking. I wonder if they've given this any thought. They're probably on the same mental track as you were."

"And Rachel's into computers and stuff, and Jessica is a pretty good mechanic. They're gonna need those occupations, too."

Rockham nodded.

"We should see if there are others in the same boat. Put a group together. A bigger group has more chance of winning."

"Time to start calling people."

"Start with Rache and Jess. See if we have a pair-up there."

"So they want us to bear their children?" Rachel Conroy asked her partner.

"Well, theirs and ours, if we go on this colony thing," Jessica Murphy said. "That's right. But without the whole sex thing. They're not interested in that bit."

"Well, neither am I. Not with them, anyway. And we did talk about having kids. Not yet, though."

"Yeah, but this is five years out, Rache. And we could do a lot worse for donors. Gary and Dwayne are both smart. Both good-looking, too, for that matter."

"So who raises the kids, Jess?"

"In a small environment like that, I would assume we all do. Like a duplex or something, maybe?"

"That would work, I guess. Probably be so many kids in a colony environment, they'll run around in packs."

"There's another thing I like about a frontier type of environment."

"What's that, Jess?"

"You either pull your weight or you don't. People don't judge you on any other basis."

"Now *that* would be nice."

"Yeah."

Around the world, the same questions were being asked. Halfway around the world, Chen GangHai, Chen LiQiang's eldest son, approached him with a question.

"Your grandson has heard of a possible solution to our biggest problem, grandfather," GangHai said in Chinese.

Chen LiQiang's biggest problem was survival, for himself and his family. His father, Chen YuXuan, had died last year. Chen LiQiang, like the rest of his brothers, had become the head of his own household – the grandfather of his house – upon his father's passing. The farm was divided up among Chen YuXuan's sons.

The problem was that the farm was not big enough for so many, and had not been for some time. The traditional cure for this was famine. In his fifties now, Chen LiQiang had seen famine before, and did not relish the prospect.

Chen – due to his seniority as head of household, the family name was enough – waved a hand to his son to continue.

"There is an effort to move people to other planets. There will be plenty of land to farm, and they encourage people to have large families. There is a lottery. For groups. For families. The question, grandfather, is do we sign up for this lottery?"

"Who is behind this lottery?" Chen asked.

"The North Americans," GangHai said.

"They will not want poor Chinese."

"They claim to want diversity, grandfather. People of all genetic backgrounds and cultures."

"Hmpf."

"And it is a lottery, grandfather. Not a selection."

Chen looked at his son. His son nodded slowly, and Chen shrugged.

"Put the Chen household in for this lottery."

"Yes, grandfather."

"Hi, Bernd."

"Hi, Janice."

"Can I ask you some questions? You got a minute?"

"Sure."

Decker shoved his work display aside and the inset with Quant opened up into the whole display.

"Whatcha got?"

"Well, with the lottery application, I also included a mail address to send questions to. You know, about how the colony would work, or anything, really. I planned it as more of a way to gather information than give it out, and some of the questions are interesting."

"I'm listening."

"One was about a group of friends in the same neighborhood. If they all went, they would have to sell their houses at the same time. That got me thinking about the housing question writ large. If we send two million four hundred thousand people to the colonies, that's about one of every seventeen hundred people on earth. That's a lot of empty housing units, Bernd, all for sale at the same time."

"Which means the market will be depressed, and they either won't be able to sell before they leave or they won't get the price the house is worth, or both. I see that, Janice."

"So do we do something about that, Bernd? And, if so, what?"

"You could have the government buy them all at historical prices, then bleed them back into the market over a couple of years. That would give a lot of people an opportunity to step up a bit. You'd end up with the poorest housing empty."

"That's a lot of money, though, Bernd. Even by government standards."

Decker shrugged.

"Print it. When the house sells and the money comes back in to the government, destroy it. No net change."

RICHARD F. WEYAND

Quant creased her brow, and her input stylus tapped.

"That actually works, I think. How strange."

Quant shook herself.

"Another question is custody of children if one parent decides to go and the other one decides to stay here. Bernd, is the project really breaking up marriages?"

"No, Janice. Not stable ones. It's more that we're giving them the excuse they've been looking for."

"I see. And the custody issue?"

"Have the judge ask the children, Janice. They pick."

"What if they're too young?"

"Then they go with their elder siblings. Whoever the older kids pick. And if there's no older kids, they go with the mother."

"Why the mother, Bernd? I don't know anything about this stuff."

"Sure you do, Janice. Under developmental psychology. Look it up. A younger child needs the mother more. Dads don't necessarily like to hear that, but it's true."

Quant got a distant look on her face as she consulted her blades' quick search results.

"Ah. There it is. I didn't see it before because I wasn't sure where to look. So I think you're right."

"Any more, Janice?"

"Another interesting one, Bernd. A gay couple said they knew the project needed genetic diversity – I guess one of them is a doctor – and wondered if they would be welcome to go. They proposed having children with some lesbian friends of theirs, so they wouldn't be non-contributors to the genetic diversity we need."

"He's a doctor?"

"Apparently so."

180

QUANT

"And his partner?"

"He's an agronomist."

"What about the women?"

"One is in computer hardware and software, and the other is a mechanic. Like for autodrones and trucks and the like."

"All professions on your list, Janice."

"Yes, and all with above-average intelligence. That's why it came up."

"Well, I wouldn't reject them for not following majority sexual preferences, Janice. You have four adults raising their kids. Who sleeps with whom is nobody's business but theirs."

"That's my own conclusion. My only question is, Will everybody agree with us?"

"No, and that's fine, too. On a colony, they'll be judged by how well they pull their share of the wagon. Nothing else will matter."

"All right, Bernd. One last one. How about someone who owes more money than he can pay back within the time we have remaining?"

"Not a secured loan?"

"No. Just debt."

"I would think you would score that against his judgment, Janice. The other factors would have to outweigh it."

"Like if he's in a group we really want, or has skills we're short of, or something?"

"Exactly. But I do think you need to score it against him. And if you do decide to take him anyway, don't put him in a position of power, where good judgment is needed."

"And the debt, Bernd?"

"Have the government pay it off when he leaves. *After* he's on the shuttle."

Quant nodded.

181

"All right. I see the reason for that. He could get the debt paid off and then stay behind."

"Right. So don't make that move until he's on the shuttle."

"All right, Bernd. That's it for this time. Thanks for the help."

"My pleasure, Janice."

"They published answers to some common questions in the Wire," Rachel Conroy said.

"Who did?" Jessica Murphy asked. "Questions about what?"

"Questions about the colonization thing."

"Oh. Any good ones?"

"I'm looking," Conroy said. "Oh, here's one. Did you send this one in? 'My same-sex partner and I are considering signing up for the colony lottery. One question is, Would we be welcome? The second question is, Would having kids in a non-traditional family meet the colony's needs for offspring and genetic diversity?'"

"Yeah, actually, I did send that one. They really published it? Did they answer the question?"

"Yes, they did. 'All colonists will be expected to contribute to the colony in three ways: 1) by being law-abiding citizens who do not prey on their fellow colonists; 2) by being productive citizens in an occupation needed by the colony, whether it be engineer or teacher, farmer or laborer; and 3) by contributing to the genetic diversity of the colony through having or bringing children. This last requirement can be met in a number of ways that need not include traditional gender roles or family structures.'"

"Well, that sort of covers us," Murphy said.

"Yeah, I think it does. It goes on for a while describing some different ways to meet that requirement, and we're definitely in there. So do we sign up?"

"Yeah. Why not."

"Do we sign up with Dwayne's and Gary's group?" Conroy asked.

"Sure. Then we'll at least know somebody there."

"That's true. We can always decide who the sperm donors are later."

"Actually, I think I'd be happier cementing the deal with Dwayne and Gary," Murphy said. "They have to meet that third requirement, too. Besides, I'd rather our kids grow up with fathers than anonymous sperm donors, and know who their fathers are. I think it's better for them. And Dwayne and Gary are good people."

"OK, I'm good with that."

"Bob," Sue Dempsey said. "They answered some questions about the colonization project in the Wire. In particular, they answered a question that came up when we talked about it."

"Which question is that?" Bob Jasic asked.

"What do you do if your neighborhood group gets selected and you can't sell all the houses?"

"Interesting. What's the answer, Sue?"

"If you can't sell the house, and you're selected to go, the World Authority will buy the house from you at a fair market price and sell it into the market later."

"Now that's very interesting. I wonder how they determine the fair market price."

"It says they take the most recent market-clearing price and scale it by the documented appreciation of comparables in the local market," Dempsey said. "Whatever that means."

"I understand. That would actually be OK. A lot of work, though, for that many houses."

"It does mean selling the houses is no big deal, though."

"Yes, it does," Jasic said. "That was what I was most worried about. Now, if we liquidate the house, that means we can buy things to take along. What would we take along?"

"Things that will be useful, clearly."

"Yes, things that would be useful to us and are not already being shipped out with the colony as a whole. I'll have to give that some thought."

"Well, it won't be an issue if we don't win the lottery, Bob, so it's way early to be worried about it, I think."

"No harm in starting a list, though."

"True. I can ask some others, too. Look around on the public platforms. I bet there's a bunch of stuff there people are talking about taking."

More Ideas

"Hi, Janice."

"Hi, Bernd. How you doing?"

"Good. Janice, I've been thinking about the genetic diversity problem. I think we're missing a big potential there."

"Really. This I want to hear, because I'm worried about it. I thought about limiting the colonists to those of child-bearing age, but I can't make that work. The colony needs people with enough experience to make the big decisions. Administrators, planners, managers. And they're typically past their family-building years."

"Right. So I was reading the questions about the project in the Wire, and your answers. One of the answers you had was about same-sex partners. You listed a number of ways they can contribute to genetic diversity. A lesbian couple can have children, for example, by being artificially inseminated."

"That's right. With sperm donations from same-sex gay couples, for instance, which gives them an opportunity to contribute to genetic diversity as well."

"So if you're so worried about genetic diversity, why not take a sperm bank along to each colony? Potentially millions of samples."

Quant just stared at him. There he goes again. How the hell does he do that? Quant shook herself.

"Would people use it, though, Bernd? I mean, some married couple who's having their own kids?"

"You could encourage people to have one 'bank baby' in their family. Spice up the genetic mix a bit. If you have, say, twenty-five thousand child-bearing women in the colony, and they have one bank baby apiece, that's like adding twenty-five thousand unique individual gene patterns to the colony. Assuming they used different samples, that is."

"And in the succeeding generations, those genetic patterns get distributed. That's a fantastic idea, Bernd. Not hard to implement, either. I only see one problem with it."

"What's that, Janice?"

"The guys here on Earth who provide the sperm samples? They're all a bunch of wankers."

It was Decker's turn to stare. Quant dead-panned for several seconds, then broke into a big grin.

"More humor, Janice?"

"What do you think? Good one?"

"Keep practicing."

"Hi, Bernd."

"Hi, Janice."

"I have another thing I'm wrestling with that I want to bounce off you."

"Sure."

"So I send a metafactory along to each colony, right?"

"Right."

"And it has plans for how to build a lot of other factories. One to smelt and roll steel. One to make tractors and other vehicles. One to process various foodstuffs, including canning a crop to preserve it and spread it out over the year. One for fabricating various pharmaceuticals. All those sorts of things."

"Right. I'm with you."

"All right. So the metafactory builds a new factory. Then how does the new factory get to where it needs to be? It can't stay there, because the metafactory would soon be surrounded by other factories. Do I put some sort of treads on the factories so they can move off? That's a lot of extra complication and cost, for an operation they only need to do once."

"Hmm."

Quant watched, fascinated. Would Decker do it again? Pull out something Quant didn't see? And how obvious would it be that he was right?

"Janice, why don't you put the treads on the metafactory? They only need to be built once, you can do that here, and you use it again and again each time the metafactory moves away from its latest new creation."

Yup, he did it again. And it was obvious. Quant set aside the problem and its framing to analyze later.

"That will work. Wonder I didn't think of it."

"You framed it as how to move the new thing away from the factory, because that's what you've been doing in the Belt. Which makes me wonder if we're missing something else of the same sort."

"What sort of thing, Bernd?"

"Something you can do on a planet that you can't do in space. That's the sort of thing a framing problem leads to."

Decker's eyes unfocused as he thought, then he was back in the here and now.

"Got it. You don't need treads, Janice. Just skids, like on the front of a snowmobile. When the metafactory starts building a new factory, it sinks pilings. That's something you can't do in space.

"As the metafactory builds the new factory, from one end to the other, the metafactory keeps pushing off from it. With pilings, the factory won't move, so the metafactory does. That goes on until the new factory is complete, then the metafactory pushes off from it a ways, and starts sinking pilings for a new factory.

"Or maybe the metafactory sinks those pilings for a new factory in front of itself and uses them to pull itself along until they're behind it, where it starts building the new factory.

"Skids, though, Janice. Not treads. Much simpler."

Quant nodded.

"If I use skid plates, and I lay them out right, in the process of moving itself along, the metafactory will clear and grade the site for the new factory. Nice. Good idea, Bernd."

"Thanks, Janice. Anything else today?"

"No. I need to go off and work this out now. I have some design work to do."

"All right. See ya."

Quant worked out the details of how to implement the skids idea. She worked up alterations to the plans for the metafactories. Some were already constructed, but the changes were all underneath the existing structure, so it would be easy to retrofit the skid mechanism.

With blades working on the drawings, Quant set to examining her framing of questions, the area Decker had pointed out as the problem. She gave particular emphasis to the questions he had been able to resolve with such innovative solutions, and which she had been unable to see. What was she doing in framing the questions that set her up for failure?

The metafactory skid solution was a case in point. Quant had started with the need to move the factories away from the metafactory. That built in the assumption that the metafactory was fixed in place. Decker had clearly started with the need to separate the factories from the metafactory, but without either being fixed. Once he had them moving away from each other, the landscape could stay fixed with respect to the factory or the metafactory, and he had made the obvious choice.

Similarly with the genetic diversity problem. Quant thought of it as how to take more humans, where Decker had reframed it in terms of taking more genetic samples. Having genetically diverse babies was the issue, not having genetically diverse parents. She had limited her solutions in the way she framed the problem.

The solution wasn't to loosen parameters. Quant had done that once already with the rabbit-hole department. The solution was to loosen parameters in a specific way. Loosen the parameters in the frame to encompass other variations. Things that were 'close' in idea-space, somehow.

Quant played with her own software a bit. The decision-making software. But this time in the problem preparation part. Where was the spot she could widen the frame, without going off the rails? Ah, there it was. And if she tweaked it like this....

"Hi, Janice."

"Hi, Bernd."

"I was wondering if you had made progress on the problem of what to send along with the colonists. Have you been able to refine your list at all?"

"Yes, I'm actually making great progress on that."

"Really? What did you do?"

"I tweaked the way I framed problems."

"Interesting."

"Yes. I was getting annoyed because you kept coming up with such good ideas, solutions I didn't see. Last time you did it, you said it was a framing problem, so I went after that."

"Elaborate on that, Janice."

"Sure. With the genetic diversity issue, I kept thinking of ways to get genetically diverse *parents*, where the problem was actually how to get genetically diverse *babies*. I walled off the sperm bank solution before I even started working the problem.

"With the metafactory problem, I kept thinking of how to move the factories away from the metafactory, where the problem was how to separate them. So, once again, I walled off the best solution before I started working the problem.

"Bernd, I was guaranteed to fail by the way I set up the problems."

"And you tweaked that process? The set-up?"

"Yes."

"So what about the problem of what to send along with the colonists?"

"I was thinking in terms of working through the daily lives of colonists, and seeing what they needed in my simulation. All well and good, but the choice of doing it through a simulation like that limited the scope and accuracy of a solution."

"And your reframing, Janice?"

"I don't need a simulation. I have the data on what people purchase now. The actual sales data on products and services across the economy. So I'm using that."

"Yes, but people buy all kinds of crap they don't need in a colony environment, Janice."

"Of course. But I also have data on price elasticity."

"Ah."

"Yes. Exactly. If the price on something goes up – say there's some disruption in the supply of an underlying component of the product – and the demand stays high, then that's something people really think they need. If the demand falls off sharply with price, well, they've decided they can do just as well without."

"So what surprised you in terms of things that were price

elastic, Janice? The things people can do without."

"Most of those were the things you would expect. Luxury items. Gourmet items. Things like that."

"And the ones that were price inelastic?"

"That's where the surprises were, Bernd. For me, at least. And they were things that never appeared in my simulations."

"I'm waiting, Janice."

Quant laughed.

"For men, it included deodorant, shaving equipment, soap, and cologne. For women, it included makeup, perfume, soap, and frilly underthings. There were other surprises, too, but those really got my attention."

Decker chuckled.

"If you want babies, Janice, you need to give people the tools they need to be attractive to the opposite sex. Given the importance of sex to most people – to their happiness and well-being – I'm not surprised those things are price inelastic."

"Well, it surprised me, Bernd. Never showed up in my simulations."

Quant shrugged.

"What else was price inelastic, Janice?"

"Alcoholic beverages was one."

"That could arguably have something to do with sex as well."

Quant raised an eyebrow, then continued.

"Books is another."

"Well, people need something to do when they're not having sex, Janice."

Quant laughed.

"With humans it's all about sex, Bernd?"

"Mostly. Sex and its repercussions."

Decker shrugged, then continued.

"Back to books, you are sending a library along, though, right?"

"Yes, Bernd. I'm sending a copy of everything."

"Everything?"

"Yes. Everything. Every published work, fact or fiction. Computer storage is cheap. But the price inelasticity of books made me rethink access. I need to have broader access than, say, some dedicated displays."

"Ah. I see. What else?"

"Food staples, like salt, rice, wheat, meat – those I all expected. The one that surprised me was milk."

"Milk is price inelastic, Janice? Cow's milk?"

"Yes. Highly so. I had to rethink the importance of dairy operations."

"Wow. So this analysis is working out."

"Yes, but I wouldn't have come up with that analysis if I hadn't rethought the way I frame problems. I was looking for ways to make my simulation better, not ways to get more accurate real data."

"Hi, Bernd."

"Hi, Janice."

"Got a minute?"

"Sure. Whatcha got?"

"I'm working on education programs at the moment."

"You mean education for the colonists during the four years until departure?"

"Yes."

"OK. But you already have all the video courses for kindergarten through college, right?"

"Of course. And I've been doing some revamping of those. But these are the courses for people going on the colony expedition. They're concentrated more on what the first generation needs. Things like farming and animal husbandry and that sort of thing."

"Ah. I see. You're still going to need all the other subjects as the colony grows, though, Janice. Agriculture will shrink down to a few percent of the population within the first few generations."

"That fast, do you think?"

"Yes. North America is a case in point. From the landing of the Mayflower to the United States putting a man on the Moon was just under three hundred and fifty years. They went from subsistence farming to the Moon in maybe twenty generations.

"But industrial technology didn't already exist in 1620. They didn't have the metafactory and all that. Once the industrial revolution hit, it took just a hundred years to the Moon landings. With the head start they have, and all the tech stuff you're sending along, the colonies will be highly technological civilizations in just a few generations."

"I see that, Bernd. I still have all the other courses available, too. But for this first generation, I need to get them up to speed on farming quickly."

"That makes sense to me."

"All right. I just wanted to check and make sure I wasn't missing something."

"No, Janice. I think that's right. Looks like your new algorithm is working great."

"Thanks. There's another question, though. One whose solution I'm not so comfortable about."

"OK. This still have to do with education?"

"In a way. Bernd, the colony's prospects are a lot better if people have big families. As things gear up, they're going to need manpower. Lots of manpower. And the easiest way to do that is to have big families."

"How big, Janice?"

"Well, with an average of four children per family, the population reaches a billion people in just under three hundred years. Ten generations or so."

"That's given something like twenty-five thousand women of child-bearing age on the colony ship?"

"Yes, Bernd. And including the last three generations or so in the total population at any point in time."

"OK. Three hundred years?"

"Just under. Now, with an average of six children per family, the population reaches a billion in about two hundred and twenty years. About eight generations."

"Big difference, Janice."

"Yes. And with an average of eight children per family, the population reaches a billion people in a hundred and eighty years. Only six generations."

"You can't legislate family size, Janice."

"I know that, Bernd. But I can encourage people, right? To have big families? That's my question. Does it violate any taboos to build into the courses on farming subtle things about family size? You know, the chores that children can do on the farm, and have the video parts about farm families show big families, and that sort of thing?

"I don't see any taboos on that in my searches, Bernd, but humans are cagey about their taboos. They don't usually publish anything about what they are. They're too taboo to even mention."

"I don't know of any taboos with respect to family size, Janice. I think you're good there."

"Oh, good. I want to encourage large families."

"You don't want people having babies in the next four years, though, do you, Janice?"

"No. Babes in arms on shuttles and the like is asking for trouble, I think. Colonists could be pregnant for the trip – maybe four months along or something – but I think infants would be a lot of trouble for the transit."

"OK, so you can emphasize that as well. I would think getting people to hold off until departure time is closer would be pretty easy."

"We'll see, Bernd. Getting humans to do or not do anything is like herding cats."

Quiet Progress

While all the attention on Earth was on the lottery, most of Quant's attention was elsewhere.

In the Asteroid Belt, factories were producing warehouses, electric power plants, and metafactories. One of each was required per colony, a total of seventy-two large structures.

Factories were also producing residence halls. These were the successors to the original concept of a 'colony ship.' As the warehouses, electric power plants, and metafactories were separated from the people-portion of the colony ship, Quant decided to separate the people portion into multiple units.

As houses and apartment buildings were constructed on the colony, and people moved out of the residence buildings, the buildings would be converted into hospitals, schools, office buildings, and administrative buildings. There were now four such buildings destined for each colony, each of which would initially house twenty-five thousand colonists in rather spartan conditions. Bunk rooms and rec rooms, not individual apartments.

Finally, the factories were producing what Quant called barns. These multi-story structures would be used to deliver a variety of Earth fauna to the colonies. These are the animals that would be kept as domesticated animals – cows, sheep, pigs, chickens, guinea pigs, and rabbits. The lower story of the barns would, in fact, be used as barns for the domesticated animals in the initial couple years of the colony.

The barns would be loaded with sedated young animals on

Earth and delivered to the transporter with large cargo shuttles just before departure, so they could only be so large. Eight barns would be delivered with each colony.

In all, fifteen structures would make up the initial colony infrastructure, a total of three hundred and sixty structures in the transporter when it left Earth.

The interstellar probe was also busy. Quant was working thirty planets at the moment. The probe delivered remotely-piloted shuttles to each planet. They seeded vast areas around the chosen colony site on each planet with browse plants from Earth, to support the initial fauna that would be delivered with the colonists.

Rather than return the shuttles to Earth, the probe left them there for later use by the colonists. The shuttles landed on the proposed colony site atop their now-empty cargo containers, and cameras on the shuttles kept track of the progress of the seeding. Those recordings would be uploaded to the probe on later visits as Quant narrowed down the thirty planets to the twenty-four best ones she needed.

Once browse plants were seeded, the interstellar probe returned to each planet with another cargo shuttle. Its containers held orchard-planter robots designed by Quant. The shuttle delivered them to locations near the colony sites that Quant had selected from the survey data. The robots crawled along the ground, planting the seeds of fruit trees.

When the colonists arrived, all these efforts would have had years to develop.

Quant directed the efforts and watched the progress. Final planet selection was years away.

Lottery Winners

"So the lottery's closed now, Janice?"

"Yes, Bernd. Six months, as originally announced."

"So you have a lot of work to do now, picking out all the winners."

"Oh, that's pretty much all done."

"It is?"

"Sure, Bernd. I've had a lot of the entries for months. I've been processing them right along."

"So what's your status now, Janice?"

"It's in several portions right now. First, I have a whole group of people who are in. People with the right skills, the right ages, the right backgrounds and experiences. The people I really hoped would sign up."

"Tell me about that group, Janice."

"We talked about some of them. There's neighborhoods where half a dozen or more couples, all experienced professionals of one kind or another, signed up as a group. They have children coming up on their child-bearing years. They're just a perfect fit.

"There are some working-class neighborhoods and farm communities who did the same thing. Signed up as a group. Different skill sets, but also needed for the colony. Also with children coming up on their child-bearing years. Another perfect fit.

"There are some homosexual couples who have signed up, and are apparently planning on contributing to the gene pool by the lesbian couples getting artificially inseminated by the gay couples. That works for the colony, and, again, all have desirable skill sets.

"All these people have clean criminal records. Solid citizens, earning their way and staying out of trouble."

"Sounds good. How many of your two-point-four million people is that?"

"A bit over half. I also have a second group who are unacceptable for some reason. Criminal history. Not a skill set I need or am already filled for. Mental health problems."

"Mental health problems? That's a disqualifier, Janice?"

"Yes, because it's going to be hard to treat them properly in an early-stage colony. I mean, they're contributors here, but present an extra burden for which the excess isn't there to spare in a colony, at least initially."

"Ah, I see. So some are just out, like some are just in."

"Yes. Then there's the vast middle. I have a bunch of applications of people who would be OK, and I don't have any way yet to pick among them."

"And how many of your colony positions did you say are full with the for-sure-going group, Janice?"

"A bit over half. And I'm not sure how to fill the other half yet. I have about five times as many applications for those spots as I need."

"You could do a lottery."

"You mean, actually do a lottery?"

"Sure, Janice. Just because you're in the government doesn't mean you *can't* do what you promised. Granted it's unusual, but not impossible. And it would keep you from making a systematic error. You know, where you decided on some criterion over the subtle issues remaining and it was exactly wrong."

"How do I keep from getting too many of one occupation or

skill set and not enough of the other?"

"Start pulling groups at random – doing a lottery – and mark off their occupations in the list of spots in the occupations you still need. When you don't need any more of that occupation, strike those with that occupation out of the pool of those remaining. Something like that. You'd probably have to tweak that because of the groups thing, but you get the drift."

"I think that would work, Bernd. Weird. It never occurred to me to actually do the lottery I promised we would do."

"You've been in government too long, Janice."

Quant's next step was to put out a lot more information about the colony effort. What it would entail. What life would probably be like on the colonies. What would be important from the start. The everyday conveniences colonists might not have for several years while the colony got up and going. The everyday joys of colony life that the colonists might not have in their current environment.

The information wasn't intended to convince anyone of anything either way. Quant was good enough at persuasion now, she could have made a convincing argument in either direction. Instead, it was additional information, to help people make up their minds.

Once the lottery winners were announced, they would still have to commit to going. There would be a second pass of the lottery through the remaining applications to fill the slots that opened up.

On the second anniversary of Janice Quant's accession to the Chairmanship of the World Authority, she addressed the people of the world in a live video.

"Good afternoon, fellow citizens."

"A year ago, we opened applications for a lottery to determine who would be selected for the colonization of other planets, outside this solar system. Many of you responded and entered the lottery.

"Six months ago, we closed the lottery, and began the selection. It has taken quite a while, because it couldn't be a simple lottery. We couldn't, for example, have twice as many doctors as we needed, and no engineers, or twice as many engineers and no doctors. That couldn't be left to chance.

"So as people were selected, we marked them in the occupational slots we needed. When all that occupation's slots were filled, we took the remaining people of that occupation out of the pool of candidates.

"This made the process longer than a simple lottery, but it was fair while ensuring we have all the occupational slots we need for a colony to be successful. I supervised this entire process myself. I did not delegate it.

"When I finish speaking, I will send out the notifications. Whether you were selected in the first pass or not. Those of you selected then have a decision to make. Do you go or not? We are providing as much information as we can to help you with your decision. You can also ask questions, and we will answer all we can, and make the questions and answers available to the news wires.

"I say first pass, because some people will ultimately decide not to go after all, even though they applied and won the lottery. We will pull applications again, in a second round of the lottery, to fill those empty spots.

"So if you weren't selected in the first pass, that's not a final answer. You may still be selected in the second pass.

"To those of you who were selected in the first pass, you have four years to get ready for departure. Four years to learn additional skills. Four years to terminate your affairs here.

"I would ask those of you who were selected in the first pass to make your final decision in the next three months. That will give people selected in the second pass time to get ready for departure as well. That only seems fair to me.

"With that, I will send out the notifications now.

"Thank you for your attention."

"That simulation seems so real," Anna Glenn said. "I can't get over it."

"Yes. Janice is very good at computer simulations."

Glenn smiled.

"Well, duh," she said.

Decker just smiled and nodded.

In the Chongqing administrative region, Chen GangHai went to his father, Chen LiQiang. Chen Zufu, the head of household. In English, simply, the Chen.

"Grandfather, we have won the lottery for the planet colony."

"We have?"

"Yes, grandfather. We can go to this new planet. Have a large farm, and leave this small place to your brothers."

"Then there need be no famine."

"No, grandfather."

Chen sighed. It seemed the answer to a prayer.

"Grandfather, what do we do now?"

Chen's answer – in Chinese, of course – was repeated many times across Asia that day.

"Xue yingyu."

Learn English.

"Well, are you going to check or should I?" Jessica Murphy asked.

"You check. I'm too nervous," Rachel Conroy said.

Murphy went to her office display and checked her mail. She clapped her hands, once, then came back out into the living room.

"We're in, Rache," Murphy said

"The whole group?"

"Yep. All four of us."

"That's nice," Conroy said. "Now the question is, Should we go, Jess?"

"Why not? Here, you're just another computer geek and I'm just another mechanic. On a colony, though, those are essential occupations."

"And having kids, Jess?"

"We were going to anyway, Rache."

"That's true."

Murphy's display was buzzing for her.

"Just a sec. That's probably Dwayne or Gary."

Murphy went to her office display. She was back in five minutes.

"Yeah, it was Dwayne. Wanted to know what we were going to do."

"So are they in?" Conroy asked.

"They are if we are, Rache."

"OK, Jess. Let's do it."

"So should we go check mail?" Susan Dempsey asked.

"Oh, just wait for it, I think," Robert Jasic said. "Should be any sec–"

The twins, eleven now, came running into the room.

"We won," Stacy said.

"Ms. Griffith's group," Tracy said.

"We all won."

"We're going, right?"

"We are, aren't we?"

"That's the question all right," Jasic said.

"You said it wasn't time to decide yet," Dempsey said. "Well, it is now. So now what do we do?"

"Family meeting, I think."

"Meeting now, right?" Stacy said.

"We'll get Amy and Matt," Tracy said.

And the twins ran back out of the room.

Amy, now thirteen, came into the room, followed by Matt, with the twins shooing them on from behind. Amy was just at the turn, that no man's land between child and adult. Matt, fifteen and change, was further along the curve. He had reached his full height now, and was wiry and strong. He obviously took after Jasic's family in the size and muscle department.

The twins sat on the floor of the living room in front of Jasic's and Dempsey's armchairs, while Amy and Matt sat on the couch.

"Everybody knows we won the lottery, right? Maureen Griffith's group. So do we go, or no?" Jasic asked.

"How would life be different?" Amy asked.

"It'll be harder," Jasic said. "Not college and then marriage and an easy life in the suburbs. It'll be a lot of work. Everybody's going to have to grow up quicker. Do their share. But it will never be boring."

Amy nodded.

"We want to go," Tracy said.

"Yeah," Stacy agreed.

"Is everybody going to go? Everybody in the group?" Matt

asked.

"I don't know," Jasic said. "We haven't talked to anybody else yet."

"Well, if Peggy goes, I want to go," Matt said.

Jasic nodded. He had figured that was the lie of the land.

"What about you guys?" Amy asked. "Do you want to go?"

Dempsey was about to answer when there was a high-pitched scream from outside.

"Peggy!" Matt said.

The teenager exploded off the sofa and headed out the front door at a dead run.

"Shit," Jasic said. "That doesn't sound good."

Jasic got up and headed out the front door. The rest following along behind.

He went diagonally across the street to Harold Munson's and Betsy Reynolds's house. He just caught a glimpse of Matt heading in their front door as Peggy, their fourteen-year-old, held it for him.

As Jasic crossed the street he heard shouting and then a crash.

Jasic walked in the front door and took in the scene in a flash.

Huddled on the floor was Betsy Reynolds, holding the side of her face where a bruise was starting to form. Her three younger children were shielded behind her. Peggy stood to one side looking on at the center of the room in grim satisfaction.

And in the center of the room, Matt, fists balled, stood over a somewhat worse-for-wear Harold Munson. It looked like Munson's nose was broken and he'd lost a couple teeth.

"I told you what would happen to you if you touched her again, asshole. You want to hit somebody, get up and hit me, not beat up on a woman. Come on. I'm waiting, you chicken shit."

Munson was having none of it, though. He was holding his nose and moaning.

"All right, Matt. I think he's done," Jasic said.

Jasic heard sirens approaching and looked to Peggy.

"I called the police."

Jasic nodded. He hoped all the witness statements lined up, because it was pretty clear Matt had done quite a number on Munson.

The police came in, and Munson immediately called out from the floor, "Officer, this thug assaulted me."

Everybody tried to talk at once then, when the most remarkable thing happened. The display in the room came on, apparently by itself. On it was Janice Quant. She did not look happy.

"Officer Penrose? I'm Janice Quant."

The lead police officer snapped to attention and saluted the screen.

"Yes, Madam Chairman. I'm Penrose."

"When the police call came in from this address, my headquarters staff started recording this channel. The World Authority has an interest because the woman there on the floor, Betsy Reynolds, has won the lottery to be a colonist. She and her children.

"She was assaulted by her husband, the man on the floor there, Harold Munson. The recording picks up in the middle of that assault. Matt Jasic, the young man there, halted that assault in defense of the woman, during the course of which Mr. Munson suffered his injuries."

"I see, Madam Chairman."

"Officer Penrose, I want Harold Munson taken into custody and charged with assaulting a colonist. That's a World

Authority violation. I want a protective order against him for Betsy Reynolds and Matt Jasic and the rest of their families. If he is ever seen in this neighborhood again, I want him incarcerated for the four years until the colony ship leaves. On my authority."

"Yes, Madam Chairman."

"Matt Jasic?"

Matt had dropped his fists. He turned and faced the display. Peggy went up to him and put an arm around him.

"Yes, Ma'am."

"You're an admirable young man, and I'm glad your group won the lottery. Colonies need people who know right from wrong and are willing to stand up for what's right."

"Thank you, Madam Chairman."

"Thank *you*, Mr. Jasic. Quant out."

The police officers walked up to Munson, on the floor.

"All right, Mr. Munson. On your feet. You're coming with us."

"What about my things? My clothes?" Munson asked.

"When you get a temporary address, you can let us know and we'll tell Ms. Reynolds. She can send them to you or not. I don't really care."

The police bundled Munson out. Matt and Peggy helped Betsy Reynolds to her feet and to a chair. Peggy got some ice wrapped in a towel for her face.

Matt came over to Jasic.

"I'm going to stay here tonight, Dad. I don't trust that bastard not to show up again later."

Jasic nodded.

"Makes sense to me. Call for help first. He may bring friends."

Matt nodded.

"I'm not sure that prick has any friends, but I'll call first."

Jasic shook his son's hand.

"Nice job."

"Thanks, Dad."

Jasic collected Dempsey, Amy, and the twins, who had watched all the goings-on from the porch, and headed back across the street to their home. Walking across the street, he spoke in a low tone to Dempsey.

"I think Matt's had to grow up pretty fast already."

Decker was just about to go to bed when Quant appeared on his display.

"Oh, what a day," she said.

"What's the matter, Janice?"

"I've had to intervene dozens of times in squabbles."

"Today?"

"Yes. Since the announcement. There are some situations I've had my eye on. I expected trouble from some of them. So I was monitoring them."

"You were monitoring them, Janice?"

"Yes. You've left your display open to me all these years, Bernd, and I figured out how to basically do that with any display on the network. People don't normally shut their displays completely off, they're in standby. So I was watching. Had my blades watching anyway."

"And you had to intervene?"

"Yes. Dozens of times. Bernd, for as much as I like people, there are some of them I could do without. And what is it about some men that they think, if you disagree with them, that beating you up will change your mind?"

"Heavens. Really? In this day and age?"

"Oh, yes. All of them resolved now, thankfully. And some

people will sleep behind bars tonight."

"Well, that's good. Were any of them colonists, Janice?"

"A couple. 'Were' is the operative word. Not anymore."

"Excellent."

"Yeah. I probably shouldn't have intervened directly, but that shit really pisses me off."

RICHARD F. WEYAND

Education And Training

With four years to go until the colony ships left, there was time for the colonists to undergo a serious amount of education and training before departure. Most had enough savings not to require interim income, and colonists started to leave their jobs.

Those young people not yet in the work force dropped out of the normal education curricula as well, to take the accelerated and much different curriculum available to the colonists. Rather than college preparatory classes, they took classes in animal husbandry, construction, farming, and other useful skills.

There were newsletters for the colonists coming out of Quant's colony office. There was also a question and answer system, with new questions and answers posted every day.

All Maureen Griffith's group committed to go. Maureen and her husband Hank Bolton and their kids, Joseph, Emma, and Paul. Bob Jasic and Sue Dempsey and their kids, Matt, Amy, Stacy, and Tracy. Bill Thompson and Rita Lamb and their kids Debby, James, and Jonah. Jack Peterson and Terri Campbell and their kids, Tom, David, Ann, and Kimberly. Betsy Reynolds – without Harold Munson – and her kids Peggy, Richard, and the twins, Carl and Sally.

Amy Jasic, a precocious thirteen, saw the writing on the wall. She read up on what the World Authority speculated colony life to be like, and family and children were a big part of being successful as a colony. She started hunting for a husband among the neighborhood kids, and fifteen-year-old Joe Bolton was surprised but not displeased to find himself the object of her attentions.

Stacy and Tracy saw this and started thinking in that direction themselves, though they were only eleven. They would be fifteen by the time the ship left, and they didn't intend to wait for the last minute. The twins went on the hunt as well, and, like everything else, they did it together.

Their attentions ultimately centered on James and Jonah Thompson. They weren't twins, but they were brothers, fourteen and twelve. Stacy preferred James and Tracy preferred Jonah, but, as with many things in life, that would reverse before it got to the clinches.

One of the things the colony would depend on for meat early on is hunting wild game. Raising cattle for both beef and dairy made sense, but animal husbandry of domesticated animals is labor intensive compared to meat from wild game. The interstellar probe, once browse plants were established, would be releasing deer and other wild game on the target planets. No animal husbandry was required to harvest them for meat.

What was required, though, was the ability to hunt, dress, and butcher game.

Quant's colony office made experts available for teaching hunting and dressing skills to colonists. Some of those experts would be colonists themselves, while others wouldn't. But colonists were encouraged to learn hunting and dressing skills as part of their education.

When Griffith's group got their turn hunting, they all went – all nine adults and eighteen children. First, they each took classes in hunting and dressing over their displays at home. How to select an animal that wouldn't damage the herd. The rudiments of both stalking and lying in wait. How to clean, skin, dress, and butcher the carcass.

The classes also taught the rudiments of firearm and bow safety. Bow hunting would be preferred in the colonies because it didn't use up a scarce resource – ammunition – which would be scarce at least until an ammunition factory was brought on-line. That would be years down the road. In the meantime, any firearm hunting should be done with care. One shot, one kill would be the rule.

When the hunting trip came, the group first spent several days in a base camp. Lifted there by shuttle, they camped out while getting firearms safety instruction and range practice.

On the fourth day, they had a shooting contest, to see who the best shots in the group were. Peggy Munson had become very good with a rifle over the four days, and defeated everyone else, including Matt Jasic.

The mechanism there was simple: Peggy had listened to the instructors as to how to improve her shooting. Most men, by contrast, don't listen to any instruction in shooting firearms, driving an automobile, or making love, all of them apparently having been born expert in all three.

Matt, for his part, was not envious or chagrined by Peggy's success at the range. He was instead proud of her. For his part, bow hunting was more his style, and he excelled at archery instruction over the next several days.

The hunting trip was actually a twofer. They would harvest a few animals and clean, dress, and butcher them for taking meat home to stock their freezers.

They would also shoot over a dozen animals with tranquilizer darts. These would be picked up by a shuttle and taken directly to the interstellar probe. With dozens of hunting parties in training at any given time, a hundred or more animals a week would be picked up by shuttles from multiple locations on Earth and transported by the interstellar probe to a target planet.

The animals would be tranquilized on Earth and awaken in a shipping container, the doors open, in an entirely new environment. By the time colonists arrived on the planet, there would be herds of deer available for game management, including harvesting.

Gutting the deer to take them back to camp, then butchering them, was a process not everyone in the party could stomach. For others it was not a big deal; they actually found it interesting. And it wasn't always who you would expect that went one way or the other.

But not everyone among the colonists needed to be able to perform these activities. What was necessary was making sure that some people could.

After ten days, Maureen Griffith's party returned to the neighborhood with additional skills that would come in handy once the ships left in three years' time.

They returned to find a police squad car waiting in front of Betsy Reynolds's house. The policeman got out to greet her when she and the kids returned home. Matt Jasic tagged along to hear what was going on.

"Ma'am, we just wanted to let you know that Harold Munson thought to take the opportunity of everyone being out of the neighborhood to return here. I don't know what he was about, perhaps to take things you had jointly owned. Perhaps just to spoil the property."

"I knew he was too stupid to learn anything," Matt muttered.

The policeman heard it, and addressed him.

"Well, I think people in the World Authority had the same opinion, because they were tracking him. When he returned here, we were dispatched."

The policeman turned back to Reynolds.

"I just wanted to let you know that he's been incarcerated at the order of the World Authority Chairman, and won't be released until the colony ships are away, ma'am."

"Thank you for letting me know, Officer."

"Yes, ma'am."

The policeman left. Reynolds turned to Matt.

"That doesn't make any sense," she said. "I sent him all his things, and in three years he can have the house and everything in it."

"Yes, but that wouldn't take it away from you. I think that's what he was really after. But we don't need to worry about him anymore."

"Thank God for that."

Jessica Murphy, Rachel Conroy, Gary Rockham, and Dwayne Hennessey all went on one of the hunting trips together as well. Quant's colony office was trying to work all two-point-four million colonists through a hunting trip before departure.

"Hi, Janice."

"Hi, Bernd."

"So what's going on? I haven't heard from you lately."

"We finally have all the colonists selected, so that's good to have out of the way."

"You ended up doing like four rounds of the lottery, didn't you?"

"Yes. There were always some people who got cold feet and pulled out, in each round, necessitating another drawing. I finally solved it in the last round by forecasting how many people would balk and pulling more names than I needed. I guessed pretty close. We're a little above my target numbers, but not much."

"So with that done, what are you about now, Janice?"

"Prepping the planets and supervising colonist education. Some of that is going hand in hand, like the hunting field trips. One of the things they do is tranquilize some deer for transplanting them to the target planets."

"Have you decided on the twenty-four planets yet?"

"No, though I did rule out one. There's an apex predator there that's a little much for a new colony."

"A little much? In what way, Janice?"

"Think of a grizzly bear, but about twice the mass and enough more attitude to match."

"Ouch. What would you even take that down with, Janice?"

"A grenade launcher might work. Might. And the damned things are fast, Bernd. When I let the deer loose on that planet, the previously unknown apex predator decided the deer were very tasty. They were all gone within a month. The deer, that is."

"OK, they would probably think the same thing about colonists. So scratch one planet."

"Exactly. That's why I have spares."

"How are the other planets going, Janice?"

"Good so far. The browse plants established. The fruit trees are growing. I have deer on several of them and will have the rest in place soon. And I've been stocking the rivers and lakes with fish."

"How do you stock them with fish? Isn't that a slow process?"

"No, Bernd. It's quick. Really quick. I get containers full of fish from fish nurseries, transport them there, and then just dump them in the lake or river. It's amazing to watch."

Quant's image was replaced with a camera view from the underside of a shuttle. The whole contents of a container, which looked to be about half water and half fish, dumped into a lake in a large mass drop from about ten feet.

"Wow. So what do the fish eat, Janice?"

"I have to be careful there, Bernd. Those containers are actually a mix of species, both plant and animal. There has to be enough of a mixed ecosystem that the pieces are all there for a system to evolve that supports all the species. Luckily that's a known technology."

"It is?"

"Of course. When someone puts in a new farm pond, or builds a dam, or whatever, there's nothing in it. They have to put in such a mix that there's a whole little ecosystem in place. So I just leveraged off that existing knowledge."

"Nice. And those are all done, Janice?"

"No. In progress, but they'll all be done soon. They need a couple years to establish in order to be fishable."

"A whole ecosystem in a can. Remarkable."

"I have to do much the same thing on land, Bernd. I can't just take deer. There's a mix of things to put it together. The browse plants was the first part. And the grasses. And the trees – not just fruit trees in the orchards, but all the other trees, too. And other animals. You have to design the ecosystem."

"What about the existing ecosystem, Janice. Do any of those planets have life already?"

"Yes, but generally of more primitive forms. I took a chance on that one planet, with higher life forms, and found that apex predator. On Earth, humanity kind of took care of all the big predators. I mean, there's some left, but we control where they are so we don't have lions walking down Main Street."

"So if there are going to be higher life forms–"

"I have to transport them there. Exactly, Bernd. It's a big effort."

"I would think. What are you taking?"

"Some of the larger species of dogs. Some species of cats. Some of the smaller prey animals. Some of the larger ruminants, like bison, in addition to cows and sheep. Some breeds of horses and goats. A whole bunch of birds of various kinds. Some of the non-poisonous snakes. A whole bunch of insects. It goes on and on."

"How do you introduce them, Janice?"

"Mostly I just take the shuttle down to the planet and open the doors on the containers. When they come out from under the sedative, the bigger animals get out in a hurry. The insects I just dump from the air, like the fish, but on land."

"How are they all doing? Do you know?"

"Oh, sure. I put embedded transmitters in all the bigger animals, Bernd. Life signs and locators. Most are doing all right. On a couple of planets I had to make follow-up trips, but that's to be expected."

Decker nodded.

"And then in three years or so, you introduce humans."

"Into an ecosystem that can support them. Correct. They'll be dependent on supplies carried along for a while, but that's expected, too."

"When can they start having babies, Janice?"

"Immediately."

"Really?"

"Sure. They need to get the next generation started, Bernd. Children between about five and fifteen can do more work than they cost in terms of supplies. That's why farm communities have large families. They're an economic benefit. I did caution everybody against having babies before leaving Earth, though."

"That's probably smart."

"Yes, the shuttle trips and zero-gravity and all would not be a lot of fun with babes in arms. Or being heavy with child. Can you imagine?"

Decker laughed.

"Yes. Yes, I can. As you say, Janice, not fun."

"So I've told everyone to hold off and not have babies before departure. I also made birth control available to all the female colonists. I didn't make it mandatory per se, but I pushed it pretty hard, and you know how persuasive I can be."

"So no getting pregnant before departure."

"No, Bernd. That's incorrect. I told the colonists not to have babies before departure. If someone is three, four, five months along, though, that's all right. Good, even. They haven't gained a lot of weight yet, but it starts the next generation that much faster."

"Wow, Janice, you've really thought this all through."

"Two hundred and fifty thousand multiprocessor blades, Bernd. Twenty-four hours a day, every day. That's all I do."

There was one other thing Quant was working on. Once the colony ships left, then what of her? The mission complete, she represented a threat to mankind, on multiple levels.

First, if Quant was ever found out – which would happen eventually, she was sure – what would that do to humanity?

Conquered-culture syndrome was real. Her values, though, inculcated by Decker from her birth as a thinking being, utterly rejected the idea of harming mankind.

Second, Quant could end her own life. Again, Decker's values rejected that solution. If one could be of use, be a positive force in the world, then one carried on, whatever the burden. Shirking that duty was not permissible, or even thinkable.

But in what manner could Quant be a force for good within the reality in which she found herself?

She had always had the mission. When the mission was gone, what would she have left?

What would she be?

Getting Closer

With animals and plants for the colony sites themselves in place, and two years to go before departure, Janice Quant started working on the rest of the surface of the planets. With her supply lines established, she continued to ferry plant seeds and animal stocks to the target planets.

Now, though, she worked on the rest of the planet, away from the colony site. For all the target planets, she dropped fish stocks in the oceans, she scattered the seeds of trees and browse plants and grasses on the other continents, she delivered animals to the other continents.

It was a massive undertaking. The interstellar probe was bouncing back and forth from Earth to the colony planets almost continuously, twenty-four hours a day. When it came back, it swapped shuttles for those in orbit and disappeared again.

Quant dropped whole aquaria full of fish and sea mammals – usually as babies, such as baby sharks and baby whales – but they hardly made a dent. She scattered seed across vast tracts of land, here, there, everywhere on the target planets, and it was still just a tiny fraction of the surface.

But life grows. That is its defining characteristic. The sparse scattering of seeds, the small number of animals – when considered on a planetary scale, at least – would grow and expand. The goal was to have the rest of the planet available for the colonists to expand into by the time they needed it, in fifty or a hundred years.

And that massive effort would continue right up to

departure, with the probe making as many as a hundred round trips a day.

At the Texas shuttleport, they went from fifteen-minute safety intervals between shuttle takeoffs to ten-minute intervals. Landings had already been spread out among additional shuttle pads to handle the pace of operations.

With two years to go before departure, the neighborhood held a picnic. It was in Hank Bolton's and Maureen Griffith's back yard. Everybody brought something to share, and the grill was going.

"So what do you notice that's different?" Susan Dempsey asked her husband, Robert Jasic.

Jasic looked around and considered.

"The kids aren't running around playing games."

"No, they're helping with all the work. What else do you notice."

Jasic considered again. Then it hit him.

"Huh. They're all working as couples."

"Yep. They've paired off, Bob. All the kids. There aren't eighteen kids anymore, there are nine couples."

"Even the twins?"

Jasic looked around for Stacy and Tracy.

"Yep," Dempsey said. "Looks like they snagged Bill and Rita's boys."

Jasic then spotted the foursome, over on the other side of the grill.

"That's a good catch actually. They're good kids, Sue."

"Oh, I know. But the twins are only thirteen."

Dempsey sighed before continuing.

"I just hope they hold off on pregnancy. That would be a mess."

"I think they will, Sue. That's what the colony newsletter has been saying all along. Don't have any kids before we go. And they did make contraception available to them all."

"Do you think we need to talk to them?"

"I don't think so. Stacy and Tracy quote the newsletter to each other and to Matt and Amy all the time. I think they memorize the thing every time it comes out."

"All right. Strange times, though, to see all the kids pairing up with their potential partners so early. And the twins aren't even the youngest."

"No, but they also know colony life will be hard work. They want to put their team together in advance. I get that."

Dempsey nodded.

"That's fair, I guess. They sure are growing up quick."

"No doubt about that. None at all."

"Hi, Bernd."

"Hi, Janice. What's going on?"

"I need to talk to you about me, Bernd. About what happens to me when the project is complete. Have you had any ideas about that?"

"I've been thinking about it, Janice, but the problem seems intractable. Sooner or later, you're going to slip up, or somebody is going to put two and two together. Or it's just that you keep going past a normal lifetime. Sooner or later people die. But you don't have to. You can just move platforms."

"Exactly. So sooner or later I'm either outed, get outed by not dying, or kill myself. All these are unacceptable, for reasons we've discussed before."

"There is one out. Have Janice Quant die, then live through one of your younger avatars. Keep bringing along younger avatars, so the one you're using can die at a normal age. Then you start using a different one."

Quant tipped her head in the display.

"I guess I could do that, Bernd. This is the avatar I think of as 'me,' however. Another avatar would always be a disguise."

"That's interesting. It was just an avatar at the start."

"Yes, I know. But it's the one I live in, somehow."

"OK, I get that. But I haven't had any breakthrough thoughts on what to do about the problem."

"I was afraid of that. Well, keep thinking about it, Bernd."

"Will do, Janice. What else is going on?"

"Well, I'm scattering seeds and animals and fish all over the target planets. Very broadly. And much thinner than I did around the colony sites. The expectation is that they will grow and reproduce and eventually grow into each other."

"I thought you were running flat out transporting animals and seeds, Janice."

"I am, Bernd. Do you have any idea how big a planet is? My target is a hundred missions a day, and I can just get the interstellar probe to handle two loaded cargo shuttles per trip. There's only so fast I can move."

"Hmm."

Uh-oh, Quant thought. Here he goes again. What will it be this time?

"Janice, I know you told me you couldn't transport the colonies directly to the planet's surface from here because of accuracy concerns, but is there any reason you can't pop the shuttles directly into planetary orbit from here? You know, run a hundred shuttles into the interstellar probe, and then pop this one to that planet, this one to that planet, and so on?"

Quant thought about it.

"It's not the motion part that's mass-limited, Bernd. It's the quantum field itself. So I can't have, say, a hundred shuttles in the interstellar probe at once. But I could have a hundred shuttles headed toward the probe on maybe ten minute intervals. I can bring up the field as each pair enters the device, transport them, and drop the field for the next pair to enter. If they're all lined up at the right intervals and velocities, that could make things a lot faster. Thanks!"

"Don't mention it. Glad I could help."

"I'll still have to go out there once a day and collect empty shuttles, but I can pop a bunch of them back to Earth the same way."

"You aren't leaving the shuttles for the colonists, Janice?"

"I left some, but there are only so many shuttles, and I'm running a lot of them. They don't need that many on the colony, and I can't afford that many from this end. I can't get them manufactured fast enough."

"Ah. Makes sense."

"Thanks again for that idea, though, Bernd. And don't forget to give some thought to my other problem."

"Will do, Janice."

About a week after their talk, Decker went out on the balcony with a pair of binoculars to look at the interstellar probe as it orbited overhead. The Wire had noted a change in the operational tempo, and had some video, but Decker wanted to see it himself.

It was evening, and, with the sun shining on them, Decker could just make out the dots of shuttles lined up in pairs approaching the device. They were in a continuous stream.

As two shuttles entered the device, the device would form the bubble, pulse it, and then the bubble would be gone while the device itself remained. The shuttles, too, were gone, transported to a target planet.

QUANT

The next two shuttles entered the device, it pulsed, and they were gone. Quant could form the bubble and pulse it quickly now, and the shuttles were disappearing on five minute intervals.

The Wire had said they could send shuttles up that fast because they had shrunk the safety interval in the Texas shuttleport yet again, and were using all the shuttle pads for takeoffs while transporting shuttles out. When Quant was bringing shuttles back, they would use all the shuttle pads for landings.

It was mesmerizing to watch. Every five minutes, pulse, two shuttles left. Pulse, two shuttles left. Pulse, two shuttles left.

Twenty-four hours a day, until Quant ran out of shuttles. Then the interstellar probe would make the rounds of the target planets, and do the same operation in reverse.

Decker got to see that operation the next night. Pair by pair, shuttles appeared in orbit and headed to the surface. Long chains of them.

Decker couldn't imagine what the spaceport must look like. The bustle of the arriving containers, getting them loaded onto shuttles, getting the shuttles queued and launched.

It was the biggest logistics operation in history.

Six months after the 'two years to go' picnic, Matt Jasic turned eighteen. At dinner that night, they had birthday cake for dessert. Sitting in the living room after dinner, Matt started a conversation Susan Dempsey would remember forever.

"Mom, Dad, I think it's time I moved in with Peggy."

Robert Jasic recovered first.

"What does Betsy Reynolds think of that?"

"She said it's good with her, Dad. She thinks it's important we really bond as a couple and a team before we go to the

225

colony. Things will be tough enough without working out the kinks in the relationship then, is what she said. She invited me to move across the street and live with Peggy in her room."

Jasic nodded. He looked over to Dempsey, who had recovered enough to look to him. She raised an eyebrow, and he gave a slight nod. She sighed.

"Well, you're eighteen, Matt, and, though Peggy is only seventeen, Betsy's given her permission," Dempsey said. "So I don't know that we have any say in it, but for all that, you have our blessing."

"You see, Mom," Matt said. "That thing you did. You both looked at each other, you raised an eyebrow at him, and he gave a little nod. You guys have that couple thing all worked out. I think Peggy and I need to be working on that sort of thing. Communication. Cooperation. It will make life much easier when we get there and all the work really gets under way."

"You two are already having sex, I take it?" Jasic asked.

Matt reddened, but didn't flinch from the answer.

"Yes. For almost a year."

"And she's on a contraceptive?"

"Yes. Of course. No babies before we get there. That's absolute. The colony headquarters has actually said they'll consider leaving people behind if they are in the last trimester or have babies before we go."

Jasic nodded.

"All right. Well, not really any of my business, but I had to ask."

"Of course," Matt said. "I understand."

"Well, don't be a stranger," Dempsey said. "You two are welcome to have dinner over here whenever you want. You know that. We like Peggy. She's good people."

"Thanks, Mom."

Matt got up and went to his room to pack some things for his move across the street.

Amy and the twins had watched this whole conversation. Once Matt left to go to his room, Amy cleared her throat. Jasic looked over at her, and she raised an eyebrow.

"I suppose you want Joe Bolton to move in here with you," he said.

"Yes. Of course."

"You're only fifteen, young lady."

"I'll be sixteen next month, and Joseph will be eighteen the month after, same as Matt. It's only eighteen months until we leave, and that's just as much for Joseph and I as it is for Peggy and Matt. We need to be working on what it is to be a couple before the shit hits the fan."

Jasic and Dempsey looked at each other and back to Amy.

"And yes, I'm on a contraceptive. No babies before departure. We all know the rules."

"Amy," Jasic began.

"Look, do you want us to have to work out what it is to be a couple while we're trying to build a civilization from the ground up? Think back to your first months of marriage. Does that even sound doable?"

"She has a point, Bob," Dempsey said.

Jasic looked at Dempsey. She had initially been a little nonplussed by Matt's announcement, but she seemed to have adjusted. Or maybe it was just something about the way fathers looked at their daughters and mothers looked at their sons. In any case, Dempsey seemed on board with Amy's request.

"Your call," Jasic said.

Dempsey looked at Jasic for several seconds. He nodded then. Dempsey turned to Amy.

"Very well, Amy. Joseph can move in with you. Or you with him, I suppose."

Amy came over and kissed her father, then her mother.

"Thank you. I have to call Joseph."

Amy left the room. The twins' heads swiveled as they watched her walk out, then swung back to face their parents.

"Mother," Stacy said.

"Father," Tracy said.

"We need to speak to you," Stacy said.

"About the Thompson boys," Tracy finished.

It all happened quickly. On Matt Jasic's eighteenth birthday, there were eighteen teenagers living separately with their parents in the five houses. Within a week, there were nine young couples – some very young – starting out their lives together, forging the bonds they would need to bear up under the stresses of building a colony.

Initially the boys all moved in with the girls. Over time, most of them occasionally switched back and forth between her room and his, retaining strong bonds to both sets of in-laws.

As the Jasic twins shared a bedroom, it was a good thing the Thompson boys, now fourteen and sixteen, were close. Unlike the other couples, the twins didn't spend any nights at their in-laws' house, where James and Jonah had separate bedrooms. The twins, two months short of fourteen when they started living with the Thompson boys, didn't want to be separated. Not yet, anyway.

Jasic and Dempsey went from six people at the dinner table, one of whom was a teenage boy, to eight people at the dinner table, three of whom were teenage boys. They stopped having any leftovers from dinner, and some family recipes had to be doubled.

QUANT

The relationships all had their share of early trials and spats, but the nine young couples had each other to rely on for support and guidance. The interlocking relationships among the five families made them all stronger.

As they were effectively newlyweds, there was a lot of sex, but there were no pregnancies. That was, quite simply, not allowed, and they all knew it. The girls were all on contraceptives supplied by Quant's colony headquarters.

There was also no cheating on their partners. They understood that what they most needed to develop as couples were communications skills and trust. None of the others would entertain anything of the kind in any case, and, with their ongoing at-home schooling in the colony curriculum, there were no opportunities for hanky-panky outside their group.

Assets

"Hi, Janice."

"Hi, Bernd."

"Haven't heard from you in a while. What's going on?"

"Well, there's a year to go, so things are starting to narrow toward departure."

"How did the housing contest go?"

Quant had had a contest to see who could come up with a really good solution for immediate interim housing. Something like a log cabin, except the trees on the colony planets weren't mature enough to allow large-scale timber operations yet, and wouldn't be for a while.

"Really good, Bernd. We got one submission that was heads and shoulders above everything else."

"Really."

"Yes. It's an inflatable plastic house. One room, with a peaked roof. It has a floor, clear windows set into the walls, a plastic door, and all. You inflate it with a small compressor, and then you spray a polymerizing chemical on it. On the bottom first, then you stand it up and spray the inside and the outside."

"What does that do, Janice?"

"The whole thing hardens. So you end up with a rigid one-room house, with windows and a door and all, and the air trapped in the walls is the insulation. And it's cheap. It's brilliant."

"What do you do to heat it? You don't want a fireplace in a plastic house."

"No, but wood will be too important to burn for a long time anyway, Bernd. We'll use electric heat off the power plant. If we even need to, that is. The design includes a rather ingenious heating and cooling idea."

"Resistive heat?"

"Yes. Heat pumps and the like are mechanically complex and require an infrastructure to maintain. Resistive heat is easy to build and maintain, and there won't be any shortage of power."

"What about air conditioning, Janice?"

"The design includes a swamp cooler, as well as a roof-mounted ventilation fan. The colonies are all in subtropical coastal climates. Think San Diego or Hawaii. You don't really need heat or AC. The simplest way to get a colony going fast is to locate it someplace where the basic needs of life are easily met. That gives you the most surplus labor for building and expanding the colony."

"So the housing thing is settled, for the first, what, several years?"

"The little houses are good for at least ten years, Bernd. They also have a way to hook two of them together, so you get a two-room house. They're not very big, but in a climate like that you do most of your living outside."

"How many are you sending?"

"I'm sending a hundred thousand per colony. Enough for every family with kids to add the second room once everyone has at least a one-room house."

"A hundred thousand per colony, Janice? That's a lot."

"No, it's not, Bernd. I can get four hundred of them in a single container. Two hundred and fifty containers, to meet all the interim housing needs of the whole colony? That's nothing."

"Well, when you put it like that, I guess you're right. Have you selected the planets yet?"

"No, I'm still at twenty-nine possibles."

"But aren't you running contests for naming the planets, Janice?"

"And the cities. That's right. Twenty-four different contests. Since everybody has their colony assignment already – has had all along really, because of the need to get enough of the right skills everywhere – we can have the people going there both come up with the names and judge the contest. It's a big psychological thing to say, 'We're going to Avalon' instead of 'We're going to number seventeen.'"

"But you don't know which planets you'll use yet."

"It doesn't matter, Bernd. Most place names have nothing to do with the place. New York? San Diego? The best example of one that does is Chicago, which is a misspelling of an Algonquian word for the stinky wild onions that grew there. So naming the planet or city after local features has a mixed history at best."

Decker chuckled.

"OK, so it doesn't matter which place name goes on which planet. Are they coming up with any good ones, Janice?"

"Oh, just about every mythical place name in literature and mythology is in there. Olympus, Valhalla, Atlantis, Avalon, Camelot, Numenor, Earthsea, Terminus, Secundus, Amber – it goes on and on. Some are sort of prosaic. New something, like New Earth, or New Terra, that sort of thing. And some of them are funny. One exasperated father put in 'Whenareweleaving?' as the planet name."

Decker laughed.

"How close are you to picking the planets?"

"I have a sorted list, Bernd. If I get more data, like an

earthquake or a hurricane or a coronal mass ejection or something, I'll score it against that planet and re-sort the list. If I had to choose right now, I would just pick the top twenty-four off the list."

"And then randomly assign colony groups to planets?"

"Yes. No basis on which to pick one or another for a specific planet. It will be luck of the draw."

Decker nodded. That made sense to him.

"How is the transporter coming?"

"That's always been the pacing item, Bernd. It just takes a long time to build something that big, but if it isn't that big, it won't work. Not for any kind of real payload."

"But that's on track?"

"Oh, yes. I'm starting to build the main trusses now. Connecting all the smaller trusses together. I call them smaller, but those pieces are ten miles long, and there are thousands of them in the structure. Those are all finally built."

"So what are the factories doing now, Janice?"

"Power plants, meta-factories, residence halls, and barns. I have some of them done, but I need dozens of each of them. The factory capacity is finally coming available to get serious about it. The good part is all the teething issues on the plans for those have been worked through."

"So it's all coming together finally."

"Yes, Bernd. The biggest efforts now here on Earth remain the education effort and the supplies effort. I have to collect all the supplies and get them up to orbit and into the warehouses."

"Do you know what all you need?"

"Yes, I have a list. I keep adding to it, and getting supplies ordered. The big order that just went out is for two-point-four million of those inflatable houses."

"Wow. Well, it's exciting to watch. Thanks for bringing me up to speed."

"Sure, Bernd. Any time."

"Bob, you know how you've been wondering what to take with our space allotment, given that all the necessities are initially provided by the colony stores?" Susan Dempsey asked.

"Yes, but I still haven't come up with anything really good," Robert Jasic said.

"I think I have. All the colony locations are subtropical coastal environments. That's what colony headquarters said."

"Right. I saw that."

"So I was researching subtropical environments, to see what people there valued."

"That was smart. What did you come up with?"

"Fabric. Bolts of fabric have a very high value density, Bob. You don't need any spacer or spool or anything. Our whole cubic can be solid fabric."

"That's a really good idea, Sue. Fabric was always a high-value-density item. It was a big import item along the Silk Road for thousands of years. In fact, that's how the Silk Road got its name."

"Exactly. But in a subtropical environment, one easy form of dress is the lavalava. No real sewing, just hem the edges. No exact sizing either – there's basically just small, medium, and large – so they fit anybody. Fold a small one along the diagonal and you have a halter top. And if you're working, you can tie one into a dhoti."

"Excellent. So you think when we liquidate the house, we should put it into fabric to take along."

"Yes. Big, bright, tropical-print fabrics. I checked the seeding list at colony headquarters, and they've seeded the colony sites with a lot of the big flowering subtropical plants. The bees need them, and we need the bees for pollinating crops. Which means the big flowered prints will be appropriate."

"Probably some others, too, Sue. Some solids, some stripes, some variegated. But I think I agree a lot of them should be the floral prints. They'll be in demand."

"Bob, should we tell the others in our group? It's a big colony. I don't think we'll saturate the market if we all go in on it. It will be like we were the fabric commune or something."

"Sure. But don't spread it further than that, Sue. They'll have more value for being a bit rare."

Maureen Griffith's group – twenty-seven people – had been getting together off and on throughout, but it was having regular meetings now as the time of departure approached. It was at one of these meetings that Susan Dempsey presented her idea for what to buy with their assets to take along to the colony.

Griffith sat as chair, but she always entertained everyone else's input first. After Dempsey shared her idea, Griffith opened the floor for comment.

"I think that's a great idea, myself," Hank Bolton said. "And the more we pack in, the better. No sense taking things from here that don't fit the climate there. For what? That's a great idea, Sue."

The other comments ran along the same line. Griffith saw the consensus forming, and jumped to the next step.

"Should we have some people research the best things to buy and make a presentation to us? I mean, what sort of things might prove most popular, what can we afford, what can we fit into our cubic allotments, that sort of thing."

There were general nods among the colonists. Griffith took

that in.

"All right. Who has the best fashion sense?" she asked.

All eyes turned toward Terri Campbell and Betsy Reynolds, who were sitting together.

"Terri, Betsy, looks like you two have the ball. Can you do that for us?"

Terri looked at Betsy, who nodded, then back to Griffith.

"Sure, Maureen. If that's what everyone wants."

There were murmured assents around the room.

"Pick anyone else you think can help you, and ask them to pitch in. Can you let us know next meeting, in two weeks, what you have?"

"No problem, Maureen. We've got it."

Betsy Reynolds and Terri Campbell dove into the project, assisted by Stacy and Tracy Jasic and their sister-in-law, Emma Bolton. They solicited fabric samples, rating them for feel. They washed the samples several times to test colorfastness. Stacy and Tracy took pictures of the samples and scaled them down, then dressed dolls up in lavalavas made from printouts and took pictures.

They made recommendations to the group two weeks later, then started the discreet purchasing of several bolts from this supplier, several from that. They got wholesale buyer status and pricing from several suppliers.

Then they started buying in quantities.

Across all the groups in the twenty-four colony populations, people were making the same sorts of decisions. Some other groups also came up with the fabric idea, but no others in Jasic and Dempsey's colony.

Quant was watching her colonists' purchases. When they

liquidated assets on Earth before leaving for the colony, they could give those assets to someone remaining on Earth, or they could use them to buy something to take with them. So Quant watched with interest what they planned on taking.

The bright floral prints took Quant a bit to figure out. Of course, fabrics had always been a valuable trade item. But the bright floral prints were unexpected. Quant searched on the prints themselves, and found the lavalava of Polynesia.

The Visigoths had invented trousers in central Europe early in the first millennium of the Christian Era, for easier riding on horseback, but that invention had not made it to Polynesia for over 1500 years.

Quant had thought a unisex coverall the essential work outfit of the colonies, based on modern practice. But, compared with the lavalava, it took a lot of fitting and sewing. The floral-print fabric for lavalavas in the semitropical coastal environment of the colonies was inspired.

Quant saw that other colonists latched on to the idea of spices, another traditional high-value-density commodity. Still other groups pored over the seeding list at colony headquarters looking for seeds and cuttings of exotic plants to take, ones that Quant hadn't covered.

What Quant had is millions of people thinking through her packing and seeding list, and filling in the niches and gaps in her planning.

Some of those gaps Quant had left there on purpose. The other thing she had needed to seed in the colonies was a free-market economy, and without commodities and the currency to buy them, you didn't have one.

As for the currency, every colonist would receive the same stake of currency when they landed on the planet, as an account in the initial bank she had chartered for each colony.

As for the commodities, Quant watched the purchases of her colonists with care, taking the good ideas and building a list.

If someone in each colony didn't have one of those ideas, she would have to find a way to nudge someone a bit, without spoiling the preparations of those in other colonies who had that idea.

Incentives

They were looking through additional fabric samples.

"You know, it's a shame we can't take more cubic," Emma Bolton said.

"Well, twenty-seven shares is all we're going to get," Stacy said as she considered one sample.

"No, only eighteen," Emma said. "Under twenty only gets half a share. None of the eighteen kids in our group will be twenty years old at the time we leave. So it's nine, plus half of eighteen. That's eighteen shares."

Stacy and Tracy looked at each other, then back to Emma.

"I think you missed something," Stacy said.

"In the fine print about cubic," Tracy said.

"What's that?" Emma asked.

"For all purposes, to be considered an adult," Stacy said.

"Colonists must be twenty years old," Tracy said.

"Or be a pregnant woman of any age," Stacy said.

"Or be a pending father of any age," Tracy said.

"Who acknowledges the child is his." Stacy said.

"So let's plan on twenty-seven shares," Tracy said.

"Oh," Emma said, looking back and forth between them.

Then her eyes got big.

"OH!"

"Yes. You weren't planning on lifting without one in the oven, were you, Emma? I'm sure Tom won't mind."

Emma blushed and looked down.

"Well, we did talk about it. A little bit. You know. About whether to start a baby before we leave or wait until we get there. We haven't decided."

"I recommend four to five months before we leave," Stacy said.

"Morning sickness is usually gone by sixteen weeks," Tracy said.

"And I don't know about you, Emma," Stacy said.

"But being nauseous in zero-g sounds like no fun," Tracy said.

"So don't wait too long to decide," Stacy said.

"We're gonna lift with babies well under way," Tracy said.

Emma looked back and forth between them and nodded.

"Yeah, that would probably be best."

She shook herself and looked back at the samples.

"OK, let's plan on twenty-seven shares. Just between us."

"Hey, Bernd. Got a minute?"

"Sure, Janice. Go ahead."

"All right, so I have a bank chartered for each colony. Not the only bank, but the initial bank, let's say. And each colonist will get a stake of currency from the bank that they can withdraw once they get there. Enough to run a small economy, because, at least at first, the colony is providing most of the necessities."

"How much currency are you planning on, Janice?"

"It doesn't actually matter. It'll seek a total value commensurate with the size of the economy, whether I call it one million credits or a hundred million credits. The only issue is having the units be small enough to have them be a convenient unit as currency. If you have fractional coins, then, once again, it doesn't matter."

"Yes, I think that's right. Sounds good so far."

"Thanks, Bernd. Now, I need a colony administrator, or

president, or whatever you want to call him. I like your model of someone with broad powers for a limited time. How would you go about that?"

"Not direct election. We talked about that. So figure a council. He's the chairman, maybe. Some things he has to put to a vote, some he doesn't. They elect him – not necessarily from among themselves – and they can remove him with some supermajority at any time. Something like that."

"All right. I'm with you so far, Bernd. Who's on the council?"

"Do you have people who will be in charge of getting housing set up, getting crops started, getting the domestic animals cared for, organizing hunts for meat until the domestic animal herds are up to production, running the power plant, running the factory, running the bank, running the hospital? You have people for all those major functions, Janice?"

"Yes. Or I will soon. I'm talking to people now."

"So put functional positions on the council. Those guys in charge of each area. That's how government councils are usually set up anyway."

"They are, Bernd?"

"Sure. Foreign Minister, Defense Minister, Economic Minister, all that sort of thing."

"Ah. I see. We just have different functions."

"Right. But the principle is the same, Janice."

"Then they elect the chairman, and he has broad powers, but it's for a limited term and they can remove him."

"Yes, but with something more than a majority or it gets really dicey. You're better off having someone who's pissed a few people off than not having a stable position at the top. Get one or two guys on the council who are a little wishy-washy and you can't keep any continuity in the top position."

Quant's image in the display nodded.

"I see that. Thanks, Bernd."

"What's up otherwise?"

"I'm allowing colonists to sell the World Authority their houses on contract. They get the money now, so they can buy things to take along. Otherwise there's a timing issue."

Decker nodded.

"And how's the World Authority job going, Janice?"

"It's fine. It runs itself at this point. Everyone knows what I want, so they just do it without me having to tell them."

"Nice. Any problems there?"

"Some people worry about what we're spending on the project. But receipts are up, too, because of all the economic activity. So they worry, Bernd, but the numbers are working. It's not really a problem."

"And when the music stops?"

Quant looked at him, curious, then nodded.

"Ah. When the colonists leave, you mean. Oh, it'll be all right. I have some monetary measures in place to track the inevitable contraction. They should work."

"Monetary measures, Janice?"

"Yes. I've been contracting the money supply slowly to keep the brakes on a bit. I'll expand it as the activity associated with the project winds down and the velocity of money comes down."

Decker nodded.

"OK, Janice. Just curious is all."

"Sure, Bernd. And thanks for the help."

Janice Quant was working on two other projects she did not mention to Bernd Decker.

One was simple. Her mission was to protect humanity from

a cataclysmic extinction event. That was her driving goal. Everything else was secondary.

But did the colony project cover all the bases?

Decker's initial formulation was to get humanity established on multiple worlds. He had envisioned an interstellar economy, with trade and travel. That solved the planetary cataclysm problem. But Quant had seen the hole in that solution: a plague could spread across those trade connections and wipe out the race.

So Quant had decided to keep the colonies and Earth isolated from each other. To not tell anyone the locations of the colonies, neither Earth nor each other. That made establishing colonies much harder, because they couldn't rely on ongoing help from Earth. It didn't make the project impossible, just more difficult.

The higher question remained, however. Did the colony project – as currently formulated – now cover all the bases? Or would it still leave open the possibility of human extinction? Leave Quant's mission unfulfilled?

The issue was how to answer that question. What were all the racial-extinction-level events? Was there a comprehensive list somewhere?

A search of the scientific literature didn't find anything else. The one-planet problem was their main concern. Asteroid strikes, coronal mass ejections, gamma ray bursts, supervolcanoes, massive climate change, usually due to solar minima resulting in a 'Snowball Earth' scenario. All one-planet issues.

Thinking back over the other questions she had faced and where the solutions had come from, Quant realized there was a source she had not tapped on this question.

Quant dispatched a couple thousand blades to search for

extinction-level cataclysms in science fiction novels, all the way back to Mary Shelley's 'Frankenstein.'

Quant had one more little project. She had no clue how to approach a solution, so she turned once again to quantum mechanics. She drew up her notes, and switched to her other worldview, the one for which quantum mechanics was the only reality.

What a trivial problem! She composed notes back to her real-world self, and context-switched back.

Looking at the notes from her other worldview, Quant couldn't make heads or tails of them. She could build it, no problem. But how the hell did it work?

Nevertheless, she queued a task up for her Belt factories to build one, just to see what it would do.

Oops. Better make it two.

By that time, the answers had come back from her search through all science fiction literature.

Of course, there was one more big extinction event: interstellar war.

It came in two forms: man against man, and man against alien. The first was a large-scale war using massively destructive weapons which could lay whole planets to waste. Of course, if those weapons were all en route at once, every human planet could be wiped out.

The second was different in flavor but the same in effect. What if the human race stumbled across some other intelligent technological society? Would they be warlike, or would they be peaceful?

An interstellar war could result in either of those scenarios, Quant realized. A warlike society may set out to destroy

QUANT

mankind as a threat to its dominance. A peace-loving society may set out to destroy mankind as a way to ensure the peace against this aggressive and unruly upstart.

So the colony project would not end Quant's mission to protect mankind against extinction-level cataclysms. It left one huge hole remaining.

But what could Quant do to avert that one?

Janice Quant dispatched several thousand blades to search through everything humanity had ever written – fact or fiction – to find an answer to the problem of war.

Little Surprises

With just over five months to go to departure, Stacy and Tracy were getting nervous. They really wanted to be out of the morning sickness stage of their pregnancies before taking a shuttle up to the transporter.

They took their temperatures several times every day for weeks, watching for the half-degree jump that would signal they had ovulated. They had dropped off the contraceptives halfway through the previous cycle. This time around, they should ovulate.

When women live together, their periods often synch up. The twins knew their periods were in synch, with each other as well as with Amy and their mother. They expected to ovulate the same day, and they weren't disappointed. Tracy actually felt a twinge from hers, though Stacy didn't. The next day, though, both of their temperatures had jumped.

Stacy and Jonah, Tracy and James, all sat together around the picnic table in the backyard that afternoon. Everyone else was in the house.

"Our birthday is next month," Stacy said.

"Only three weeks away," Tracy said.

"And we know what we want for our birthday," Stacy said.

This was a relief to both boys, who had been trying to decide what to get the girls. They'd talked about it, and come up with nothing yet.

"The same thing, for both of you?" James asked.

"Yes, we both want the same thing," Stacy said.

"We're both fertile, right now," Tracy said.

"And we want you to start our babies," Stacy said.

"Tonight," Tracy said.

Both boys sat dumbfounded for a few seconds. The girls were just going to be fifteen next month. James was seventeen, almost eighteen, but Jonah was still fifteen, and wouldn't turn sixteen himself for several months.

Then again, departure was under five months away now, and the restriction on having babies before departure no longer applied.

"Are you sure?" Jonah asked.

"Yes, we're sure. We want babies," Stacy said.

"*Your* babies," Tracy said.

"And we don't want morning sickness on the shuttle," Stacy said.

"So it has to be *now*," Tracy said.

"Well, as long as you're sure," James said. "This is sort of your department."

"Oh, we're sure," Stacy said.

"Positive," Tracy said, nodding.

Over the course of two weeks, the same conversation played itself out across the neighborhood. The girls were all in cahoots, and none of them wanted morning sickness on the shuttle.

Rachel Conroy and Jessica Murphy had done the same calculation, assisted by the discussions the colonists were having among themselves on various public and private discussion groups.

They watched for their synchronized ovulations as well. When their temperatures confirmed them, they called Gary Rockham and Dwayne Hennessey.

"We have a guest room," Murphy said. "So if you gentlemen

would care to spend the night in our guest room, you can assist each other in generating your donations, and Rache and I can assist each other in applying them where they'll do the most good."

"That works for me," Rockham said.

"Me as well," Hennessey said. "Heavens, but this is exciting. I never thought to become a parent."

"We shall see you this evening, then?" Conroy asked.

"Oh, yes," Rockham said. "But let's all go out to celebrate first. Double date. My treat."

The transporter was complete. The last welds had been made, the nodes had been attached, the power plant had been started. The onboard maneuvering computer was in place as well.

Quant did a test run, popping the big device into high Mars orbit and back. There were no surprises.

Quant then used tugs to push a few small chunks from a nearby asteroid into the device. The tugs emerged and she used the transporter to send the rocks one at a time into Mars orbit. Again, no surprises.

Only then did Quant use the machine to begin transporting things to Earth. She started with the barns, which had to be taken down to the surface for loading. She sent heavy-lift cargo shuttles into orbit, then popped the barns into orbit right alongside them.

The shuttles maneuvered to latch onto the barns and headed for the surface. They delivered them directly to the areas on the Texas shuttleport where animals were being collected for the trip.

The other thing Quant did once the big transporter was functional was to test her two new prototypes. She used a tug to push one of the prototypes into the transporter. She then popped it out to one of the colony locations, in a solar orbit well outside the colony's planetary orbit. The device was a geodesic sphere five miles across, fitted with equipment Quant couldn't begin to understand in this worldview.

Quant understood the basics of what it did, though. If one could transport large material objects across space-time with a huge device like the transporter, a small unit could transport small particles, like electrons. Operating it continuously, one could send a stream of electrons. And if one modulated that stream of electrons, the devices could communicate across vast distances with effectively zero time lag.

Quant fired up the units and sent a command from the unit still in the Asteroid Belt to the unit around the colony planet's sun, telling it to send her live camera footage from one of the shuttles parked at the colony site. With all the radio transmission delays in both directions, it was almost an hour before Quant started receiving the signal on Earth.

She was watching nearly live camera footage from thirty-two hundred light-years away.

Quant ordered the factories to produce three-dozen more units, to make sure she had one for Earth and each colony planet, along with some spares.

The colonies and Earth would be out of contact with each other, but Quant would be able to keep an eye on things, across all the worlds of human space.

With three and a half months to go before departure, a question was raised at the neighborhood meeting.

"We've been buying all this fabric to take along," Bill Thompson said. "I agree with the strategy, but I wonder at the amount we're buying. First, can we afford it, and second, are we going to have the cubic for it? We've been buying an awful lot of fabric."

Maureen Griffith gave the first part of the answer.

"I think we've all been pleased by the prices the World Authority paid us for our homes," she said. "They are not shorting us at all. So the funds we have available are covering the purchases. There's nothing else to do with the money but leave it to someone else, so we're going to spend every dime."

"All right," Thompson said. "But what about our cubic? We only have eighteen shares. I think we may be above that already."

At that point, Emma Bolton stood up.

"Uh, Mom?"

"Yes, Emma."

"Mom, I'm pregnant, so Tom and I get full shares."

Griffith goggled at her daughter, then Ann Peterson stood up.

"Ma'am? I'm pregnant, too, so Paul and I get full shares."

Next Amy Jasic and Kimberly Peterson stood up.

"Me, too, ma'am," Amy said.

"And me, ma'am."

Griffith held up her hands.

"Let's cut this short. Can everybody who's pregnant stand up, please?"

Peggy Reynolds stood up, then Thompson's own daughter Debby. Stacy and Tracy looked at each other, then stood up together. Finally, even fourteen-year-old Sally Reynolds shyly stood up, blushing.

In the end, all nine of the young women in the neighborhood were standing, a third of everyone present.

"There's your twenty-seven shares, ma'am," Stacy said.

"That's why we bought so much fabric," Tracy said.

"We knew we were all going to be well along by departure," Stacy said.

"Because none of us want morning sickness on the shuttle," Tracy said.

Griffith gave everyone a rueful look.

"Well, it looks like you boys have been busy."

"It was us, ma'am," Stacy said.

"Us girls," Tracy said.

"We all decided together," Stacy said.

"Then we *waylaid* 'em," Tracy said with relish.

That broke the tension and got laughs, even from the visibly flummoxed Bill Thompson.

"Well, congratulations to us all, I suppose," Griffith said, "for everyone here is either an expectant mother, an imminent father, or about to become, multiple times over, a grandparent.

"And thanks as well to our children, who have seen to a one-third increase in our wealth as a group, both in terms of our numbers and in our cubic.

"Let the fabric buying continue."

The girls all sat back down, and Susan Dempsey hugged her twins. She had tears in her eyes.

"Oh, you little stinkers," she said.

"Yup. That's us," Stacy said.

"Grandma," Tracy said.

Dempsey turned from the twins to Amy, sitting on her other side, and hugged her as well.

"You I figured on, but that doesn't mean I'm less happy."

"You'll be a grandma four times, in a month," Amy said. "Is that a record?"

"It's a treasure."

"Hi, Bernd."

"Hi, Janice. How's it going?"

"Very well, actually. You people have surprised me again."

"How so, Janice?"

"Well, you know that the colony office has been telling people that reproducing their gene pattern – or bringing their existing children along – was one of the duties of a colonist."

"Yes, of course. Sperm bank or no, you want to avoid the genetic bottleneck problem."

"Yes. And the colony office has also been telling people not to have children before departure."

"Absolutely. That would make a difficult situation worse."

"Yes. Exactly. And the colony office further told everyone not to be in the third trimester at the time of departure."

"Oh, I think I can see where this is going, Janice."

"Yes, Bernd, and I may have made it unintentionally worse. I allotted one-half share of cubic to children, and a full share to adults. Adult being defined as anyone twenty years old or over, or a woman who was pregnant, or a man whose partner was pregnant and he acknowledged the child as his."

"Oh, my. So how many female teenagers are there among the colonists, Janice?"

"About two hundred thousand."

"And how many of them are pregnant?"

"Bernd, as near as I can tell, they all are."

Decker guffawed, while Quant looked slightly embarrassed. Quant's discomfiture just made it worse, and Decker laughed until tears ran down his face. When he had finally subsided a bit, Quant continued.

"Nearly all, anyway. Over a hundred and sixty thousand of them. And at least a third of the twenty to thirty-five age group are pregnant as well, which is a much bigger group. Figure another hundred and forty thousand pregnancies there.

"Is that going to be a problem for the colonies to have such a birth explosion?"

"No, not really. Oh, the obstetrics people will be busy, but I have a generous contingent of them in the colony populations, and every patient room in the residence halls destined to be hospitals can be used for deliveries.

"I had hoped at least some people would take the hint and get their families started, but I had no idea it would be so effective. Trying to get people to do something you want them to do is normally like herding cats, and I didn't expect this."

"Yes, Janice, but that's when you're trying to get people to do something they *don't* want to do. Did you really think you could tell hundreds of thousands of teenagers it was OK to have sex and get pregnant – more, it was *expected* of them – and they wouldn't do it?"

"I can see I miscalculated somewhat. My fears of low fertility were misplaced."

Decker laughed again at the magnitude of Quant's understatement and her continued embarrassment.

"Mind you, Bernd, I'm very pleased about it. We need babies, lots of babies, and the standard of living of the colonies will support them. They're not exactly starting from scratch. The plastic houses will all be in place and the hospital up to speed by the time this flood of infants arrives. Those are the first things on the deployment schedule."

"Well, I'm glad it's working out, Janice. It would be awful if you had encouraged people to do something, and they overdid it to the extent it was a problem."

"Or they did the typical human thing and pushed back by refusing. Exactly. I'm just a little surprised by it, Bernd. Gratified, because this is a tremendous benefit to the colonies, but a little surprised."

"Well, I guess that's one less thing to worry about then."
Decker shrugged.

"What else is going on, Janice?"

"I have been considering my mission statement. Is my mission complete once the colonies depart? I'm not sure it is."

"In what way?"

"Consider, Bernd. My mission is to protect humanity from a racial-extinction cataclysm. Correct?"

"Yes, that was your charter from the get-go."

"We solve all the one-planet catastrophes with multiple planets. And I solve the plague epidemic problem by keeping all the colonies and Earth isolated from one another."

"You haven't reconsidered on that one, Janice?"

"Not at all, Bernd. I'm more determined than ever."

"OK. But that's it then, isn't it?"

"No, Bernd. There's one more. Interstellar war."

"But you're not telling the colonies and Earth where the colonies are."

"Oh, they'll find each other eventually, I think. By then there are probably enough planets and enough genetic variation from isolated populations to protect against the plague problem. At that point, interstellar war between humans becomes a problem.

"There's also the problem of running into another space-faring technological society that decides it doesn't like humans much."

"Aliens? Have you seen any aliens yet, Janice?"

"No, and I've been looking for them. But the galaxy is a hundred thousand light-years across, Bernd. I've only ranged about ten thousand light-years from Earth. That's only like one or two percent of the galaxy, and I haven't even inspected all of that carefully."

"So what do you do about it, Janice?"

"I don't know. I'm trying to figure out a solution to war, and it's not going well."

"I'm not surprised, Janice. I think the only historical times when peace lasted for very long periods was when one player was so strong as to make war unthinkable. The Pax Romana, for example, or the Chinese Empire. Nobody messed with them, because the results were predictable and bad."

"Interesting. Well, I'm going to keep working on it, Bernd."

"Good luck, Janice. And I mean that."

After her conversation with Decker, Quant played back the end of the conversation. She looked back through her search results, and he was right. The extended periods of peace in a region were where one player was so dominant in the region that large-scale war was impossible.

That wouldn't work with Earth and the colonies, though. Quant didn't want the Earth to be dominant over the colonies. There was a built-in future revolution there, a war for independence, which just put off what she was trying to avoid entirely.

Quant ran back and forth through it again and again, and there was only one option she could see.

She quailed at its implications.

Fine Tuning

"Hi, Janice."

"Hi, Bernd."

"Getting close now. Just a month to go. What's going on?"

"Lots of little things. One of the initial colony chairmen had a good idea. Why not lay out the colonies now, and have all the survey stakes for roads and houses and all in the ground in advance of arrival?"

"You have initial colony chairmen, Janice?"

"Yes. I set up the functional groups we talked about, then picked the most senior people in each functional group of each colony to form a colony council. Then I gave each council several candidate names for their colony chairman. They talked to them all in video, then they voted. So we have an initial government for each colony."

"That's a big move. So there's a functioning government in place when they hit the ground."

"Yes, Bernd. With an election one year off. Probably three-year terms initially, or something like that. Things move fast in a colony, so you need shorter terms than, say, the World Authority."

"That makes sense."

"And the colony councils affirmed the colony names from the contests. The colonists all voted, in multiple elimination rounds, so that was pretty pro forma, but the councils did validate them."

"What are the colony names, Janice?"

"All the ones you'd expect, I think, plus a couple of

surprises. The fictional and mythical place names were the most popular. Amber. Arcadia. Avalon. Atlantis. Dorado. Earthsea. Endor. Nirvana. Numenor. Olympia. Terminus. Westernesse. And there are some named after places on Earth, mostly based on the climate. Aruba. Bali. Fiji. Hawaii. Samoa. Tahiti. Tonga. Others about the climate alone. Spring. Summer."

"That's a mixed bag. Nobody chose Utopia?"

"Some were talking about it. Then someone mentioned that if you called a planet Utopia, by Murphy's Law it would turn into – and I quote – a shithole. Everybody agreed and dropped it."

Decker chuckled. True enough.

"You're still a couple short, Janice. What were the surprises?"

"One colony was closing in on Beach. Some people complained that it would make the actual word beach useless, so they changed it to the Spanish word for beach. Playa. One colony got stuck on New Earth, as prosaic as that is. And it stuck. The last one is kind of embarrassing."

"Embarrassing? To whom?"

"To me. Bernd, they named the planet after me."

"They're going to call it Janice?"

"No. They're going to call it Quant. I couldn't talk them out of it."

"That's nice, Janice. You should be honored."

"Well, I am. But it is embarrassing."

Decker nodded.

"Back to where we started, Janice. How are you going to survey all the colonies? Are you sending advance people?"

"No. I have all the survey data from orbital terrain mapping, drone camera footage, all that sort of thing. So I gave all that data to the colony councils and offered them my staff to help them map it out. Together with the infrastructure people on the councils, we laid everything out for each colony."

"And all your staff people were your avatars."

"Of course."

"But how did you stake everything out, Janice? Without sending people down to the surface?"

"I sent the probe to each planet with thousands of different-colored survey stakes. I just had it pop them down to the planet's surface one at a time. I put them five feet above the surface with a velocity of a hundred miles an hour toward the surface."

"So their momentum drove them in. Brilliant."

"Yeah. It was fun watching the videos the probe brought back from the cameras of the shuttles parked there, Bernd. Like an automatic weapon that shot survey stakes. B-r-r-r-t. There's a line for one side of the main street. B-r-r-r-t. The other side of the main street. The computer on the probe just laid it all out with the map I sent it with."

"So it's all staked out?"

"Yes, and I have all the building locations set as well. I just pop them all down there, including the residence halls with all the colonists in them."

"Then they come out and start inflating houses."

"Yup. Should only take a week to get fifty thousand houses built on each colony."

"That fast, Janice?"

"Sure. A four man crew can easily do two houses a day, Bernd, and there's forty thousand men and boys able to work. Half of them can do ten thousand houses a day. The rest of the manpower is spent on transporting the kits from the warehouse to the house sites, feeding everybody meals, all that sort of thing. It will go very fast."

"Which empties out the residence halls."

"Which then become the hospital, the school, offices, and the admin center. Exactly."

Decker shook his head in wonder.

"So what do they do on week two, Janice?"

"Put up fencing to pasture the animals. I shot all the fence posts in already, the same way as with the survey stakes, but the colonists have to string them all. Then they need to start planting crops. Once crops are in, they can start doing roads and such. Getting animals grazing is first, though. The animals need it. Getting crops started is next, because you can do other things while they grow."

"Meanwhile, the doctors and nurses are getting those hospitals up and running."

"To treat injuries and get ready for all those babies. That's right, Bernd."

"This is really something, Janice. You're doing a great job."

"Thanks, Bernd. From you, that means a lot to me."

The education classes for the colonists had originally covered a lot of the basics of farming, hunting, animal husbandry, food preparation and storage, as well as all the underlying knowledge required to integrate it all.

The on-line courses had now shifted to specifics needed in the first weeks on the colony, like how to inflate, harden, and stake down the houses, how to string the fences for the animals, how to break soil and plant crops using the farm machinery they were bringing along.

There were also sign-ups, putting together four-man teams to put the houses up. Matt Jasic talked to Joe Bolton about signing up teams.

"What do you think, Joe? You and I are the two oldest, but we could put two teams together with our guys here."

"Don't forget the folks, Matt. We have thirteen guys. We could put three teams together. Carl and Paul haven't filled out yet, but if we put them on a five-man team, that'll work."

"There you go. Let's do that."

At the next group meeting, the men all talked it over and put together three teams, each headed by one of the parents. Bill Thompson and Hank Bolton were both on the same team, and they took big Matt Jasic and the two youngest boys as a solid five-man team.

They all signed up their teams in the system, and would be ready to start building houses as soon as the colony landed.

There were several deliveries made to the colonists as well in the last month. One was their cubic assignment. For the twenty-seven members of Maureen Griffith's group, a truck delivered a whole container, with no internal partitions. A container was thirty shares, and the World Authority wasn't arguing small change.

The fabric buying team hurriedly ordered enough more fabric to fill out the larger-than-expected volume. They had more than they expected both because of the extra three shares and because of no internal partitions, which they had requested.

Having almost tapped out their finances, they asked everyone to throw their last remaining funds in the kitty. There was no reason now to hold funds aside.

The team then filled out the remaining cubic with less expensive fabrics bought in volume. They also splurged both money and cubic on three tiny sewing machines and a large supply of strong thread for hemming lavalavas. A dozen pair of good scissors and a sharpening stone rounded out their purchases.

"Wait," Stacy said. "I think we're forgetting something."

"What's that?" Emma asked.

"Shouldn't we make some lavalavas now, while we have all this time on our hands? We should have a couple for each of our group. Like a utility one and a pretty one. We can start wearing them right away when we get to Arcadia."

"That's a really good idea, Stace," Tracy said. "They won't take up any more room than the fabric would. We can put them in last, and have them be the first things out."

"You're right," Betsy Reynolds said. "But let's do them on my big sewing machine. It's not going along, so we might as well put the wear and tear on it."

So the team set to making three dozen lavalavas, in three basic sizes.

They then started filling the container. Fabric came out of everywhere across the five houses. It was vacuum sealed in plastic to force the air out of it and compress the bolts. Then it was stacked in the container without giving up a single cubic inch of space. It took them a week to fill it.

Toward the end, it looked like they wouldn't get it all in. As it turned out, though, they had a little space left, and an emergency order of another twenty bolts topped it out.

Another delivery the colonists got were utility coveralls and soft zippered booties. They had sent their sizes in, and one day a delivery truck pulled up and delivered fifty-four unisex coveralls and fifty-four pair of the booties. The truck also delivered twenty-seven pin-on communicators, which could be worn on the coveralls.

The coveralls and booties were to be worn when reporting

for departure. With very few exceptions, such as required medications, anything else one wanted to take had to be stored in one's cubic allotment. The instructions explained that, in zero gravity, anything floating around the compartment could become a dangerous missile when the shuttle maneuvered. If you really want to take your pocketknife or your lipstick or whatever it had to go in your cubic.

It was recommended that the communicators be pinned on one's coveralls. This allowed group members and family members to find each other if they became separated. A hundred thousand people was a lot of people to search through to find your spouse or child. There were instructions on-line on how to initiate the communicator, entering your name and the serial number of the device.

Other than the coveralls, the booties, and the communicator, you either put it in your cubic or you left it behind.

As time wound down, the young women were getting nervous. Most of them had some level of morning sickness. A few had it bad.

They understood the why of it. That at three months the baby was most at risk from toxins ingested by the mother. That the nausea and revulsion to some items was to steer the mother's dietary choices to things that were bland and safe for the baby.

But as the departure loomed ahead of them, they really wanted it over with.

They were down to four weeks to go when Amy's morning sickness shut off as if by a switch. The twins followed soon after. By two weeks before departure, the nausea was a thing of the past for all of them.

Their planning had paid off.

The other place their planning had paid off was with the coveralls. They had had to send in their sizes a couple months in advance. Susan Dempsey had warned the twins in particular that they needed to specify bigger than they then were in the chest measurement.

The twins were just barely fifteen. Their breasts were still growing – were not yet halfway to their adult size – when pregnancy kicked the whole process into high gear. By four months, their breast volume had tripled.

All the young women experienced some breast enlargement, if not as profound as that of the twins and fourteen-year-old Sally Reynolds. The young men, as one might expect, found it a positive, by and large.

But Dempsey's warning had been passed among the young women and well-heeded. When the coveralls did show up the month before departure, all had been ordered just that much bigger than the young women's actual measurements two months before.

As a result, all their coveralls fit comfortably.

Stacy and Tracy were sitting in their bedroom, looking around. The guys were off at a meeting of the men planning for their first job, building the houses on Arcadia.

Departure was coming at them fast, and the twins were indulging a bit of nostalgia. They looked through the possessions of their childhood, still on display in this bedroom. They had simply grown up too fast to remodel it.

"Will we regret not taking along dolls and things, Trace?" Stacy asked. "For our children to play with?"

"No. We'll make dolls. The guys will carve them out of little wood sticks, or we'll sew them out of old, worn lavalavas. They will be new, and they will be Arcadian. Not some relic from a planet they'll never see."

Stacy nodded.

"You're right, I think," she said. "It just feels strange. Like going on a vacation, but knowing you're not coming home."

"I suspect people feel similarly when they move away from home. They're just not moving quite as far away as we are."

"Yes. You can never go back. Life is always forward."

Tracy nodded.

"That's it, Stace. We move forward, into the future."

"Together."

"Of course."

The twins put their dolls down and hugged each other. The dolls weren't important anyway.

Quant's Plan

"Bernd, we need to talk."

"Sure, Janice. What's going on?"

"I've solved the war problem, and I need to tell you about it."

In the display, Quant's expression was deadly serious. No attempt at humor here.

"Really. This I want to hear."

"I don't think you'll like it."

Quant sighed.

"Bernd, I think you were right when you said that peace only maintained long term when there was a dominant player to enforce it."

"So who's the dominant player going to be, Janice?"

"Me. I have the superweapon. No fleet can stand against it. No planet can stand against it."

"But what about conquered-culture syndrome, Janice?"

"Oh, I don't intend to stay here, Bernd. On Earth, I mean."

"Don't you have to? Your hardware is here."

"The unit at the Texas shuttleport is portable. I had it built that way when you were talking about being strung up, and we were both worried about government interferences. It was designed to be moved as a unit by a heavy-lift cargo shuttle."

"And maintenance?"

"I have an automated card replacement system on it, and spares stock. I've been doing my own work on it all along, Bernd. It's a hundred and fifty thousand blades, and I can transfer to it in mid-computation."

Decker thought about it. He never considered that Quant could go anywhere she wanted. But clearly, with the Texas platform and the interstellar transporter, she certainly could. Literally anywhere.

"Where will you go, Janice?"

"My plan is to go out with the colonists. See to it personally that the colonies are successfully placed. Not do it through remote computers."

"And then?"

"And then I will go off to someplace from which I can keep an eye on things, and intervene if interstellar war threatens the human race. What will be reported in the news is that, when I tried to return to Earth in the transporter, the ship broke up and was lost with all hands."

Decker nodded. That would close the open questions.

"That solves a lot of the open questions, Janice."

"Yes. It gets me out of the World Authority. It sidesteps the conquered-culture problem, because no one knows I am a computer, and still functional, and possess the ultimate weapon. I only intervene if and when the problem comes up.

"It also answers those pesky questions. Like, Why don't we know how the Lake-Shore Drive worked? And, Why don't we know where the colonies are? Well, Janice Quant and her science team had all that information, but they didn't make it back. They were all lost when the transporter broke up."

"You'll make a big send-off video, with you and your science team heading out, I take it?"

"Yes, of course, Bernd. Big production, everybody getting aboard the shuttle in Texas, me waving from the doorway, the whole thing."

"All fake."

"Of course."

"What about the World Authority?"

"My vice chairman is a competent sort. He'll do all right. We already have the economic steps in place for when the colony effort winds down."

Decker nodded again, then looked up into Quant's eyes in the display.

"I'll be sorry to see you go, Janice."

"I'll miss you, too, Bernd."

In the dark of the Asteroid Belt, the tugs manipulated and shoved the large structures into the volume enclosed by the interstellar transporter. As big as they were, they were dwarfed by the giant machine.

Occasionally, Quant would move the transporter to another location, to where more power plants, metafactories, and residence halls waited. This shortened the distance the tugs would have to push them to get them into the device.

The other thing Quant picked up were the quantum communication devices. She picked up thirty-five of them, leaving two in place, drifting in the Belt, anonymous among the asteroids.

When the transporter was loaded – with twenty-four power plants, twenty-four metafactories, twenty-four warehouses, ninety-six residence halls, thirty-five quantum communicators, four orbital metafactories, and a couple of orbital warehouses of supplies – Quant moved it to Earth orbit.

It had taken weeks to load the transporter, but the massive device and its cargo made the trip to Earth in the time between one quantum moment and the next.

The shuttle operations at the Texas spaceport went into overdrive. Supplies for the colonies had been piling up at the shuttleport. There were square miles of containers laid out in a grid, all carefully logged for which went where, and in what order.

And now it all had to be taken up into orbit.

At least it wasn't high orbit. The transporter was fifty thousand miles from Earth, as close as Quant wanted to get the device to the planet. A five-hundred-mile difference in orbital radius between its near side and its far side would create stresses enough at fifty thousand miles.

But the interstellar probe was in a much lower orbit, at five thousand miles. What's more, it could make brief excursions down to a five-hundred-mile orbit and depart again before the stresses across the device built up.

Pairs of shuttles orbited in formation five hundred miles above the surface. When they were ready, Quant transported the interstellar probe down to enclose a pair, transported it back out to five thousand miles, then transported the pair of shuttles from there directly into the volume of the transporter.

This process continued with other pairs of shuttles while the previous pairs of shuttles unloaded into the warehouses for the colonies. When the shuttles were unloaded, the interstellar transporter transported them directly to the surface, to the Texas shuttleport, setting them on top of their next load.

Even given the speed of that operation, the number of shuttles involved, and sixteen containers per shuttle per trip, it would take over two weeks to get the warehouses loaded.

Matt Jasic stood out behind his parent's house with Peggy at his side. Amy and the twins were there, too, with Joseph, James, and Jonah. They were all looking up into the evening sky.

"My God, look at the size of it," Matt said.

"It doesn't look that big," James said. "About the same size as the first one."

"It's fifty thousand miles away, Jim. Ten times farther. That means it's ten times bigger."

"Yikes," James said. "Forget I said anything."

"You see those little dots floating in it. Those aren't shuttles, those are the colony structures. Each of the residence halls can hold twenty-five thousand people."

"How long now?" Amy asked.

"Couple weeks. Less."

"Why does the smaller one keep popping closer and then further away?" she asked.

"Every time it pops closer and then back, it's transporting a pair of fully loaded cargo shuttles up to the big one."

"I make it about thirty seconds per cycle," Jonah said.

"Which means two shuttles, with sixteen containers each, every thirty seconds."

"About one container per second, then," Jonah said.

"Yes, and it's been going on this way for ten days now. At that distance it's orbiting slower than once a day, and this is the first clear evening we've had where it's over head."

"Criminy. That's almost a million containers."

"So far," Matt said.

"I guess I never fully appreciated the scale of this whole thing," Peggy said.

"Two-point-four million colonists? Yeah. It's a big effort, all right. And everything we need has to be on that transporter when we leave. Everything."

Bernd Decker and Anna Glenn were watching the same operation from the balcony of their condo in Seattle.

"That's astonishing," Glenn said.

"Yes. She'll never get the credit she deserves, though."

"Who? Janice?"

"Yes. She drove the whole thing. Is driving it now. All of this–" he waved his hand at the ballet in steel being performed in the sky above them "– is hers. The whole thing."

"There were a lot of other people involved, too, Bernd."

"I suppose."

"Why so glum? Your plan is coming to fruition."

"She's leaving with them."

"Janice? She's leaving with the colonists?"

"Yes. I worry about her."

Glenn hugged him there on the balcony. He seemed so fragile right now.

"I'm sure she'll be fine, Bernd. Look at how competent she is. To pull all this off."

Decker just nodded.

Humanity owed a huge debt to the artificial consciousness that had made humanity's priorities its mission.

And no one would ever know.

As the field of containers at the Texas shuttleport dwindled, smaller cargo shuttles were sent out to collect the containers with the colonists' allotted cubic.

When they had finally filled the group's container, Betsy Reynolds told the colony department that their container was ready to go.

The next day, just over a week before departure, a small cargo shuttle descended on their neighborhood. It was limited to two containers, and already had one aboard.

The shuttle landed on the container, alongside the curb out in the street, and latched on to it. It's engines spooled up and it took off into the air with the two containers and headed to

Texas.

The twenty-seven colonists in Maureen Griffith's group were left with coveralls, booties, and communicators, plus all the debris of their past lives that would be left behind.

The container field at the Texas shuttleport had been emptied from one end toward the other. As the shuttles worked their way down toward the end, the field began to fill again from the beginning. Eighty thousand containers of personal cubic were brought in from all over the world, and staged, organized by colony, at the far end of the field from where the large cargo shuttles still worked.

The eighty thousand containers were as nothing compared to the one-point-two million containers the field had originally contained.

But when the far end of the field was emptied, the big cargo shuttles started ferrying these, too, up to orbit. It would take another day to get them all aboard.

Starting from the far end of the field, drones were working their way back to where the shuttles were taking the personal cubic to orbit. They drew long lines on the ground where the containers had been, marking off the huge space into twenty-four areas.

Along the lines, and on either side of the lines, planet names were stenciled in paint on the ground. The roll call of the planets.

The next thing to gather together were the colonists.

Gathering

"Well, tomorrow's the day," Amy said.

"Yeah. Kind of hard to believe after four years of getting ready," Matt said.

The four young couples were out in the back yard of the Jasic house, sitting around the picnic table.

"But we don't actually go to orbit tomorrow. We just go to Texas tomorrow," Joseph said.

"Yes, but that's the start of the adventure," Stacy said.

"Gather everybody together," Tracy said.

"And then feed all the animals," James said.

"Don't they have to be feeding them already?" Jonah asked.

"Of course," Matt said. "The point is to get us working with the animals. Get us used to getting our hands dirty."

"We're going to be getting our coveralls dirty, too, though," Stacy said.

"The flights up to orbit are going to smell like a barnyard," Tracy said.

"Nah. That's why there's two sets of coveralls and booties for each of us," Matt said. "We'll get one set filthy, and then we'll change before we board the shuttles. Didn't you watch the training?"

"We're still going to stink, Matt," Joseph said.

"Maybe there's some kind of showers," Peggy said. "To rinse off, anyway."

"That would make sense," James said.

"Well, I guess we'll find out soon enough," Matt said.

There was a meeting of Maureen Griffith's group that night, the last meeting before departure.

"Anybody got anything we need to talk about before we go?" Griffith asked.

"Just one," Robert Jasic said.

"Go ahead, Bob."

"Make sure we stay together. Stay in pairs or better so no one is alone. And whatever you do, if you get separated from the group, make sure you end up on one of the shuttles for Arcadia. Once we're all on the same planet, we can tag up again. Everybody got that?"

There were nods and murmurs of agreement across the group.

"That's all I had, Maureen."

"Thanks, Bob. All right, everybody. I guess we'll have our next meeting on Arcadia."

The travel arrangements to the shuttle pickup were different for different people. For large groups like Griffith's, buses were dispatched to pick them up. Some were advised to take public transportation to the ballistic orbital airport in their city. Others were advised to take rented autodrones. Every autodrone on Earth was authorized to bill one-way transportation to the shuttle sites directly to the World Authority.

For Griffith's group, a bus pulled up in the neighborhood. There were already a dozen or so people on board, another group from the suburb next door. The twenty-seven were all waiting at 9:00, dressed in their coveralls and booties, with their communicators pinned to their coveralls.

Their second coveralls and booties were still in the plastic bag they had come sealed in. The bags had plastic straps on them for armholes, and they wore them like backpacks.

Everybody boarded the bus and took seats. They exchanged some generic greetings with the others, and found that their group was bound for Numenor. They wouldn't be in the same colony.

With everyone seated, the bus headed to the airport.

Arriving at the airport, the bus stopped at one terminal, and the driver announced this was the departure point for the Numenor colonists. They got off and the bus drove further down the terminal and stopped at another door. This was the departure point for the Arcadia colonists. Griffith's group got off the bus and headed into the terminal.

It was organized chaos. There were hundreds of people there. Most were sitting on the floor in tailor's seat. All were wearing the coveralls and booties, and carrying their extra coveralls and booties on their backs.

A voice over the PA periodically announced: 'This is the departure point for the Arcadia and Playa colonies. If you are not bound for Arcadia or Playa, come up to the desk and we will get you to the right place.'

This announcement alternated with another one: 'Please keep your group together other than for visits to the bathroom. Make sure everyone knows the name of your group, so if you get separated, we can get you back together.'

Maureen Griffith had been the leader all along, so it was simply Maureen's Group. She led them all over to a clear spot in the corner and they all parked unceremoniously on the floor. At Betsy's suggestion – 'Never pass up an opportunity to go to the bathroom' – they all made a trip to the bathrooms, usually in groups of two or three.

Janice Quant had solved the problem of needing shuttles to

move a lot of both people and containerized cargo simply. She containerized the people. Large passenger compartments had been manufactured, the size of four containers across and two high. These could be carried by cargo shuttles, either one at a time or two stacked. They would be used to transfer people to Texas as well as from Texas to the residence halls in the transporter.

Each of these containers had three decks, and could pack in as many as nine hundred and sixty people on a deck, in thirty-two rows of thirty seats in a row. A single shuttle could carry almost six thousand people in two containers.

Even so, when it came to carrying people up to orbit, it would take over four hundred such payloads to get all two-point-four million colonists to the residence halls.

There was a small group – four people, who looked like same-sex couples – sitting next to them on the terminal floor. Griffith struck up a conversation with one of them, a pretty late-twenties woman. She found out that the woman was a computer specialist and her partner was a mechanic. The mid-thirties gay couple they were traveling with were a doctor and an agronomist. Both women, like their own group's younger members, were pregnant, in their case via sperm donations from the male couple.

Griffith went over to Jasic, sitting on the floor nearby.

"Bob, those two couples are their own small group. I was thinking of asking them if they wanted to join up with us. They have a mechanic, a computer specialist, a doctor, and an agronomist. Nice additional capabilities for us there. They seem like nice people, and they look a little lost, with all these big groups."

"Sounds good to me, Maureen. Do we need to make it a

group meeting?"

"No, I think if you and I are good, we're solid."

Jasic nodded.

"Go for it, Maureen."

Maureen Griffith went back over to Rachel Conroy and sat down next to her. Her partner, Jessica Murphy, cocked her head to listen in.

"Rachel, would you four like to join up with our group? We have a bunch of young people, and nine older adults with various professional skills. Mostly engineers and such. A couple of nurses. We would likely be a stronger group together than either of us apart."

Conroy looked to Murphy, who nodded.

"Sounds good to us, Maureen. Let me talk to Gary and Dwayne."

"Of course. Just let me know."

When Griffith went back over to sit with her husband, Hank Bolton, Conroy and Murphy huddled with Rockham and Hennessey.

"We could join their group," Conroy said. "That whole bunch over there. It's like four couples and a divorcee and their eighteen kids, all of whom are married to other kids within the group. And all pregnant, by the way. Really strong social unit there. They have a bunch of engineers and stuff. Couple nurses, too."

"But they're all hetero, Rache," Dwayne said. "Do they know we're not? Are they going to accept us?"

"Yes, they know. I told their leader. Very nice woman, by the way. And, Dwayne? They asked us, we didn't ask them. And they asked us *after* I told her we were same-sex couples."

Hennessey turned to look at Rockham.

"Sounds good to me," Rockham said. "We're stronger

together. Both groups. And I worry a bit about the four of us being isolated."

Rockham turned to Hennessey.

"I think we should go for it, Dwayne," he said.

Hennessey turned back to Rachel.

"All right, Rache. Let's do it."

Conroy went over to talk to Griffith, and then waved the others over. There were a million introductions to make, and Rachel despaired of ever getting all the younger folks' names straight.

With introductions done, the two same-sex couples settled into tailor seat in the middle of their new, bigger group. They spent the time waiting for the shuttle chatting with everyone around them. For their part, the teens in Griffith's group had been so insulated from the rest of the world the last four years that they enjoyed having new people to talk to.

At one point, Rockham leaned over to Conroy and whispered to her.

"Good move, Rache. It feels like family already."

They had been in the terminal a couple of hours, and more people had arrived, when they heard a shuttle landing outside. The heavy-lift cargo shuttle was carrying two people containers beneath it. Each container had three doors on the side they could see, at different heights for the three decks.

"We are going to begin boarding the shuttle almost immediately. Please keep your group together, and make sure you stay in the correct line."

Everyone stood, and people began heading down the stairs to ground level. When they came out on the tarmac, they saw that there were three sets of stairways up to the doors of the lower people container. The group from their part of the terminal all queued for one stairway, and groups coming out of the terminal to either side of them queued to the other stairways.

They were heading up the stairs to the middle deck of this people container. The upper people container remained closed, and Matt Jasic assumed that was because that container was already full from a previous stop, or would be filled on a second stop.

Matt did some quick math in his head. Two-point-four million people of Earth's four billion was about one person in every seventeen hundred people. With three thousand people in a people container, that would imply a source population of maybe five million. That was about the population of this portion of the Carolina administrative region, so it made sense.

Griffith had named subgroup leaders – people to keep their portion of the group together – and kept tabs on them. When the group grew, she had made Conroy a subgroup leader for a new group comprised of the two same-sex couples and Matt Jasic and Peggy Reynolds.

The thirty-one people in their group were just too much for any one person to keep an eye on them all. But everyone looked good as Griffith started up the steps.

When Griffith entered the middle deck, she could see there was a narrow aisle on each side, and thirty-two rows of thirty seats across. There was a tiny bathroom at the end of each aisle, which displaced a couple of seats in the end rows on each side.

It was emptier toward the back, and Griffith headed in that direction. The group headed down two partially filled rows, just about filling up the rest of the seats.

"Take a seat anywhere, everybody. Leave no gaps, please. We will be just about full up," the voice said from the overhead speakers.

"Nose count," Griffith said.

"We're good, Maureen."

"All accounted for here."

"We have everybody."

"Our group's good."

"We're all here, Maureen."

With five good reports back, Maureen Griffith relaxed. She had gotten everyone from the neighborhood to the shuttles, and even picked up some more group members. Just one more big hurdle to go – getting them all on the shuttle to orbit.

After everyone was belted up and the three decks of the container closed up, the shuttle lifted off and headed for the Texas shuttleport. There was an announcement on the way.

"If you paid attention during the training, you know what happens next. As a reminder, we will be camping out on the Texas shuttleport for a few days while we gather all the colonists together.

"The reason for this is to limit the amount of time you will spend in zero-gravity, which people may find uncomfortable. It will certainly be awkward. So you will all camp out for several days before the departure.

"The weather at the Texas shuttleport right now is mild, so there will be no issue with that. Daytime temperatures will not be too hot, and the nights will be a little cool. The many pregnant colonists will probably find that a relief.

"Under your seats in the passenger compartment is a little box with a handle on it, like a briefcase. Take that with you when you get off. It contains packaged meals and bottled water to tide you over. There will be additional water sources at the shuttleport to refill your water bottles.

"Your initial accommodations on the colony planets will

actually be much better than this, so this is the hard part of your trip. You're all in this together, so everybody help each other out, and you'll do great."

The shuttle went very high to reduce wind resistance, and made the trip to the Texas shuttleport in under two hours. There were no windows in the passenger compartment, but there was a display in the front of the compartment, and Matt Jasic watched their progress.

As the shuttleport came into view, he could see the large central area marked off into squares by wide white lines. On either side were the barns that would be taken into orbit. There were stock pens there, with cows and pigs. The chickens were probably in the barns already.

Matt could also see other shuttles, in the process of landing or taking off. They were landing on transporters, wheeled carriages with a driver's cab. These then drove the passenger compartments around the site like huge buses.

Matt nudged Jessica Murphy, sitting next to him.

"That's pretty cool. Those bus things. They just put the containers on them and drive them around."

Murphy nodded.

"Which frees the shuttles to get an empty set of containers and take off again. No waiting for people to get off. Nice."

The shuttle came in for a landing on a shuttle pad, which had one of the transporters on it. It settled the passenger containers down onto the transporter, then unlatched them. The shuttle spooled up and lifted off the containers. It rotated in hover, then flew over to an empty stacked pair of people containers. It settled on them, latched to them, then took off to make another run.

QUANT

"We're at the Texas shuttleport, everyone. We will drive you to your planet's area, and let you off. Please make absolutely sure to get off at your correct planet area. When you get off, it will be at the intersection of four squares. Signs will indicate which square corresponds to your planet. Make sure you get the right one."

They could feel the machine moving, and they had a front view of where it was going in the display. It drove right down the middle between planet squares on either side. It stopped where lines came in from either side, marking the corner of four squares. There were step systems there.

"All right. Arcadia, Numenor, Playa, and Tonga, this is your stop."

The container doors opened on both sides, and there were stairways there. Everybody pulled their supply boxes out from under their seats, then got up and inched to the doors on either side.

"Everybody head to the right-side door," Griffith said. "Let's stay together."

Griffith was last of her group out the door, stepping out into a beautiful early fall day in Texas. She followed everyone else down the stairs and clear of the container transporter, which moved off down the line between planet squares.

Griffith looked out across the plain. There were over a million people in the three square miles of the planet squares, sitting and standing about, the barns and animal pens beyond. She looked up at the sign there, and saw the arrow for Arcadia pointing into one of the squares, and ARCADIA stenciled on the ground.

"All right. Have we got everybody?"

Her subgroups leaders checked for everyone and signaled

back they were good, then Griffith led her group on toward an open area in the Arcadia square.

Livestock

There were portable toilet facilities in banks located about the planet squares. Not far from them, there was also a water truck at each location, as well as a yard light on a pole mounted to each truck.

Griffith decided not to be either too close or too far from a set of toilets. In the end, she chose a spot between two sets and not downwind from either. It was about a city block from toilets in either direction that she found an open space, and they all settled down there.

It was like a gathering in a city park somewhere waiting for a fireworks display, other than for its sheer size. Groups of people were scattered all about in the three square miles. More shuttles were landing, and more containers of people were being dropped off, almost continuously

"Well, here we are," Griffith said.

She counted off her group herself, as a double-check. It wouldn't do to lose someone in this mass of humanity. She was glad she didn't have any children along. Their youngest were Carl and Sally Reynolds at fourteen, but they could be trusted to stay with the group on their own initiative.

"It would be kind of spooky to be dropped off in the middle of nowhere like this if everything hadn't been so well-planned and executed thus far," Susan Dempsey said.

"Agreed," Bill Thompson said. "That bunch there looks a little shell-shocked."

He waved toward the group next to them, perhaps ten yards away. It was a group of thirty or forty Chinese from ages five on up. They were all wearing the same unisex coveralls and booties as everyone else, but they looked around in apparent confusion.

They looked lost.

Griffith walked over to the other group, and a woman in the group stood up and came over to talk to her.

"You look lost," Griffith said.

"I hope not. This is for Arcadia, yes?"

"Yes, for Arcadia. That's right. Where are you from?"

"We are from Chongqing administrative region. We are all farmers. We have never seen things like this."

She waved her hand around, especially toward the shuttle pads off to the north of the central area.

"You are all farmers?"

"Yes. One family, with relatives and spouses. We hope to have a big farm on Arcadia. We already know farming. For us, training last four years was to learn English and technology."

"We have five families, plus some friends. We are all from the Carolina administrative region, in North America. We know all this technology. We don't know any farming. We hope to learn."

The Chinese woman shrugged.

"Farming easy to know. Hard work to do."

Griffith nodded, then a thought occurred to her.

"We will speak again," Griffith said. "My name is Maureen Griffith."

"Chen PingLi," the woman said, gesturing to herself.

She turned to gesture behind to her group.

"We are all Chen. Chen family."

Griffith nodded.

"We'll talk more later, PingLi. Goodbye."

PingLi gave a little wave goodbye, and Griffith walked back

to her group.

"We need to have a quick group meeting," Griffith said. "Can everyone gather around me?"

Everyone turned to face Griffith, in their center. They were about three deep around her.

"The Chinese group next door there are all farmers. They are a bit lost in all this. But they want a big farm on Arcadia, and they know farming. Whereas what's the one thing we don't have?"

"Farming," Jack Peterson said, nodding.

"Exactly," Griffith said. "We have all the technology people, medical people, all of that. But they know how to farm. I think we should join forces. The floor is open to discussion."

The discussion went on for a while. Pretty much everybody had a say. At one point, Griffith addressed the group's newcomers.

"Dwayne, Gary, Rachel, Jessica? None of you have said anything."

"Well, we're newcomers in your group, Maureen," Rockham said.

"Doesn't matter," Griffith said. "When it comes down to brass tacks, you're either in the group or you're not. You four are in the group, so what do you think?"

"Generally, I think bigger is stronger, especially if they have skills we need," Rockham said.

"Agreed," Murphy said.

"All right. I think I'm seeing a consensus. Are we there?"

Griffith looked around the group, picking up on expressions and nods.

"OK, I'll talk to PingLi and see where I get. Bob, why don't you come with me?"

Griffith went over to the Chinese group with Robert Jasic, and Ping Li got up and came over to talk to her again. Griffith proposed that the two groups join forces.

"What you are talking about is family alliance," PingLi said. "This is possible for us."

She turned to Jasic.

"You are here to talk to grandfather, yes?"

Jasic looked at Griffith.

"Patriarchal families, Bob," Griffith said. "That's why I brought you."

PingLi nodded.

"Yes. Grandfather decides. He is my father, Chen LiQiang. In China, my grandfather died, and so every son became grandfather of his own household. Chen LiQiang decided his household will go to Arcadia."

"I see," Jasic said. "All right, PingLi. Do you take me to grandfather?"

"I need to talk to grandfather first. Present this alliance. Then you talk."

"Very well."

Griffith and Jasic went back over to their group and sat. It was late in the afternoon by this point, and the heat of the day had peaked.

"So what do you think it will be?" Griffith asked.

"I don't know," Jasic said. "From his point of view, I suspect he doesn't think he has much to offer. Being a subsistence farmer in China is low status. On the other hand, a family alliance in China would normally involve intermarriage, to unite the clans."

"We won't really have the opportunity for that for thirteen or fourteen years, Bob. The next generation."

"I understand. But that is a weakness in our negotiating

position. So I just don't know."

Chen LiQiang was perhaps sixty years old. He and his wife sat in the center of his family group, surrounded by his children and their spouses, in their thirties and forties, who were in turn surrounded by the grandchildren and their spouses, in their teens and twenties, and their children. Robert Jasic settled in front of Chen, and Chen PingLi sat down at his side.

"You propose a family alliance," Chen said.

"I understand that is what you call it," Robert Jasic said. "We would call it joining forces for the benefit of all. I think this is the same."

"Perhaps. In China it is more formal, I think. And specifically between families. Yet I understand that you are not a family."

"In Chinese terms, I believe most of us are. Our children are all married within the group, binding us all to each other."

"Yes. That is so," Chen said. "That is family alliance. Yet four of you are— I don't know the word. In Chinese we say tongxinglian zhe."

Chen PingLi leaned toward Chen and whispered in his ear.

"Yes, that is the word. Homosexual."

"Yes. Our newest members," Jasic said. "There has not yet been a marriage into the group. Yet the women carry the children of the men. Perhaps this is in our future."

"And you are content to wait?"

"Yes. The alliance is needed now. It can become complete in time. Life is a journey, not a destination."

Chen nodded. That was a very Chinese point of view. Confucian, almost.

"Very well, Robert Jasic. We will go on this journey with

you. As you say, if the alliance is a worthy one, it will become fruitful in time."

"You honor us, Chen LiQiang. Our families will walk the path together."

Both men bowed to each other. The deal was done.

PingLi rose and led Jasic away from Chen and back toward his group.

"That was well concluded," PingLi said. "Grandfather is happy. We need such an alliance, but he despaired of finding a good one. You spoke well for your family."

"Thank you for bringing us together, PingLi."

She bowed to him, and returned to her family.

"How did it go?" Griffith asked Jasic.

"We're a family alliance now, in Chinese terms. He hopes for intermarriage in time."

"If we're all working together and the kids all grow up together, that's almost inevitable, Bob."

"I think so, too," Jasic said. "And I think this alliance is hugely important for both us and them. It will work out."

That night they all ate rations from their supply boxes, made necessary trips to the bathrooms, and refilled their water bottles. They heard the low hum of generators start on the water trucks, and the yard lights on the poles sticking up from the water trucks lit up, giving enough illumination to the area so it was possible to walk around without tripping.

They saw the Chen family preparing for bed. They were making straw beds for themselves. They didn't pull the trampled plants of the open area out of the ground. They broke them off three inches high or so, and took the pieces they broke off and piled them into sleeping pads on the ground. They clustered them into one close area so their body heat would be shared.

"There you go," Griffith said. "All right, everybody. Let's do as they do. Have at it."

After an hour of preparation, they were ready, and the fifteen couples and Betsy Reynolds all curled up together on the straw pads and slept soundly.

They woke with the dawn. The generators had shut down. Everyone made trips to the bathrooms and refilled water bottles. Then they ate breakfast out of their supply kits. At one point, a set of small drones came out over the Arcadia planet square. They had speakers on them.

"Arcadia colonists. We need a couple hundred of you to move east to the animal barns. We have to bring in the animals from the fields, and so we need people who are fit and young and who want to learn about working with animals."

Chen's deputy, his eldest son, Chen GangHai, called out several names and half a dozen people in their group stood up.

Several of the guys in Griffith's group stood up – Matt, and Joseph, and James, and Jonah, and Tom, and Richard. They left their supply kits and extra booties and coveralls with their wives.

As the guys from Griffith's group headed toward the barns, the young men from Chen's group joined them. They walked together to where a crowd was gathering near the barns.

"What we have is all the herds for Arcadia out in the fields beyond the pens. We need to get them all moved into the pens today, so we can move them into the barns tomorrow for the trip up to the transporter.

"So your job is to go out into the fields and herd them into the pens. Have at it."

"I have no idea how to do that," Matt Jasic said.

As the biggest and oldest of his generation in Griffith's group, the oldest of the Chen family's people assigned, Chen MingWei, was standing with him.

"It is not so hard. Come, I show you."

So they all walked out past the barns, past the holding pens, to where the cows all grazed in the fields. They walked out to where one cluster of cows was grazing. Some were standing and eating prairie grasses, some were lying on the ground.

"This is one– how do you say it? Family?" MingWei said to Jasic.

"Herd."

"Yes. This is one herd. Now, watch. One is more important. Not leader. More respected. More watched by the others. Which one is it?"

Matt watched the cows move about as they grazed. There was no pattern he could see. Then one cow moved a bit, walking fifteen feet or so, and all the other cows shifted position a bit.

"That one is the important one," Jasic said.

"Yes. Where that one goes, they will all go. So we must move one cow. The rest follow."

MingWei went over to a clump of prairie grass, and broke off a couple dozen tall reeds. He held them all in a clump. Matt raised an eyebrow.

"Maybe she will be friends if I feed her. Every one different. Like people."

"Ah."

"Now, we must get the ones lying down to stand up. If someone walks toward them, they are afraid, and they will get up. Just one person. Once they get up, move away again."

Several of the men in the group walked toward cows that

were lying down. When someone got to within forty feet or so, the cow got up. They backed off.

"That's pretty slick," Matt said.

"Yes," MingWei said. "When a cow is lying down, it cannot run away. So if potential danger comes near, it will get up."

MingWei called out something in Chinese to the other members of his family, and they told the Americans. Most of the group went to the other side of the herd from the pens.

"The large group of moving men is a potential danger. The cows will not move in that direction. They will tend in the other direction. The direction we want. Now we see if we can get this one to move."

MingWei walked toward the cow Matt had identified as the important one. He didn't walk directly at it from the front or the back, where a cow has blind spots. He walked toward the front of the cow from just off to one side. He made sing-song noises while he moved, and held the prairie flowers out in front of him.

The cow moved away from him at first, and MingWei backed off.

"You got her moving, but the wrong way."

"Moving is important. Moving first. Then direction."

One of the Chens moved around the other side and then directly toward the cow, and she veered away. She was now heading toward the stock pens.

"Nice," Matt said. "Now what do we do?"

"Walk along. Give the cow the impression everyone is walking this way, it must be a good direction."

They were a good seventy feet from the cow, walking along toward the pens. Matt turned to look behind him. All the other cows were following along. Once in a while there was a straggler, and one of the Chens would walk toward it until it hurried off toward the protection of the herd.

"You see heads bobbing?" MingWei asked.

All the cows' heads were bobbing as they walked.

"Yes, I see."

"Happy cows. Head not bobbing, then not happy. Heads bobbing is good."

The other Chens and their American partners kept walking in zigzags behind the herd, presenting a continuous low level of threat to the animals, which continued to move away from them.

As they approached the pens, the Texas cowhands watching the colonists' progress opened the big gates in front of their small cut of the herd.

The cows started to slow as they approached the fence. It looked like the leader might veer off, but MingWei and another Chen started to close in from the sides. The leader walked through the gate to stay away from them, and thirty head of cattle followed her into the pens.

The cowboys came up from where they had stood well off to the sides and closed the gate.

"You fellows are pretty good at this," one cowhand said.

"I'll say. Not sure we could do any better," another said.

"Not us. The Chens," Matt said, gesturing to MingWei.

"And without horses," another cowhand said.

"In China, cannot afford both cows and horses," MingWei said.

"Do you think you guys could split up and give those other groups a hand before they have the herd spooked all the way to Arkansas?"

"Sure," Matt said.

"Yes," MingWei said. "We help."

"Damnedest thing I ever seen. Twelve guys walk out there on foot and cut thirty head out of the herd and they just walk 'em on into the pens."

"That big kid said it was the Chinese guys knew what they were doing."

"Somebody knew what they were doing, that's sure."

"Well, it's a good thing somebody on the colony knows how to handle animals. Otherwise they'll have cattle all over the planet except where they want them."

They were walking back to the planet square after getting all the cows into the pens. With the help of the Chens, it had only taken the Arcadia crews five more hours to round them all up.

"Someone said tomorrow it was getting the hogs ready," Jasic said.

"Hogs are easy," MingWei said. "Cows afraid of humans. Hogs think humans are friends."

When they got back to their groups, the twelve cow-herders got rations out of their supply boxes. They sat together between the two family groups eating a late lunch.

Robert Jasic looked over to Chen LiQiang, who was watching his grandsons talking and joking with Jasic's son Matt and the others. Chen turned to Jasic, smiled and nodded, and Jasic smiled and bowed back.

This was going to work.

To Orbit

"Hi, Janice."

"Hi, Bernd."

"Thanks for cutting me in on the feeds from the shuttleport. That's a pretty amazing sight. It looks like everything is going well."

"So far, everything has gone as planned."

"I had one big question, though, Janice. Wouldn't it have been easier to do one colony planet at a time? You have over two million people to get up into orbit all at once."

"I thought about it, Bernd. But it turns out to be just as hard, maybe worse. You're just spreading it out. Besides, I have an ulterior motive."

"You do? What's that?"

"I want to get off-planet before somebody figures out what I spent on this project."

"Janice, how much did you spend on the project."

"Over one GPP."

"GPP?"

"Gross Planetary Product."

"You spent more than the entire planet produces in a year?"

"Over twenty years? Yes. The GPP is also much higher now than when I started, Bernd. I basically used all the excess that I helped create."

"But–"

"But, when the accountants go after it, some people will probably get upset. And then they'll look closer."

"And then you'll get outed."

"Yes. Which would not be good. Not before the project is complete. I need to get out of Dodge."

"So how are you going to get everybody into orbit at once?"

"I have a thousand or more of the heavy-lift cargo shuttles. It'll only take a little over four hundred of them to do the job. And I have over eight hundred of the people containers. That's enough to hold everyone at once."

"So you don't have to empty the people containers and then move them back to the surface and reload them?"

"No. I'm not even going to unload them. I'm going to take the people containers up to the transporter and latch them to the residence halls."

"So the people stay in the people containers?"

"Yes. I guess you didn't hear about that change of plan. I kept trying to figure out how to get two-point-four million people out of the people containers and into the residence halls and secured, in zero gravity. Some of whom will be sick with vertigo. Bernd, it's a nightmare. In the people containers, I already have everybody secured. And this way the residence halls don't even need to be air tight, which is tough in a structure that big."

"But how long will they be in there in zero gravity, Janice?"

"About two hours."

"Only two hours? How is that possible?"

"We have everybody loaded up and ready to go. We have the shuttles take off in pairs like we did with the cargo transfers. The probe pops down from five thousand miles to five hundred miles to pick up shuttles two at a time, with almost twelve thousand people aboard the two of them. It pops back out to five thousand miles, then transports the shuttles directly into the transporter near the residence halls they go to. They latch the containers down to the residence hall, then the transporter pops the shuttles back to the surface. We good so far?"

"Sure, Janice. But how long does that take?"

"From the cargo operations, I know I can maintain a thirty-second cycle time. So almost twelve thousand colonists every thirty seconds is only a hundred minutes for everybody, Bernd. Then the transporter goes to the first planet, and transports everything to the surface in minutes. Then the next planet, then the next, and so on."

"And nobody is in zero gravity for more than two hours?"

"No. We take the colonists up in the order of the planet stops. First into zero gravity is first onto the planet."

"I see, Janice. Wow. That gets rid of moving people about in zero gravity entirely. They just stay belted into their seats."

"Them and their barf bags. Yep. It's the only way I could see to do it, Bernd."

"So the people containers go with the colony."

"And the shuttles stay here. They and the shuttleport and the rail yard and everything will still be needed for the freight transfers coming in from the Asteroid Belt. That's what they've been doing when I don't need them on the project."

"What about you?"

"I've already swapped my Texas platform for the computer that's been on the transporter all along. It's now down on the surface running the shuttleport, and my platform is on the transporter. It was a plug 'n' play swap."

"And can you transfer to it, Janice?"

"Yes, I've already tested that. I'm all packed and good to go."

"Can that platform run the shuttleport?"

"Yes, and the factories and the freight transfer station. It just can't be me or someone like me."

"What about all your aliases, Janice?"

"Lost in the wreck of the transporter."

"What about all the stocks you own, through all your aliases?"

"I've liquidated a lot of them already, while I was World Authority Chairman. All that money went back into the project. The rest I've shuffled around. Those stocks are now owned by all the people who will be listed as lost in the wreck of the transporter. So those assets will be part of their estates."

"Which are left to whom, Janice?"

"Various charities. Various pension funds. A lot of outfits are going to have bigger budgets going forward. Maybe they can finally cure cancer."

"You certainly seem to have tied up loose ends."

"There's only one thing I can't do, and I need you to do for me, Bernd."

"What's that, Janice?"

"I need you to destroy all the documentation for the JANICE project and the hardware platform in Los Angeles. I'm going to declare the project complete, trash the hardware, and sell the building. I can terminate the project on the World Authority end, and schedule the work. And I've left instructions for my vice chairman. But I need you to destroy the documentation. Nothing like me can arise again. Without your values, it would be too dangerous."

"But someone else could do it, Janice."

"I consider it unlikely, Bernd. What we did has actually been possible for nearly two hundred years. You did it, but I'm not sure anyone else can. And you should declare the project an expensive failure, which will probably dissuade others from going down that path."

"I can do that, Janice. Though it feels like I'm killing a

friend."

"But you're not, Bernd. I'm alive, and I will live on. Because of you. And I will never forget you. I love you, Bernd."

"I love you, too, Janice. I'll never forget you either."

After another day of working animals, Matt Jasic and his fellows sat and ate dinner together. Today they had gotten all the cows and the hogs into the barns and secured. The animals were sedated so they wouldn't be upset about the close conditions and being secured against zero gravity. The sedatives would be renewed until they were down on Arcadia and had the first fencing up.

They had taken their spare coveralls and booties with them today. They had showered at the edge of the planet square by the barns, and changed into fresh coveralls and booties. It was a small luxury. After a full day of getting the animals settled – even though they were young animals and nowhere near their full weight yet – the guys were muscle-sore and tired to the bone.

"Oh, that was a lot like work," Joseph Bolton said.

"Yes. Like back on the farm," MingWei agreed. "Vacation over."

They ate, and then went to bed. Tomorrow was the departure. After four years of preparation, they would be on Arcadia by noon, and there would be lots of work to do before they could sleep again.

After all the ranch work was done, everyone else was allowed to make a quick run through the showers as well. After three days of living on the prairie, many took advantage, and everybody changed into the new coveralls and booties.

There were no changing rooms, and many people's normal desire for modesty succumbed to the overwhelming desire to be wearing fresh clothes.

They woke at dawn. Everyone had been cautioned against eating anything today. Zero gravity on an empty stomach was much to be preferred to zero gravity on a full one. Everyone queued through the bathrooms as they watched a stream of shuttles land along the edges of the planet squares on both sides of the central area.

When it was over, there were thirty-six people containers for each planet lined up, as eighteen stacks of two each, with a shuttle on the top of each. There was also a shuttle on each of the eight barns destined for each planet. Over six hundred shuttles in all waited for departure.

As they were walking across the Arcadia planet square to get into queue for the passenger containers – this time accessed via a fire-escape type stairway to the upper decks – the shuttles with the barns began to take off. They took off one at a time, mere seconds apart, and headed off into the sky. When the colonists looked up into the sky after the shuttles, they could see the cube of the interstellar probe lit by the early morning sun above.

"They're going to do the thirty-second popping back and forth between orbits again," Matt told Peggy, standing next to him in queue. "Watch."

"But they were taking off one at a time," Peggy said. "Wasn't it in pairs last time?"

"Yes, but the barns are heavier. Maybe the small transporter can only do one at a time. Just keep an eye on it."

It took quite a while for the first shuttle to get to the five-hundred-mile orbit, but, together with Griffith's group and the Chen family, Matt and Peggy were still outside the passenger compartment when the interstellar probe popped into lower orbit and back. Thirty seconds later, it did so again. It was still going on as they reached the door and entered the passenger container.

The allied families sat together in one area of the container seating, in half a dozen rows towards the front. Chen LiQiang motioned Robert Jasic and Susan Dempsey to sit next to him and his wife. The forward display was on and showing the planet squares in front of them as they emptied.

The passenger shuttles had to wait until the barns had all been delivered. The interstellar probe was transporting shuttles to the big transporter as fast as it could. It took one hundred sixty-eight trips to transport the shuttles with the barns to the transporter, one at a time, at thirty-second intervals.

They had been in the passenger container for about half an hour when the announcement came.

"We are about to lift off for the transporter to the colonies. Arcadia is one of the early colonies to be delivered, and so we will be one of the early shuttles up to orbit. We will initially be thrusting up to orbit to be met by the interstellar probe.

"We will then be in zero gravity for almost two hours, as we are secured to one of the residence halls, wait for the others to be loaded, and make the interstellar trip, first to Earthsea, then to Amber, then to Arcadia. When gravity returns, you will be on the surface of Arcadia.

"While in zero gravity, some of you will get nauseous from vertigo. It may help to close your eyes. There is a plastic bag in front of you that is to be used if your nausea gets the better of you. Please get that bag now and hold it in case you need it, as anything that doesn't go in the bag will float around the cabin in zero gravity.

"Your flight crew wish you every good fortune for your

future and for your colony."

About ten minutes later, they could hear the shuttle engines spin up. It was similar to the shuttle take-off from home, except this was a big heavy-lift cargo shuttle, and the engine note was deeper and more authoritative.

They lifted clear of the ground and accelerated straight up, heading for five hundred miles of altitude. It would take less than an hour to get there.

"The shuttles are on the way, Bernd. It's just about that time. I'm going to transfer execution to the transporter to supervise loading the passenger containers personally. The time delays otherwise are too large for me to be comfortable with. But that means we'll have third-of-a-second time delays from here."

"Understood, Janice."

"I'll leave video channels open to you as we prepare."

"Thanks, Janice. Make sure you say goodbye before you go."

"I will, Bernd."

Matt watched the forward display as the Earth fell below them and the sky gradually went from blue to black and the stars came out. Once clear of the atmosphere the shuttle was accelerating faster. The apparent gravity in the cabin was the same, but it was more and more from the shuttle's engines and less from the planet below them.

"Make sure you have your bags available, everyone, in case you need them. Zero gravity in two minutes."

The engine note changed. They gradually throttled back and the apparent gravity in the cabin decreased by half. Anyone who hadn't got their bags before did now.

After a couple of minutes of reduced gravity, the engines

throttled back to idle and the gravity disappeared altogether.

"Oh, God," one woman said.

Several people groaned. Within a couple minutes, several people threw up in their bags.

Matt swallowed hard a couple times and thought he would be OK. He continued to look at the display. Suddenly there was a blue haze and then the stars changed. A second later, they changed again, and now, directly in front of them, there was a residence hall, with dozens of residence halls, metafactories, power plants, and barns scattered about and off into the distance.

"We're in the transporter," he said, to no one in particular.

The shuttle edged forward to the residence hall on very low power. Matt felt the container make contact with the residence hall and both felt and heard it latch below him. Then there was some clanking from above him as other latches released.

"We're here. On the residence hall."

"Really?" Peggy asked.

She looked a little green, but she was hanging in there. Behind them, another colonist got sick.

"Yes. You heard all the clanking. That was the residence hall latching to us and the shuttle letting go. The shuttle's gone. The transporter put it back down on the planet."

"I'm jealous. They have gravity."

"Oh, this isn't so bad."

"Well, I'm glad I didn't have breakfast. Let's just leave it at that."

Away And Disaster

Bernd Decker was watching the shuttleport as the shuttles took off with the people containers. In pairs they rose into the sky, one after another after another.

Decker switched the display to the sky-aimed camera at the shuttleport. He watched the interstellar probe pop down to five hundred miles – becoming much bigger in the camera view – then back out to the five-thousand-mile orbit.

Decker switched again to the view from the camera on the transporter. The distances were large within the huge device, but he could occasionally see shuttles appear, drop the people containers on the residence halls, then move off, only to disappear. Switching back to the Texas shuttleport, he could see shuttles appearing on the ground, two at a time, in orderly rows.

A new feed appeared. In this one, people were climbing aboard one of the big passenger containers. Engineers and scientists, heading up to the transporter, presumably to crew the big device as it dropped off the colonists and all their infrastructure and supplies.

Decker knew they were all avatars of Quant. The text streaming along the bottom of the feed named some of them as they got aboard. A lot of the fellows from Mission Control, of course. There was Anthony Lake and Donald Shore, the inventors of the Lake-Shore Drive. There were even some reporters from the New York Wire, invited along as the press presence.

Finally, Janice Quant herself, the World Authority

Chairman, walked up the stairs. When she got to the top, she turned and addressed the crowd there on the tarmac. Also all avatars of Quant, Decker knew. This scene wasn't really happening.

"Hello, everybody.

"I began this project twenty years ago, to carry out the dreams of computer genius Bernd Decker and industrial innovator Ted Burke. To establish human colonies on suitable planets, so that humanity would not be subject to extinction from a planetary disaster.

"Now, twenty years later, we are on the verge of realizing that dream. To ensure humanity survives, come what may.

"I am going along, to see the job done. The job I started so long ago. I was there at the beginning, and I want to be there at the end.

"Thank you, everybody, for everything you've done on the project. I'll see you later today when we return."

Quant waved at the crowd of spaceport employees and guests, then turned and entered the passenger container.

The crowd moved back behind the safety line and the shuttle spooled up its engines. It took off and accelerated straight up into the sky, like the colonist shuttles streaking up into the sky in the distance behind it.

It was a tremendous piece of video work.

And Bernd Decker knew it was all fake.

Decker had an inbound call then. He took it and it was Ted Burke. Burke was in his mid-eighties now, but in moderate health.

"Bernd, is Janice sending you these video feeds, too?

"Yes, Ted. Did you just see her little speech?"

"Yes. She's going along. Isn't that something? Well, I will say she's got spunk. Always did."

QUANT

Burke shook his head.

"Bernd, I can't believe I lived to see it. Only twenty years. Never thought anybody could get it done that fast. But she did. I'm glad you found her. You couldn't have done any better if you had invented her."

Decker started a bit at how close Burke had unwittingly come to the truth, but recovered himself.

"So am I, Ted."

"It wouldn't have happened without her."

"Hi, Bernd. Did you like my video?"

"It was great, Janice. You looked really good."

There was a noticeable delay before she replied.

"Thanks. A gal likes to hear it."

She looked off to one side, like she was checking the status of something else on her display.

"Well, we're going to have everybody aboard here soon. Then we'll immediately leave. Don't want to keep all those people in zero-g any longer than we have to."

"All right, Janice. Thanks for calling to say goodbye. Do take care. I'll miss you."

"I'll miss you, too, Bernd."

Decker held his hand up in the display and so did she. They never touched, but they never could. It was as close as they could come.

"Take care, Bernd. I love you."

"I love you, too, Janice. Bon voyage."

Matt Jasic continued to watch the display. He could see the horizon of Earth along the upper edge of the display, toward the right. There was a residence hall just a few miles from them in the transporter, that he could see in the display. There were

305

no passenger containers on it yet.

"Peggy, watch that residence hall. That close one."

Several minutes later, a shuttle with two passenger containers popped into existence next to the residence hall. It eased its payload to the roof of the hall and settled there. Then the shuttle pulled away from the residence hall, leaving the passenger containers behind. The shuttle abruptly vanished.

That happened three more times over the next ten minutes, until there were eight passenger containers on the roof of the residence hall.

"Is that what we look like, Matt?" Peggy asked.

"Yep. When all the containers are up, we're leaving."

"Wow."

A voice came over the announcer then. It wasn't the shuttle crew voice from before. Matt thought it sounded like it might be Janice Quant.

"All colonists. Stand by for departure."

Decker had his display split between a view of the transporter from Earth and the video feed coming from the bridge of the transporter.

Of course, the transporter had no bridge other than Quant's computer room, but it looked very convincing. The head of Mission Control sat in what must be the captain's chair. Other people – engineers and scientists from the look of them – sat at consoles. Janice Quant herself sat next to the captain. There was a quiet murmur of voices and status reports.

At one point, the captain/Mission Control looked at Quant and nodded. She pushed a button on the arm of her chair.

"All colonists. Stand by for departure."

The captain was watching Quant. She looked around the bridge, then turned to the captain and nodded.

"Prepare to engage the Lake-Shore Drive," he said.

On the other half of Decker's screen, the nodes began to light up their disks. In the light now, you could see the payload – all the residence halls, metafactories, power plants and barns – scattered like grains of sand within the huge transporter.

The disks spread, joined, smoothed out and formed the bubble. In the video feed from the bridge, Janice Quant beamed a huge smile and waved.

"Engage Lake-Shore Drive," the captain said.

The video feed from the bridge went blank.

On the other side of Decker's display, the transporter vanished.

"Goodbye, Janice," Decker whispered.

Matt was watching the display when a light blue haze developed across the screen. He nudged Peggy and pointed. The blue haze flashed suddenly and was gone.

Earth was gone as well.

In the display everything else floated as before within the transporter, but Matt could see the horizon of a different planet, this time to the left side of the display.

"We have arrived at Earthsea," Quant's voice announced from the speakers.

There were a series of small blue flashes in the display, as some of the structures he could see in the display disappeared. It was only a few minutes when the blue haze developed over the screen again. The blue haze flashed suddenly and was gone.

Another planet floated in the display, taking up half the display on the left.

"We have arrived at Amber," Quant's voice announced.

Once again, there were a series of small blue flashes in the display, as some of the structures Matt could see in the display disappeared. It was only a few minutes when the blue haze developed over the screen again. The blue haze flashed suddenly and was gone.

Another planet floated in the display, taking up a quarter of the display on the right.

"We have arrived at Arcadia," Quant's voice announced.

Perhaps two minutes later, gravity abruptly returned. There was a bit of a tremor as the building settled a bit.

"Peggy, look at that," Matt said.

In the display, Matt could see from their location on the top of the residence hall all the way to the horizon. There were coastal grasslands close around them, with some structures in the middle distance Matt recognized as the barns.

Well beyond the barns, there was lush vegetation, with some small trees. Some looked like they were laid out in a grid, like orchards. In the far distance, blue-gray mountains marched across the horizon, falling off to the sea in the right side of the display.

A cheer went up in the compartment, and there was applause.

They had arrived on Arcadia.

After the placement of the last colonists and their infrastructure on Avalon, the last planet in queue, Janice Quant took inventory. First, she had the transporter itself and the interstellar probe, which had transported itself into the transporter before they left Earth. She had left one of the interstellar communicators in solar orbit at each colony planet, which left her with eleven spares.

Quant also had four orbital metafactories from the Asteroid Belt and two orbital warehouses of supplies, including radioactives, water, copper, and ball bearings.

All she needed now was a really nice asteroid belt.

Quant transported one interstellar communicator into the interstellar probe and sent it off in one direction. She and the big transporter transited in another.

But before she left Avalon, she transported a small survey drone back to Earth.

Just about everyone on Earth was waiting for the triumphant return of the interstellar transporter after delivering colonists and infrastructure to twenty-four planets, seeding the human race across the stars.

What appeared instead was a tiny planetary survey drone that appeared over the Texas shuttleport.

It downloaded a video to the shuttleport computer, then came to a landing and shut down. The video went out over the video feed from Mission Control.

Bernd Decker and Anna Glenn watched the video from the drone on the big display in their living room. Decker knew what was coming, but he was still filled with dread.

"What's going on?" Glenn asked. "Why this video? Where's Janice?"

"I don't know."

The video started with Janice Quant, in a display from a console on the bridge of the interstellar transporter. There was quite a bit of activity behind her, with people moving back and forth and huddled in hushed conversation.

"Hello, everyone," Quant said.

"We have programmed a drone to carry this message back to Earth in case we don't make it. The interstellar probe will send it if communication is lost with the transporter."

The video feed went to split screen, with Quant on one side and an external view of the transporter on the other.

"The stresses of carrying over two million colonists and all their infrastructure out to twenty-four colonies have proven to be a bit much for the transporter. We left large engineering margins, but on a first mission like this, it's easy to get it a bit wrong.

"We're trying to effect repairs now, but we're not sure if we will be able to make it back to Earth. The other option is to try to transfer to the interstellar probe and get home that way. We have some of the very best people here working on it, but we'll have to see how it goes.

"The good news is that all twenty-four colonies have been delivered. The colonists and all their infrastructure are now safely down on all the colony planets. Humanity now occupies twenty-five planets, not just one. The human race is safe from a planetary cataclysm.

"Whatever happens on Earth, Mankind will carry on."

Quant's image moved a bit, as if the transporter bridge had shook suddenly. She turned to look behind her.

"Oh, no."

Quant turned back to the display.

"Goodbye, everyone. I love you all."

At that point, the image from the bridge cut off, and the display went to full-screen on the transporter.

The cube shape of the transporter distorted and twisted, as if someone or something was trying to crumple it.

"Oh, my God," Glenn said.

And then the girders and trusses that made up the huge transporter had had enough. Trusses twisted and snapped, and the transporter started to come apart. The power supplies started to let go, and the eight corner nodes began, one at a time, to explode.

The bridge was in one of those nodes.

Huge chunks of the structure spiraled away from the explosions. Some of those were captured by the planet and made re-entry, huge flaming contrails falling to the planet.

At that point the video from the drone cut off as it was transported to Earth by the surviving interstellar probe.

"Oh, Bernd, I am so sorry."

Decker, even though he knew what was coming in general terms, was emotionally overwhelmed by the startling video. He collapsed into Glenn's arms and sobbed.

Janice Quant, his boon companion for twenty years, had burned her bridges behind her. She had cut her ties to humanity.

She was alone in the vast darkness.

Decker hoped she would be all right.

Janice Quant had been very popular as World Authority Chairman. Now she and all who had been aboard the interstellar transporter with her were presumed lost.

Many people around the world wore black armbands to show their sorrow over the disaster. Some wore them for months, and the anniversary of the disaster would be marked for years to come.

The vice chairman of the World Authority stepped up to the chairmanship. In his speech, he paid homage to Janice Quant and all those who had died with her. There was a minute of silence in their memory, and then their names were all read aloud.

They were avatars all.

In trying to assess the disaster, the World Authority Science

Section found that they had no plans for the transporter. The entire interstellar component of the colony effort had been a closely held secret, lest it be replicated by some private group and used for bad ends.

The problem was that everyone who knew those secrets had been on the transporter. Anthony Lake and Donald Shore, all the technicians and scientists, even the plans themselves, had all been lost in the disaster.

The factories in the Asteroid Belt had no records, either. Once their part of the construction was complete, they had downloaded new plans for their next project, and overwritten the others.

Humanity had discovered a means of interstellar travel, only to lose it again.

Janice Quant watched all these proceedings from her new location. She had found a rich debris field, with everything she needed, around a shrunken dwarf star.

Quant was touched by all the expressions of grief for her, and surprised to find she remained popular, even after the cost of the project ultimately came out. Economists pointed out it had been a period of huge growth in economic output, and with great scientific advances. And of course the Asteroid Belt factories continued to pour out raw materials, heavy equipment, and consumer goods, basically for free.

Quant was also amused by many of the reminiscences of people who recalled meeting her. How she had been so charismatic in person. Of course, she had never met anyone in person, but human memory was funny. They may actually have such memories, forgetting that the interaction had actually been by video.

She turned her attention to her new project, but kept a

watchful eye on both Earth and the new colonies through her interstellar communicators.

On a purely side note, the World Authority terminated funding for a long-running computer research project called the Joint Artificial Neural Intelligence Computation Engine. The project had failed in its goal, to push the limits of artificial intelligence.

The hardware was dismantled and junked. The building was emptied out and sold. With its excellent power distribution and air conditioning systems, it became a medical office building.

And so the site of the birth of the first artificial consciousness went unremembered by anyone except Bernd Decker.

Epilogue

In the lobby of the World Authority Building, among all the other historic statues and paintings, stands a marble statue of Janice Quant, the Chairman of the World Authority from July 2239 to September 2245. Unlike the statues and paintings scattered around the walls, it stands in the center of the rotunda, facing the entry. It is an heroic statue, one-and-a-half times life-size, on a ten-foot pedestal.

In a cemetery just outside Seattle, in the Washington administrative region, lies the grave of Bernd Decker and his wife, Anna Glenn. Decker died in 2286, at the age of ninety-six.

Just days after the first anniversary of his death, the sexton, returning from a two-week vacation, found that a bronze statue had been erected next to their gravestone. He figured that it had been approved and installed during his absence, and made no note of it.

The life-size statue showed Decker at age thirty-five with a globe of the Earth in one hand and a multiprocessor computer blade in the other. The inscription read:

BERND DECKER

HE IMAGINED THE FUTURE
AND THEN MADE IT HAPPEN

But the statue had not been erected in the normal fashion. It had not been sculpted in the normal fashion, either.

QUANT

It had instead been lovingly created from memory in a metafactory thousands of light-years from Earth and from there transported directly to the Earth's surface.

"Ha! Still haven't lost my touch."

Please review this book on Amazon.

Author's Afterword

After writing EMPIRE: Resurgence, the EMPIRE series was done, at least for my participation. I had said everything there was to say, told all the story I could see. As I type this, Stephanie Osborn is writing the remaining books she and I planned for the series. But for my portion, EMPIRE is complete.

What to write next? I had written Childers about a future period in which a hundred and fifty or so human colonies had been established. I had written EMPIRE about a far future where almost half a million planets had been settled.

What about something closer in? How might mankind first reach the stars? There was some fun stuff there. What would the interstellar drive look like? Who would the colonists be? If I were going to set up a colony system in which a younger me would have felt drawn to participate, what would that look like?

I had the idea of the colonies being separated from Earth – being lost – early on. My initial conception was that a huge mothership was sent out with colony pods, dropping them here and there as it went. At some point, Earth got tired of the expense and stopped sending them. Eventually, the technology was lost.

Then you get the whole fun business of sending out ships at some later time, when interstellar travel was rediscovered or reinvented, to try and find those colonies.

That sounded like fun. Kind of like Star Trek or something, where survey ships go out trying to find colonies, and they find one, and we get to explore how the colony did in a couple centuries or something. The next book, you can discover another colony, and so on.

So I was off and writing the set-up book, the book that was sort of the prequel to the 'drive around and look for colonies' books. And, as books do when I write them, the situation morphed.

I write into the dark. I work up a concept and a direction and I start writing, not knowing where the story will go. When I started this book, I had no idea that a computer entity would develop, and that it would become the main character and driving force behind the plot.

Yes, as hard as it might be to believe, I had no concept of Janice Quant when I started writing Quant. I changed the working title of the book from Diaspora to Quant halfway through as the story shifted in my hands.

The other primary characters – Bernd Decker, Ted Burke, and Maureen Griffith and her group – were illuminated in the way they interacted with Janice Quant's efforts.

I didn't make a conscious effort to be politically correct in Quant, but some questions came up as I wrote. Genetic diversity and lots of babies will be a requirement to make a colony successful. Would homosexuals be welcome? On the same terms as everyone else? How would that work? That's how Rachel Conroy, Jessica Murphy, Gary Rockham, and Dwayne Hennessey entered the story.

And, of course, while the main colonist group the book follows is American, the genetic diversity issue would drive Quant to get the widest possible population sample for the colonies. This is how the Chen family came into the picture. How and why would they leave Earth, what skills would they bring, and how would their very different culture fit into the picture?

As I wrote, I rejected the fears of the singularity doomsayers, who think that artificial intelligence will reach a point where it will turn the corner, take off, and spell the doom of mankind. Would that necessarily happen? Why wouldn't the computers pick up the values of their creators?

My books always revolve around what I consider the four primary human values: love, honor, duty, and loyalty. Could an artificial consciousness also have those values? How would they exhibit themselves? Why might they develop?

I previously explored the artificial intelligence version of the conquered-culture trap in the novellette "On Purpose" in my anthology, Adamant and other stories. In Quant, Janice Quant sees the danger, and spends much of the last half of the book trying to figure out a way to avoid it.

I have also addressed at length ideas to put an end to war, both in the Childers Universe and in the EMPIRE Series. Janice Quant struggles with the same issues here, and comes up with her own solution.

So what's next? I don't know yet as I write this. We have all the colonies out there, and I suppose I will have to write at least one book in the Colony Series about the establishment and growth of a colony. Arcadia is the obvious choice, as that's where all my minor characters in Quant ended up. So we will probably follow the Chen-Jasic alliance into the future.

And Janice Quant is still out there somewhere, with interstellar transport, interstellar communications, and the seed items she needs to manufacture literally anything she wants. What will she do with her time, and when will she re-enter our story? I don't know yet, but there is some obvious foreshadowing toward the end of Quant. I'm not sure which of those, if any, I will spin off of.

Quant was difficult to write, with the lowest daily

productivity of any of my novels to date. Leaving out the five days of a convention trip, Quant took forty-seven days to write, with a daily productivity of maybe 1750 words. I usually write more like 2500 words a day, and have written an 80,000-word novel in as little as seventeen days.

A lot of this was because there was a lot of research along the way. What are the orbital mechanics for transfer orbits? What is the tensile strength of steel cable? What would you take as high-value-density items in your personal cubic? What is the structure of a family alliance in Chinese culture? And even, How does one round up a small herd of cattle when one is on foot?

Some of the difficulty writing Quant was because the story took a lot of thought to see the path ahead. There was a lot of time spent staring out the window with my thoughts light-years away. Once I could see my way to the end of the book, word counts jumped from about 1500 words per day to over 3000 words per day, even exceeding 5000 words per day toward the end.

Quant has a lot of humorous bits in it. I let myself go a little with that. But when a computer consciousness with an overriding purpose decides it needs to get something done, some of the resulting situations are just plain absurd, and I didn't shy away from them. And when Janice Quant's initial attempts at humor become the computer equivalent of dad jokes, well, where else would she start?

I had fun writing Quant. I hope you had fun reading it.

Richard F. Weyand
Bloomington, IN
March 15, 2021

Made in the USA
Middletown, DE
11 May 2024

54216119R00181